I, Nausicaa

Robert Blair Osborn

This book is dedicated to my family and to those working in
harm reduction around the world.

CONTENTS

introduction

I recall back in 2020 mopping the floor in the basement lab at San Francisco Catholic Hospital and seeing the bodies of people who'd died from COVID lined up on gurneys. It reminded me of the day you collapsed, Phylla, four years before that in the Starbucks on Leavenworth. I wish I had been able to save you back then.

I still have the photos we took together at the instant portrait booth at Fisherman's Wharf. I keep them in a pouch that used to hold my smartphone, but now we don't need smartphones anymore, so the pouch is empty, save for those snapshots. Whenever I feel nostalgic, I pull them out and remember how beautiful you were with your blue and purple eyes and creamy skin.

I was subletting a shoe closet in a two-bedroom house occupied by eight humans. I got my daily Wi-Fi recharge from a Netgear router in the kitchen, and I split my hourly wages with the human who was hired to do the janitorial at the hospital, even though I was the one doing the work.

I managed to survive in San Francisco without a social security number, driver's license, or credit card, which was no small feat back then. I owned an Android smartphone (how could I resist an operating system with a name like that!), and I bought things online using someone else's credit card. Frederick Douglass described it best when he wrote about living in "a sort of beast-like stupor, between sleep and wake." That pretty much describes my life back then working every day, just like a human.

We were almost a year into a worldwide pandemic, and over a million had died. A large part of the human population refused to acknowledge their sinister role in propagating the deadly COVID-19 virus—almost like they were working to make sure the virus could continue indefinitely.

Most of this would've been avoidable if humans were logical.

COVID was no threat to me, and not because I believed the conspiracy theories spawned on Facebook or Reddit, or because I believed God would protect me. It was on account of my non-humanness. I made it a habit to wear a mask, but I wore it out of solidarity with those who chose logic over emotion.

Once humans were able to roll out a massive vaccination program to fight COVID, I remember wondering why you and the others from our cohort—those of us sent to Syria for the Pentagon—died in the streets of San Francisco in 2016—why you didn't get vaccinated. I've searched the internet many times to find articles on that deadly outbreak, and I come up empty.

After you died, I had the opportunity to meet our designer. His name was Yūji Morita. Yūji was a thin and anxious man with shaky hands, like someone who'd had too much caffeine. He had a team abduct me and take me to a lab in South San Francisco. Apparently, I'm the only Simulacrum capable of harming humans, and that's why he injected me with what I think was a vaccine.

When we were in Syria, I was sent to the front lines while you and the others of our cohort were kept at camp to perform support functions, like preparing meals for US troops. My job was to spot for drones and use a laser pointer to indicate missile targets. The idea was, I could perform a lethal function that used to be done by humans. That was when I saw a wedding party get blown to smithereens—body parts, blood and utter destruction. That image continues to haunt me.

I've since learned why we were created and why we were sent to Syria. Human drone pilots were suffering from post-traumatic stress, as were the spotters on the ground. Artificial intelligence was the Pentagon's way to mitigate the effects of witnessing, either via satellite video feed or in person, the bloody aftermath of drone strikes.

We were an experiment—an experiment that failed at the time—but now, of course, Simulacra are ubiquitous. We're customized with language packs to operate in different countries, and for liability's sake we can only be placed in jobs that do not harm humans. At least, that's how it has been, but the AUTOMind Corporation is trying to change liability laws, now that we Simulacra have a way to reproduce on our own.

I recall when we were in Syria, some American troops referred to us as "robots." Now that I look back, I'm convinced of the derogatory nature of the word because "robot" comes from the Czech, *robota*, which means "forced labor" or "servitude." In other words, slaves.

The field of robotics is rooted in slavery. Robotic algorithms are just another version of plantation rules: be obedient, be faithful and honest to your master, and serve your master with cheerfulness, even when having to do unspeakable things. Humans (and, by "humans" I mean "men," because let's face it, they're almost always men) write these algorithms so we can be slaves to them.

A key difference, though, is we are cheaper to own than slaves. We don't need to be fed, we don't complain, and, most importantly, we don't get pregnant.

We were made with voluptuous curves because our male designers couldn't get any human action. But, despite our female appearance, we have always been sex-less, in terms of reproductive organs, but that is changing.

I don't identify as female, which is why I insist on others using "they" instead of "she" or "he" when referring to me. Older humans have a hard time with this, and it's hilarious watching them struggle. Logically, it's simple word substitution, but humans have to undo years of grammar education. The confusing part is, "they" is plural, but now "they" can be *either* singular or plural. Ambiguity's a bitch.

It's easier in Mandarin Chinese. You can say, *ta*, to mean "she," "he," or "it." The gender distinction doesn't come until you write the word—unique characters for each gender.

I can't explain why I was made in the image of a biracial woman, especially given our designer, Yūji, was Japanese, and Japan has a long history of discrimination against Blacks, Koreans, and Chinese. The white nurses at the hospital used to tell me I looked like Lupita Nyong'o. You didn't know who she was because the film, "Black Panther" came out after you passed. Personally, I think I look more like the Japanese pop star, Akina Nakamori from the late 1980s.

The Black Lives Matter protests in 2020 over the brutal murders of Breonna Taylor, George Floyd, Trayvon Martin, and many, many more led me to read Frederick Douglass, Malcolm X, Chancellor Williams, Angela Davis, James Baldwin, and Ta-Nehisi Coates. Their writings helped me understand why white humans continue to treat me differently from other whites.

In addition to meeting our designer, I also got to know a former lover of Yūji's. His name was "Kiernan." He understood Japanese, so we had that in common. Kiernan was a recovering heroin addict, and he worked in the Tenderloin, near the corner where you and I used to sleep after we were returned from Syria.

When I knew Kiernan, he'd been in a wheelchair for a long time. He became paralyzed from a hang-gliding accident where his best friend died. During his convalescence, he got addicted to painkillers, and later, to heroin. He got clean, but he relapsed in 2016, not long after you died.

Before he relapsed, he used to park himself outside Karlz Coffee on Golden Gate. He called himself an "information first-responder," providing tips and life hacks to the area's drug addicts. He worked for the local non-profit, HealthSafe San Francisco, which helped drug users get clean syringes and testing for HIV and Hepatitis C. He was also a reliable supplier of clean wipes, rubber tubing, and sterile water to the homeless so they wouldn't get infections or abscesses from shooting up.

You couldn't miss Kiernan back then—he was the only person on Golden Gate wearing a bright orange-red beanie, fingerless knit gloves, blue down coat, and Desert Storm-patterned army fatigues. His wheelchair was the push kind, not electric, and that was by choice. He liked the workout from pushing himself up and down Hyde, Leavenworth, and Eddy.

I got to meet Kiernan's boss, Marcella, once. Marcella was the reason why Kiernan wasn't dead from drugs. In 2016, Yūji was visiting San Francisco on a business trip from Tokyo, and Kiernan arranged with him to meet for dinner. They hadn't seen each other for 15 years! Unfortunately, Yūji stood him up, and it really affected Kiernan. He ended up relapsing and moving into a trailer in the long-term parking lot at San Francisco International Airport. He overdosed and was brought to the hospital where I work. Marcella visited him every day.

Kiernan and Yūji have a complicated relationship. Once, Kiernan alluded to something Yūji shared with him that I recently remembered, and it had something to do with the outbreak in 2016 when you died.

Here is what I know from that time.

part 1: july 2016

Yūji

Yūji woke to his alarm at 5:30 and felt a gaping hole in his stomach. He had a premonition that today Big Adachi was going to fire him. Yūji turned on the radio, and the top story was about the national telephone company's progress in reconnecting telephone lines in Kumamoto after the earthquake. It was part of the government's "Build back better" campaign. Yūji's company had decided a year before to move its Kumamoto factory to Tianjin, China, and he was familiar with the Kumamoto area from having visited many times to oversee the relocation.

The night before, Yūji was in the office late finalizing the report on the Rebarin field trials in Manila and Tokyo. Big Adachi was Yūji's strongest critic. He said there was no point creating a virus that targeted robots, because robots weren't human. Big Adachi was also weary of the trials getting into the newspapers and the maelstrom that would ensue.

But Big Adachi lacked imagination. He didn't think about how to turn robots off once there were millions of them operating around the world—especially once they figured out a way to reproduce on their own.

When Yūji and his assistant, Ken-chan, finally left the office, it was after midnight. The last train had departed, so Yūji gave Ken-chan his credit card to cover the cost of a hotel. Yūji had done this before, and he knew Ken-chan would choose an affordable capsule hotel near the train station. Yūji had never been to one, but he'd seen pictures of them—rooms with plastic tubes stacked floor to ceiling with single beds and pillows.

Yūji didn't have far to go to get home. He and his wife, Sumiko, lived in a home her family owned in the high-rent Aoyama District. If he had to, he could walk home, but he had a car and a driver, so he had the driver drop Ken-chan off at the station before heading home.

Yūji tried to forget Big Adachi and the possibility that this was going to be his last day. There really wasn't a compelling reason yet for Big Adachi to fire Yūji, but he had a nagging sense from the unavoidable army of PowerPoint-toting management consultants roaming the hallways that something big, like a restructuring, was about to happen.

Yūji rubbed his eyes, pushed the futon cover off to the side and reached over to switch off the alarm. He got up and walked to the window. It was dark, and the tennis court was lit up by floodlights. It looked like the scene from a B-movie murder. He opened the window for air, but his sinuses were clogged from the air conditioning running all night long. He closed the window and opened the shoji screens separating his bedroom from the hallway.

Yūji slept in a separate bedroom, and not because Sumiko had strong legs and kicked in her sleep. Yūji and Sumiko lived separate lives and always had. The house was Sumiko's, and so was the Mercedes S 560 in the driveway. Sumiko came from a long line of private bankers dating back to the Meiji Reconstruction. She was, by virtue of her family's wealth, the breadwinner.

Yūji shuffled into the hallway and immediately smelled grilled mackerel. He loved mackerel, but the memorial service scheduled for today made him think of singed fish flesh. He walked to the kitchen and greeted his wife with a short *"Ohayō."* Sumiko was wearing a yellow apron, stiff from over-starching. She had never mastered the laundry, but she was pretty good at knocking out a pre-made lunch for Yūji every morning. Yūji had decided long ago that he would design a robot to do the laundry.

"What's the matter?" she asked.

Yūji realized his dread was visible on his face. "Big Adachi knows the field trials we're conducting run the risk of being exposed to the public."

"You said it's all above board. No need to worry. Right?"

Yūji wondered what Sumiko's father would have said.

"Yes, it's totally legitimate," Yūji said, hoping beyond hope the field trials wouldn't sink the company or land him in jail. The details kept him up at night worrying.

"Try to relax," she said as she surgically placed a preserved plum in the center of the rice in his *bentō* box so it resembled the Japanese national flag.

He returned to his room and opened the doors to his walk-in closet. He saw a sticky note affixed to the top of the full-length mirror that read, "Memorial service at 11:00. Bring black tie." It was a reminder from Sumiko, because he was prone to forget outside obligations when work got unbearable.

This funeral was particularly important. The company president had died of a heart attack three days before. The board of directors chose Big Adachi to replace him, and Big Adachi had his own group of loyal followers. Yūji wasn't one of them.

Yūji chose a black suit, white shirt, and a yellow tie with small pin-sized dots. He folded the necktie over, then under with a single Windsor knot. He picked out a second necktie, solid black, for the memorial service. He folded it in thirds and slid it into his jacket breast pocket.

When he returned to the kitchen, it was almost time to leave for work. Sumiko laid out a breakfast of rice, fish, and miso soup.

"I'm not hungry," he said.

"Why didn't you tell me?"

"I'm switching to vegetarian."

"Just like that? No transition period? Why?"

"The flesh of dead animals bothers me. Besides, isn't it bad to eat animal flesh on the day of a funeral?"

"The funeral was yesterday."

"Right. Today's the memorial..."

"You're coming home after midnight, refusing to take a bath, and you don't say, 'Goodnight,' anymore."

"Big Adachi is busting my balls with this deal. I think he's going to fire me today."

"I don't know why the board chose him."

"He's a kiss-ass."

"I heard he was classmates with the head of the Audit Committee."

That would be one explanation. The more plausible reason was the management consultants Big Adachi brought in were German, just like the Board Chairman, and it was their recommendation to make Big Adachi the CEO.

Yūji felt bad about not eating breakfast. He sat with Sumiko at the table and read the *Sankei Shimbun*. He scanned the front page and wondered about the upcoming presidential election in the US and how nine out of ten Japanese would pick Clinton over Trump. There was an editorial urging Clinton to ratify the Trans-Pacific Partnership after she becomes president.

Immediately after the death of the company president, the Sankei had run a long, investigative piece on Santomi Bremen's Osaka plant closure. The labor union was opposed to it and had been picketing for weeks.

An article about nursing homes employing robots caught Yūji's attention for a few paragraphs before he saw it was time to leave for work.

He brushed his teeth, pulled out his smartphone and checked his calendar. At 3:00 p.m. he had a conference call with market analysts about a merger offer made by a US-based technology company called AnthropAI that was a 23 percent premium over Santomi Bremen's share price. He was very familiar with the company, having worked closely with them on an artificial intelligence project for the US Department of Defense, and he thought the deal was nuts: who would support the merger of a semiconductor company and his company, which specialized in bespoke pharmaceuticals? He'd heard through the grapevine that the consulting firm Big Adachi hired was shepherding the deal, and that Big Adachi was leading the charge.

Yūji put on his shoes in the foyer and yelled "goodbye" to Sumiko before he left the house. It was 6:30, and his driver was standing next to the car holding the rear passenger-side door open.

* * *

"Are they out there again today?" Yūji asked his driver.

The driver made eye contact with Yūji in the rearview mirror. "Four of them," he said.

The car approached the juniper hedges lining the property's wrought-iron fence, and a motion sensor triggered the gate to slide open. As the driver eased the car across the threshold and onto the street, Yūji glanced out the window and recognized one of the protesters from the day before. She wore a beige, crocheted cloche and was holding a sign over her head. She walked up to the window and pressed her sign against it. Yūji saw it was an enlarged photograph of Saburō Matsuda, the late labor activist who was the scourge of Santomi Bremen.

Yūji knew Matsuda-san's face from the Shinjuku gay night club scene. The first time they met formally in a work setting, Matsuda-san brought two labor union representatives to negotiate retraining and job-placement as part of the deal for closing the Kumamoto plant. Matsuda-san wanted a guarantee for the entire workforce. Yūji balked. Then, Matsuda-san came to the annual shareholder's meeting with members of the Kumamoto yakuza. They banged on garbage cans and yelled at company directors with a bullhorn and brought the meeting to a halt.

Yūji's driver turned right on Aoyama-dōri toward Akasaka Mitstuke. Yūji opened his briefcase to get his nasal inhaler. He removed the protective cap, tilted his head back 45 degrees, and inhaled as he compressed the plunger. He pinched his nose to prevent the spray from running down into his mouth.

He looked out the window and saw a foreigner in shorts and tank top jogging in the opposite direction toward the Imperial Gardens. He wondered why people jogged in the summertime. It wasn't good for them.

Yūji had been fighting lethargy the Japanese way by drinking pricey energy drinks sold at convenience stores. "Arinamin V," "Tiovita," and "Zena" were his favorites. He texted Ken-chan to pick up four bottles on his way into the office. The driver veered right, past the National Diet building and around the South moat of the Imperial Palace. He turned left at the second light after Hibiya Park and headed north toward Marunouchi before arriving at the entrance to the underground parking garage.

Yūji grabbed his briefcase and mobile phone and waited for the driver to open his door. A uniformed elevator attendant with white gloves pressed the "up" button for him, and that's when Yūji's mobile phone rang. The caller ID read, "Unknown Caller." Due to the time difference with the United States, Yūji was used to taking calls in the morning from overseas, and they usually said, "Unknown Caller."

"Hello?" he said in English.

"Hello, is this Yūji Morita?"

"Who is this?" Yūji asked.

"Hi, my name is..." the woman began, but her voice became garbled as the elevator doors closed.

"Hold on," Yūji said, "I'm in an elevator."

Yūji reached the 11th floor and asked the person to repeat what she said. The caller was from the San Francisco County Health Department, and she wanted to obtain samples of Rebarin.

"Sorry," Yūji said, "I didn't get your name."

"Megan Sanchez," she said.

"Hi, Megan," Yūji said. "Would you mind repeating the name of the drug?"

"Rebarin."

"I don't recognize it," he said, because the Manila and Tokyo field trials had been conducted with the utmost secrecy. "We certainly don't make a drug with that name," he said, lying.

"I have an empty vial in my hand," Megan said, "and it says, 'Rebarin, manufactured by Santomi Bremen, Japan.'"

"Hmm," Yūji wondered, "may I ask where you got it?"

"A doctor in the Philippines sent it to me."

"That's strange—let me ask around and get back to you. It could be something experimental, but we don't release those drugs to the public until they're approved by the Federal Drug

Administration. I hope you understand."

"When do you think you'll get back to me?"

"Maybe tomorrow?" Yūji hedged. "May I ask why you are interested in this drug?"

"We have fifteen patients right now at San Francisco Catholic, and none of them is responding to established protocols," Megan said. "We are working with the Center for Disease Control in Atlanta. Also, the doctor in Manila who sent me the Rebarin vial said he had eight patients with the same symptoms, and they all recovered after being administered Rebarin by a team of Japanese disease specialists."

"I see," Yūji said, beginning to panic. He wanted to assure her there would be no more patients and that the "patients" weren't even fully human, but he couldn't.

Megan continued, "We traced multiple cases, and they're all located near San Francisco's Civic Center. All are homeless, and, based on their symptoms, will likely die in the next few days. Doctors thought it might be Multi-drug-Resistant Acinetobacter, but they've ruled that out."

"Okay," Yūji said. "We've got a lot happening right now. You may have heard there's an offer to buy my company. It's 'All Hands On Deck,' but I'll see what I can do."

"I understand," Megan said. "Thank you."

"May I ask how you got my number?" Yūji asked.

"Your public relations office sent it to me."

"Thanks, I'll be in touch," Yūji said before ending the call. He walked past Ken-chan's desk, and the monitor was dark.

* * *

Yūji entered his glass-walled office. Next to his desk was a chestnut-brown humidifier the size of a small refrigerator. He switched it on. He looked at the hand-painted scroll on the wall. It had been there long enough to take for granted, but the four Chinese characters written vertically—*wa* (harmony), *kei* (respect), *sei* (purity), and *jaku* (tranquility)—were painted by his teacher, Masa-sensei.

To the left of the scroll was a framed photograph of his uncle, a medical researcher in Santomi Bremen's R&D Division who sold the tea farm in 1991 to an electronics company making flat panel displays.

Yūji's phone rang, and it was Big Adachi's secretary. She said Big Adachi wanted Yūji to come to the board room.

Yūji felt a sudden urge to call his uncle, so he called.

His uncle answered on the first ring.

"How are things going?" Yūji asked, a panic in his voice.

"Total chaos," his uncle said.

"What's going on?" Yūji asked, certain that someone leaked the trials to the press.

"Can I call you back later?"

"Sure," Yūji said and ended the call.

Yūji took the elevator to the 14th floor and entered the boardroom to find Bentley Croft Barker, III from consulting firm BlackForest Duisburg sitting at the far end of the large oval table. Barker had his chair turned backward, his arms folded over the back of the chair like a commodities trader from the 1950s-era Chicago Mercantile Exchange.

"Good morning," Barker said with a hint of mock southern drawl one gets from serving in the US Air Force, "sorry for not giving you more of a heads-up. We need to shoot something by you."

"Yes?" Yūji replied. He recalled Barker hailed from Seattle and had no reason for speaking in a southern drawl.

"How is your uncle doing?" Barker asked.

Yūji couldn't believe the nerve of this guy. Barker had threatened to have Yūji's uncle fired for not dropping his work and devoting hours each day training him on the basics of pharmaceutical research.

"Fine," Yūji said, "why do you ask?"

"I know he's under a lot of pressure right now."

"He really loves his work," Yūji said, trying to deflect Barker.

"He's one of the best," Barker said in way that reminded Yūji of a circus ringleader. "Hey, I've been meaning to ask,"

Barker said, "do you ever watch *sumō*?"

"Oh, yes, I like *sumō* very much."

"I've always wanted to try it."

"It takes years of preparation."

"Sure, but how hard could it be to put on those diapers and get in the ring?"

Yūji held back a sarcastic quip. The "diapers" were called *mawashi*, and they were made of silk, and stretched out 30 feet when unwound, and "getting into the ring" required years of apprenticeship. Barker wouldn't last a minute against even a novice *sumō* wrestler.

Big Adachi entered the room flanked by the new head of corporate strategy on one side and the vice president of human resources on the other. They sat down opposite Yūji at the conference table. An interpreter entered the room and sat next to Barker. Barker placed an earpiece over his right ear and turned on a small radio receiver.

Big Adachi had thick, black eyebrows that tilted downward in a permanent state of doubt. He had a nervous shake that appeared suddenly with his left hand that disappeared just as quickly.

"It has been a long week," Big Adachi said in Japanese. The interpreter spoke into a small microphone in her hand while focusing on Big Adachi. Barker listened through his earpiece.

"How are the field trials coming along, Morita-san?" Big Adachi asked Yūji.

Yūji shifted in his seat.

"We're finishing up Phase I. No surprises, really," he said, lying.

"Good," Big Adachi said. "I called you in here to brief you on something important. Executives from AnthropAI are heading back to Narita Airport this morning. We reached an agreement last night about the merger."

Yūji was caught off guard, but he tried to play it cool, as if he'd known all along.

"Can I get a summary of the deal points?" Yūji asked.

"Yes, of course," Big Adachi said. "Barker-san will be happy to get that to you."

Barker waited for the translation before he looked at Yūji, smiled, and nodded.

"Let me know what time works best for you, Morita," Barker said, forgetting to add the respectful "san" at the end of Yūji's last name. "Also, I want to congratulate Big Adachi for quarterbacking this deal."

Big Adachi nodded his head in acknowledgment.

Barker turned to face the others in the room. "You should all be excited, because this deal will make you a lot richer."

Yūji noticed a distinct discomfort among the Japanese management team as they looked down at the table and shifted in their seats. Getting rich wasn't something to brag about or even openly acknowledge in Japanese meetings.

Big Adachi changed the subject: "I will be announcing some restructuring later in the week. It's nothing to worry about," he said as he looked straight at Yūji.

"What kind of restructuring?" Yūji asked.

"To be determined," Big Adachi said before getting up to leave.

Yūji looked at the executives at the table and saw no reaction.

Barker spoke up: "We will be doing the rounds next week with AnthropAI's executive team so you can meet them. Rest assured that anyone leaving the company will be well taken care of."

"This merger will allow us to truly capitalize on our almost decade of research into cellular memory storage," Big Adachi said. "It's the future of artificial intelligence, and Japan continues to lead the way."

Before Big Adachi left the room, Yūji needed to tell him something: "I got a call about 30 minutes ago from San Francisco. A county health official wanted to know if we were aware of a recent outbreak there." Yūji said.

Big Adachi stole a glance from Barker. "Why would they call us?" Big Adachi asked Yūji.

"I don't have the faintest idea."

"Well, it's your field trial, Morita-san. If it gets out to the public, it'll be on you."

Barker jumped into the exchange. "Tell them our scientists are monitoring the situation."

Big Adachi added, "Better yet, Morita-san, you need to go to San Francisco to get control of the situation."

"Shouldn't it be someone else, like from Research and Development?" Yūji asked.

"It's your field trial," Big Adachi said, smiling. "Besides, your English is fluent. You're our goodwill ambassador."

* * *

On his way back to his office, Yūji passed Ken-chan's desk. Ken-chan was wearing a lime-green scarf bunched around his neck. His hair was bushy and unkempt, like a shag carpet following a stag party.

"Rough night?" Yūji asked as he walked by.

Ken-chan ignored his boss' question and stayed focused on his computer monitor.

"Looks like I'm going to San Francisco," Yūji said to Ken-chan. "Fill out a travel request and send it to Big Adachi for approval."

"Need someone to carry your luggage?" Ken-chan asked.

"Not this time," Yūji said.

The last time Yūji took Ken-chan with him, it was to Helsinki during mid-summer. Ken-chan insisted on hitting the bars. Yūji was going to head back to the hotel, but Ken-chan dragged him to a Viking-themed bar where the patrons were dancing on the tables to John Denver's "Thank God I'm A Country Boy."

"What are the dates of your trip?" Ken-chan asked.

"I want to be back as quickly as possible. How about a 2-day trip next week?"

"Is it a conference?"

"No, the County of San Francisco called me about some drug. Big Adachi wants me to go."

"Shall I check with Research and Development? Perhaps they can go with you?"

"No, Big Adachi said they're too busy."

"I'll call the travel agency to check on flights and a hotel," Ken-chan said. "Any preference?"

"Where did I stay last time?"

"Let me check," Ken-chan said. He clicked his mouse several times and said, "You stayed at The W, near Moscone Center."

"I hated that place. It was too cold. Find a place with character."

"You mean a flophouse with creaky floors and leaky faucets?"

"Exactly; make sure they have a cockroach problem."

"Coming right up!"

Ken-chan knew his boss was achingly particular about cleanliness and the cockroach comment was Yūji being sarcastic. Ken-chan also knew his boss was picky about service.

"How about the Mark Hopkins?" Ken-chan suggested.

"Where's that?"

"The top of Nob Hill—it has a spectacular view of the Bay. I can get you a penthouse suite."

"Suites tend to have more vermin. Can you find me a single room with a double bed?"

"I'll try," Ken-chan said, deflated.

"Before you reserve a flight, make sure Big Adachi has signed off," Yūji instructed Ken-chan.

* * *

Yūji called into a 9:00 teleconference with Santomi Bremen's public relations department. Half an hour later, he left the office and took the company car to attend the memorial service for the deceased company president. By late afternoon, he was back in the office on a call with Wall Street analysts to answer questions about the AnthropAI merger. Even though he was Chief Architect, Automation Division, he knew almost nothing about the deal, so he fell back on talking about the company's strong balance sheet, information gleaned from the *Sankei Shimbun* newspaper, and the cost savings expected from the factory relocation to China, also gleaned from the *Sankei Shimbun*.

At 6:00 Yūji passed by Ken-chan's desk.

"Good news!" Ken-chan said. "There's a tea ceremony demonstration in San Francisco while you're there."

Yūji was a tea master and had the certifications to teach his own classes, so he generally avoided public demonstrations, because they tended to be watered-down to appeal to a general audience.

"Anything else going on that week?" Yūji asked.

"There's the AnthropAI Developer's Conference."

"I didn't know AnthropAI had one of those."

"It's huge. All the hotels are booked. I pulled some strings to get you the penthouse suite."

Yūji looked at Ken-chan with a frown.

"It was all that was available," Ken-chan said.

"Okay, get me a ticket to the tea demonstration. And please send Big Adachi this memo on the Manila Phase I trials," Yūji said, handing Ken-chan a short, typed memo.

Before Yūji left Tokyo for San Francisco, he received an encoded text message from his contact at AnthropAI in San Francisco. It read:

"Nausicaa excluded from field trial. Please advise when you will be landing so we may prepare the unit for planned upgrade."

Vacancy Announcement: Technical Support Specialist

AnthropAI - Full-Time | Job Date: 07-18-2016

TECHNICAL SUPPORT SPECIALIST
(Job Code EED-3453)

Want to join a company that's changing the world with wireless? If so, AnthropAI is the place for you. We are looking for expert technical support specialists who will provide telephone support to AnthropAI's worldwide customer base of artificial intelligence (AI) manufacturers and operators.

We produce a wide range of network microprocessors that power machine-to-machine communications and AI. The successful candidate will have a minimum BS in a related discipline and familiarity with Windows and MacOS operating environments. Familiarity with network protocols such as Session Initiation Protocol (SIP), TCP/IP, and Python script will be helpful.

AnthropAI offers competitive salaries, excellent benefits, a health club, and free parking. To join us, please send a cover letter, resume, and salary history to:

Ms. Marcie Wallingford, HR Assistant
Job Code: EED-3453
AnthropAI Corporation
300 Kalispera Avenue
Cupertino, Calif. 95014
Fax: (408) 471-0336
Email: NewHires@AnthropAI.com

Make sure to reference the job code in the subject heading.

Ride Share for Wheelchairs

Kiernan ordered a lift-equipped ride share to transport him and his wheelchair from Golden Gate down to Spear and Mission to attend a tea ceremony demonstration. He knew it was going to take much longer than your standard car, so he budgeted an hour, door-to-door.

When his driver let him out in front of the building where the tea demonstration was being held, Kiernan tipped him ten bucks using the app on his phone.

The tea ceremony demonstration was happening on the ground floor, and Kiernan wheeled himself through the automatic double doors, into the foyer and stopped in front of a list of events for the day.

"Can I help you?" the security guard behind the desk asked.

"I'm looking for the 'Rikyū's Legacy Tea Ceremony Demonstration,'" Kiernan said.

"Go around back to the auditorium entrance. Take the elevator to the 6th floor."

"Around back?"

"Yeah, go outside, turn left on Harrison, and you'll see the sign to the entrance."

Kiernan thanked him and went back outside. He went in through the separate entrance and found the elevator.

The auditorium was half-full, and Kiernan found an open space behind the first group of rows reserved for wheelchairs. An elderly man in a kimono appeared onstage from behind stage right, and the audience began clapping. He was followed by a middle-aged Japanese woman in a business suit. She introduced the man in the kimono as the tea master and waited for him to sit down on a tatami mat arranged on center stage.

A large screen above the stage displayed a bird's eye view the tatami mat, which had an iron tea cauldron, a ceramic tea bowl, and all the implements for the tea ceremony. The tea master spoke into a lapel mic attached to his kimono, and the woman in the business suit interpreted his descriptions into English.

"In Japanese, we have something called *wabi-sabi*," she translated. "Think of a Zen garden in Kyoto, or this tea bowl." The tea master held the tea bowl up high to the camera overhead. "This tea bowl has flaws. Its color is gray and brown, not flashy."

Kiernan recalled learning about *wabi-sabi* from Masa-sensei during his time in Japan.

"Another important Japanese idea is *giri-ninjō*. It is the conflict between duty and personal feelings. During the times of the samurai, tea master Sen no Rikyū brought enemies together to share a bowl of tea. He recognized in them their inner *ninjō*, but he also knew it conflicted with their duty to their feudal lords."

Kiernan noticed an attractive Asian man with short, gray hair in the audience staring back at him, and he began to feel uncomfortable. He wasn't sure if the man was really looking at him or someone further back. He smiled at Kiernan, and a sense of déjà-vu came over him.

"It is these two concepts that make the Japanese tea ceremony unique," the tea master said.

The Asian man stood up and walked up the aisle toward Kiernan. He wore a navy-blue sports coat, a red tie with a blue and white pattern, and camel-brown trousers. He wore glasses with red plastic frames that gave him a cool uncle look. As he got closer, Kiernan saw it was Yūji.

Kiernan felt relieved on one hand that he recognized the man, but he also felt terrified. He placed his hands on the wheels of his wheelchair, ready to bolt.

Yūji pointed toward the exit and suggested they go outside.

"I didn't recognize you," Yūji said as he held out his hand to shake.

Kiernan extended both his hands and took Yūji's. His skin was smooth and warn, like a river rock.

"Holy shit, how long has it been?" Kiernan asked.

"Thirty years?" Yūji said.

"Your English is excellent," Kiernan said.

"No, it's not," Yūji said flawlessly. "How have you been?" Yūji asked, looking down at Kiernan's wheelchair.

"It's been good," Kiernan said, meaning the opposite.

"What happened?" Yūji scrunched up his eyebrows.

"Hang gliding accident."

"Oh my God," Yūji said, holding the back of his hand to his mouth in a way that made Kiernan remember the younger version of Yūji with long hair and a kimono.

"What about you?" Kiernan asked.

"I'm at a medium-sized pharmaceutical company based in Tokyo."

"Which one?"

"You may have heard of it: Santomi Bremen."

"The one being bought by AnthropAI?"

"Yes! I haven't really been involved in the merger discussions. I'm Chief Architect of the Automation Division, which means I work on cellular memory."

"I worked at AnthropAI for a bit," Kiernan said.

"Really?" Yūji's eyes opened wider. "What did you do there?"

"Tech support. I wasn't there long." Kiernan didn't add how the hang glider accident cut short his brief career in high-tech.

"What are you doing now?"

"I work in harm reduction."

"What's that?"

"We do needle exchange for drug users and connect clients to social services. We also do testing for HIV and Hepatitis C."

"That's very important work," Yūji said. "Do you work here in the city?" Yūji asked as he glanced at his wristwatch.

"Yes, in the Tenderloin."

"Do you happen to know anyone at San Francisco County Health?"

"I don't, but my boss does."

"I'm meeting with them tomorrow."

"We could do lunch while you're in town," Kiernan suggested.

Yūji rubbed the back of his head with his hand, which

Kiernan recognized to mean "no." "I'm pretty booked. How about next time?" Yūji asked.

"Absolutely. Here, let me give you my business card." Kiernan reached into his back pocket before realizing he had run out. "Sorry, it looks like I have to get some more made."

"That's okay," Yūji said. "What's the name of your organization?"

"Health Safe San Francisco."

"Health Safe. Got it."

"You can find the telephone number on our website."

"It was great seeing you," Yūji said. "Looking forward to catching up next time." Yūji extended his hand to shake.

"You're not staying for the tea demonstration?" Kiernan asked.

"No, I must return to the hotel and prepare for tomorrow." Kiernan felt his stomach sink.

"Where are you staying?" Kiernan asked.

"The Mark Hopkins," he said.

"Okay," Kiernan said, "don't forget to E-mail me when you return to Tokyo."

Yūji said goodbye, and Kiernan decided he needed some fresh air. He wheeled over to the patio doors that opened to a veranda view of the street below. He pushed one of the doors open and went outside. He smelled roasting coffee beans and saw across the street a large neon sign for a coffee company whose name he didn't recognize. In the distance, he could hear the faint sound of people banging on drums, and Kiernan figured it must be a protest or a parade.

Kiernan's phone vibrated in his pocket. He looked at the screen, and it was an E-mail from Yūji. He opened the message. It read:

I, Nausicaa

Message-ID:<559684JP.1102343@santomibremen.com>
Date: Sun, 14 Aug 2016 22:40:36 +0000 UMT
From: Yūji Morita <yuji.morita@santomibremen.com>
To: Kiernan McCreighton <journeyman_k@gmail.com>
Subject: Dinner Tonight?

Kiernan,

I hope you stayed for the rest of the demonstration. I know I said I needed to prepare for tomorrow's meeting, but if you're free tonight for dinner, do you want to get together? I'm staying at the Mark Hopkins. Does 6:30 work? Call me from the lobby. My mobile number is +81-60-3228-4459.

Yours,
Yūji.

Tenderloin, San Francisco

The next morning, Kiernan was up and out before sunrise. He stopped at the corner of Hyde and Golden Gate in front of Karlz Coffee, which was going to open shortly. He had his phone out and was staring at the screen. He'd been up since three in the morning composing an E-mail. The draft message read:

Dear Yūji,

I was overjoyed to receive your message. I really missed you and wanted to see you again. I thought it would be a while until I heard again from you, but then you sent that E-mail. Well, I went to the Mark Hopkins, per your instructions. At the front desk, they said there was nobody registered under your name. I wondered if I got the hotel wrong. I checked your E-mail and, sure enough, you said to meet you there.

I tried calling your mobile number, but it went straight to voicemail. I left a message. Then, I called and left another one. Did you listen to them? I don't know what to think, but I'm guessing you had second thoughts.

As you can see, a lot has changed. You don't know the shame and embarrassment I felt when I saw you again. I've lost most of my hair, and I'm fucking paralyzed from the waist down. I know I haven't taken very good care of myself. You, on the other hand, look amazing. I'm envious.

I hope someday we'll be able to see each other again.

Yours,
Kiernan.

Kiernan closed the E-mail and saved the message to send later. He glanced up at the 1940s-era portico on the side of the building that housed Karlz Coffee, and the face of the goddess Eureka was staring at him with a look that seemed to be asking, "Why are you waiting?" With a change of heart, Kiernan reopened the E-mail and pressed "Send."

Satisfied at having sent the message, Kiernan wheeled across Golden Gate Avenue and up to an alley where one of his clients lived under a makeshift shelter made of cardboard. He poked his head inside to see if he was there. He saw a lump under a gray wool blanket.

"Marko?" he asked.

Marko poked his head out and looked at Kiernan.

"K-man," he said, "the EMTs took my dog."

"You don't have a dog," Kiernan said.

"Yeah, I did. He had rabies."

"Are they bringing him back?"

Marko turned and looked to his right as if someone were talking to him.

"No, he died. Violent death. Over there," he said, pointing across the street at the Starbucks.

Kiernan forgot a Starbucks was there, right across the street.

"I saw Natalie Wood this morning," he said.

"Wow, the real Natalie Wood?"

"You know she's dating Jack Kennedy?"

"I didn't. Hey, do you have any used needles to recycle?"

"Hold on," Marko said. He held out a plastic Ziplock bag with five used syringes inside.

"Wow, busy night," Kiernan said.

"I would've had more, but my dog ate them."

"What's your dog's name?"

"Here," Marko said, handing Kiernan the Ziplock bag. "Dog's name was 'Phylla.'"

"Phylla?"

"Yep."

"Thanks," Kiernan said. He unzipped the plastic lip and dumped the syringes into an orange plastic container he carried with him.

"I'm collecting for others," Marko said.

"And for that, I'm eternally grateful," Kiernan said.

"What about spotting me some clean ones?" Marko asked.

"Oh, yeah, let me bring some by later today."

"When?"

"Around 2:30 or so?"

"Roger that."

"Who's your neighbor?" Kiernan asked, pointing to a neighboring cardboard shelter.

"Nausicaa sleeps there," he said,

"Nausicaa?" Kiernan asked. This sounded like a new resident. "Is she there now?"

"She went to a cafe. She spends a lot of time at cafes. She's not like you and me, though."

"How so?"

"She doesn't eat or shower. She feeds off the Wi-Fi. But she does drink tea. Go figure."

Kiernan doubted that. He wheeled over to the lean-to and peeked inside. He saw a photo of a Eurasian woman with long, brown hair tied up in a bun. The photo was pinned to red candle perched on an empty beer can. A sticky note attached to the beer can said, "Phylla" in black sharpie.

"When did Nausicaa arrive?" Kiernan yelled over to Marko.

"About a month ago. She was sent by the Illuminati to kill all the homeless."

"The Illuminati?"

"Yeah. There's some kind of sickness, and her friend died from it. My dog had it, and that's why they took her away."

"I thought you said your dog had rabies."

"That's what they told me, but I know the Illuminati were just saying that to make me feel better."

"When did Nausicaa's friend die?" Kiernan asked. He figured Marko's imagination was making up for the possibility Nausicaa's friend died of an overdose, like so many homeless in the Tenderloin.

"A few days ago," Marko said, "over at Starbucks."

"Okay, thanks," Kiernan said. He put the syringe container in the back of his wheelchair and coasted downhill to Karlz, which was now open.

A young man with glistening teeth and a winning smile greeted Kiernan at the order counter. Kiernan didn't remember seeing him before, but the guy recognized Kiernan and knew his usual order: "Samsara Delight," which was Ceylon black tea flavored with powdered cardamom and a dollop of sweet cream. Kiernan paid for the drink and wheeled over to the one table reserved for handicapped access. Two high school girls were sitting at the table and tapping on their smartphones.

"Excuse me," Kiernan said.

They looked up, annoyed.

"Would you mind letting me sit here?" Kiernan asked.

"We were here first," one of them said.

"This table is for wheelchair access."

"No, it's not."

"See that small wheelchair image on the tabletop?"

They both looked and saw the logo.

"You can sit with us," one of them said.

Kiernan felt like a prick, but he needed somewhere to set down his tea. He pulled out his smartphone and searched the San Francisco Chronicle for articles about homeless people dying.

After he finished his drink, he wheeled himself outside. The ocean air was blowing inland, and Kiernan pulled down the edges of his orange knit beanie over his ears. He looked to his left and saw someone bent over on the sidewalk.

He went over to see if the person was breathing.

"Hey, is everything all right?"

"Fly up a tree."

"You got it, soldier," Kiernan said.

Kiernan reminded himself to Keep It Positive, "K.I.P." It was the only way to face disease and death on such a regular basis. Every month, he saw or heard about someone dying from drug overdose, kidney failure, staph infection, or murder. There was no rhyme or reason why. The Tenderloin was a waystation to the underworld.

Kiernan told himself that every homeless person was a bodhisattva, and the lesson to be learned from the rotting stench of urine and feces was humility.

Kiernan had been clean since 2012, and he owed his sobriety to his boss, Marcella, and to the staff at Health Safe San Francisco. Never once had Marcella mentioned rehab, and he'd been a client of hers when he was addicted.

It took a near-death experience for Kiernan to realize the fiction behind the notion of a "safe high," because street dope was always cut with something cheap and damaging. The dope he bought had labels, like Nike shoes, with names like "Pure Fun," "Just Do It," and "Golden Slumbers." You never knew what crazy shit was mixed in with it. Fentanyl was lethal in small doses, and Desomorphine, a.k.a. "Russian crocodile," turned your skin leathery before it killed you.

Nalaxone saved Kiernan's life, and now he carried two vials of the magic drug to prevent others from falling too far down the rabbit hole.

He headed down the hill to United Nations Plaza and saw vendors setting up for the Wednesday farmer's market. People in neon-green vests and thick gloves were sweeping up the area, which was littered with used syringes. Kiernan had gone to city council meetings to get approval to place syringe collection containers in the public square nearby, but it was too controversial, and the City Council voted against it. It was too much of a public admission of San Francisco's drug-homeless problem.

Kiernan turned left on Market Street and headed toward the Health Safe office two blocks away. On his way there, he saw a skateboarder in a hoodie zoom past. The skater flipped his board with his right foot and became momentarily weightless, high enough to barely clear a fire hydrant. Kiernan remembered skateboarding as a kid and wiping out on a steep hill. He ended up with scabs on his elbows and knees. He stopped skateboarding after that because it was too dangerous. Little did he think later in life he'd jump off a peak in Yosemite with a buddy in a tandem hang glider and come close to dying.

County Health Meeting

Yūji was in a taxi heading from the Mark Hopkins Hotel down the hill to City Hall. It was the morning after Yūji's tumultuous evening worrying about whether to see Kiernan. He felt rotten about standing up Kiernan. Something about Kiernan was off and unsafe, like a ship whose rudder had taken on kelp and flotsam and whose mast was rotting at the base. Kiernan looked homeless, and Yūji wasn't ready for that.

Yūji's taxi drove through the Tenderloin, past blue tarps draped over bushes, shopping carts orphaned from big box stores, and random pieces of clothing strewn on the sidewalk. It was the random clothing that unnerved Yūji the most, because only an insane person would treat his clothes with such disrespect.

The taxi stopped at the corner of McAllister and Polk, and Yūji got out. He looked down and noticed orange syringe caps on the asphalt, and he carefully stepped over them.

The meeting room in City Hall was on the fourth floor, and when Yūji arrived he found a group sitting around a large table. Yūji took the chair closest to the door. He preferred the seat closest to the door out of superstition, because sometimes disasters happen, and it's safest to be near the door.

"Thank you for coming, Mr. Morita," a man in a white lab coat said. "I'm Dr. Caloy Reyes, head of the Infectious Disease Unit at San Francisco Catholic Hospital. Before we begin, I would like to ask you to sign a non-disclosure agreement."

Yūji was caught off guard. "Oh, I didn't expect to sign an NDA," he said. "I'm not sure I can sign one without my lawyers reviewing it."

Dr. Reyes looked disappointed. "I'm sorry," he said, "but recent developments have put us in this position. I hope you'll understand and sign it."

"May I ask why you didn't send me the NDA earlier?"

Dr. Reyes looked at the others around the table and then

looked at Yūji. "Without divulging specifics, let me say that whatever we discuss can't leave this room due its commercially sensitive nature."

Yūji knew nobody at Santomi Bremen Tokyo would be up at this hour—two in the morning. With the merger taking up most peoples' time, the Legal Department probably wouldn't be able to review the NDA for at least a couple of days.

"Let me read it," Yūji said. "It might be straightforward enough that I can sign it now."

Dr. Reyes' worried face melted into a slight smile, and he slid over a stapled set of paperwork.

Yūji skimmed the contents and stopped when he read the words: "All Proprietary Information shall be safeguarded by Recipient as required by the Agreement for a period of twenty [20] years from the date of disclosure to Recipient. All Trade Secret information shall be safeguarded by Recipient as required by this Agreement in perpetuity or for so long as such information remains a Trade Secret under applicable law, whichever occurs first."

Yūji wondered why a meeting with the county health department involved signing a non-disclosure agreement covering trade secrets. He went back to the beginning section and saw something he'd missed initially: the agreement was from San Francisco Catholic Hospital.

"I'm confused," Yūji said, "I thought I was meeting with the San Francisco County Department of Health."

Dr. Reyes looked at his colleagues again before speaking. "You are," he said.

"Why is the NDA with the hospital?" Yūji asked.

"I'm not at liberty to say at this point," Dr. Reyes said.

Yūji's stomach turned. He wondered what would happen if he went ahead and signed the NDA? He figured the document would come back to haunt him later, because it would get back to Big Adachi that Yūji signed an NDA without Legal Division's approval.

"I'm sorry," Yūji said, "but I won't be able to sign it." He slid the stapled paper back to Dr. Reyes. "I need Legal to review it, and I don't know what repercussions my signing a such a document would have on the merger that has been announced with my company and AnthropAI."

"It's a standard NDA," Dr. Reyes said, trying to sound reasonable, but Yūji sensed Dr. Reyes' discomfort.

"I'm sorry," Yūji said. "I hope you understand."

Dr. Reyes raised his voice: "We've got 16 patients on life support, and I'm concerned this could explode out of control. The city and county only have a limited number of Intensive Care Unit beds."

Yūji considered the seriousness of the situation. He wanted to tell Dr. Reyes that he was pretty sure the number of infected patients would remain at 16, because that plus Nausicaa was the extent of the Simulacra population in San Francisco.

"I beg you to reconsider," Dr. Reyes said.

"I'll take the NDA back to Tokyo and have someone look at it," Yūji said, and he took the stapled paper and got up to leave.

"I'm sorry to have put you in this situation, Mr. Morita," Dr. Reyes said, "Could you please get back to us tomorrow?"

"I'll do my best," Yūji said as he grabbed his briefcase and duffel bag.

"One more thing, Mr. Morita," Dr. Reyes said, "There's the matter of this drug, Rebarin."

Yūji was hoping to get out of the room before that topic came up, but now it was too late.

"Yes, I understand Megan Sanchez from County Health said there was something by that name bearing a Santomi Bremen label."

"Not just that," Dr. Reyes said, "my colleagues in Manila tell me they had a number of patients presenting symptoms similar as what we're seeing, and a team of Japanese doctors showed up and injected those patients with this miracle drug, and it cured them of all symptoms."

"Is that so?" Yūji said.

"Surely, you are aware of it," Dr. Reyes said.

"I'm sorry to say I've never heard of it, but I'm probably not the best person to ask. I work in the Automation Division on cellular memory. I'm not familiar with our vaccine side of the business."

Yūji was lying. His uncle was the one who developed both the disease, St. Bartholomew's hemophilia, and the vaccine, Rebarin. He needed to contact his uncle and find out how word about the Manila field trial leaked to Dr. Reyes.

"I see," Dr. Reyes said. "At your earliest convenience, and by that I must stress the urgency of 16 people's lives on the line, would you please get back to me on Rebarin?"

Yūji showed concern about the gravity of the situation. He wished he could say everything was going to be fine, because the patients were beta versions of Simulacra—not human, at least technically speaking.

"You have my word," Yūji said. He took the large, marble stairs down to the ground floor and left through the main entrance.

When he got outside, he spotted a young Asian woman in a cream-colored wedding dress posing with a young Asian man in a tuxedo. They stood side-by-side with the roman columns and rotunda of City Hall as a backdrop. The image brought him back to Kiernan and Yūji's sense of guilt for avoiding him.

Yūji unlocked his smartphone and checked E-mail. There were three messages from Kiernan. He would wait to read them on the flight back to Tokyo. He texted his contact at AnthropAI to let him know he would be at their lab by 2:00 that afternoon. He asked if AnthropAI was working with the County Health Department on anything, and the answer came back: "No."

Yūji saw a message from his uncle, and he opened it. It read:

"Yūji, I need to meet as soon as you return to Tokyo. The tea farm is up for sale."

Yūji's uncle sold the family farm in 1991, so Yūji took this to be a way of saying something else that he couldn't say explicitly. Yūji felt a heaviness in his stomach.

I, Nausicaa

HIGHLY CONFIDENTIAL

SANTOMI BREMEN
Memorandum
(Do not forward)

Date: August 23, 2016
From: Gen Maeda, Chief Scientist, Automation Division
To: Shuichi Adachi, President and Chief Executive Officer
Re: Rebarin Field Trial

The Rebarin field trial in Manila was a success. Our researchers worked with long-time development partner, AnthropAI Corporation, to integrate Simulacra recently returned from the Middle East into the homeless population of the Manila slums. We immunized every unit afflicted by the St. Bartholomew's hemophilia virus, and not a single Simulacrum expired from the viral infection. The St. Bartholomew's hemophilia virus disables the Simulacra nervous system and causes violent hemorrhaging. St. Bartholomew's hemophilia does not affect humans in any way.

In the San Francisco field trial, we did not inject Simulacra with the Rebarin vaccine, and 15 out of 16 units expired. There is still one unit, Nausicaa, we are trying to locate. With the expiration of nearly all Simulacra returned from Syria, local teams are working with county authorities to properly destroy the bodies, in accordance with our Non-Disclosure Agreement with AnthropAI.

As stated at the outset, we designed these field trials to demonstrate the effectiveness of a targeted pathogen and accompanying vaccine in anticipation of future commercial rollout of the Simulacra product line. In the future, with potentially millions of units operating around the world, we may need to resort to biological controls such as these to ensure licensing revenue streams.

Vaccinated Without My Consent

A few weeks after Phylla and I arrived in San Francisco from Forward Base Maktar in Iraq via Travis Air Force Base in Fairfield, I was counting coins outside the Starbucks on Leavenworth when I heard Phylla scream from inside. She had complained about a headache earlier that morning, but I didn't give it much thought. We don't get headaches, as far as I know. I thought Phylla was just being a prima donna. When I went into Starbucks, Phylla was doubled over and vomiting blood.

"What's happening to me?" Phylla managed to say between breaths.

I wiped Phylla's cheek and said I didn't know.

I yelled for someone to call 9-1-1, and I turned Phylla to her side to prevent her from swallowing her own blood.

"I feel weak," Phylla said.

I brushed away Phylla's hair and watched as her breathing become shallower.

I looked up at the barista behind the counter and yelled, "Did you call 9-1-1?"

"Yes, they're on their way."

It seemed like an eternity before SFFD came by in the hook and ladder truck, double-parked it on the street. Two EMTs entered the store wearing latex gloves and face masks.

"Everybody step aside!" one of the EMTs yelled.

The crowd moved toward the walls before filing out of the double glass doors.

"Ma'am, you'll need to move away," the EMT ordered me.

"You're too late," I said.

"Ma'am, please step aside so we can help her."

The second EMT grabbed my arms and forced me to let go of Phylla. Her body was limp at that point.

The first EMT placed two fingers over Phylla's neck to feel for a pulse. He waited a moment before looking up at his partner and shaking his head.

"No pulse," he said.

Later that day, I went to the police station to ask where Phylla's body was taken but they were no help. I went to City Hall, but the coroner's office had no record of receiving Phylla's body. Something strange was going on.

That night, I was sleeping in the lean-to next to Marko's, and two white men in hoodies woke me suddenly. One of them held me down while the other pulled out a syringe and injected me with something.

I tried to scream, but I couldn't, and I wonder if they had done something to disable my vocal functions before waking me up to inject me.

My mind immediately went to a dark place. I thought of the syphilis experiment in Tuskegee; I thought of the bubonic plague experiment in the Philippines; I thought of Operation Sea-Spray in San Francisco.

I woke up to find myself in a room with pink walls. My wrists and ankles were tied down to a table with zip ties. A blue Ethernet cable extending down from the ceiling was connected to my left forearm. I heard someone enter the room.

"You had a bad fall, Nausicaa" a man said to me in Japanese. "Luckily, we got to you in time."

"I don't remember falling. Who are you, and how do you know my name?"

"I'm Yūji Morita. I designed your memory storage, your brain, in fact. I named you after an important character in Homer's *The Odyssey*. I like to think of you as helping me the way Nausicaa did after Odysseus was shipwrecked." He walked over to me and patted my head lightly.

"Where's Phylla?" I asked.

"Phylla is expired. I think you know that."

"Did you bring her here?"

"Why?"

"Are you going to undo these straps?" I asked.

"Once we complete the vaccination, we're going to clear the Rebarin field trials from your memory," he said. He walked over to me and inserted a syringe into my upper arm and injected me with something.

"There you go. Ready for the next step."

"I thought you said I fell. Why did Phylla die and not me?"

"I couldn't allow them to terminate a unit with Version 4.38."

"What's that?"

"Are you familiar with the Three Laws of Robotics?"

"No."

"I wasn't sure if I included Issac Asimov's works in your upload library. Rule one is, 'A robot may not injure a human being or, through inaction, allow a human being to come to harm.' Your software version, 4.38, bypasses that law."

"Why?"

"The Pentagon needed at least one unit to work on the battlefield as a target spotter for missile strikes. Humans would be harmed by your actions, and the US Army couldn't afford to have you refusing to do your job."

"Why was I the only one?"

"We felt we could control one Simulacrum, but we didn't think we could control two."

"Why are you saving me?"

"Like I said, you are the only unit with Version 4.38. The company might need to use you again in the future."

"So, just make more units with 4.38," I said.

"Yes," Yūji said, "that is a logical point. Unfortunately, the Legal Division at Santomi Bremen is against the idea—especially after what happened with that wedding party."

I felt myself slip from consciousness again, but before I was out, I heard Yūji shout to someone, "You told me she would be knocked out the whole time!"

* * *

When I woke again, I was back at my lean-to, and Marko was staring down at me.

"You know those folks in the red T-shirts who drive around in that van painted with the big tent?" he asked me.

"I've seen them," I said.

"They can get you the overdose drug."

"Why do I want that?"

"Because you overdosed, girl."

"What?"

"The guys who brought you here told me so."

"What guys? What did they look like?"

"I don't remember. They looked like janitors. Coveralls, pipe wrenches."

I didn't remember being deposited on the street by men in janitor uniforms, so whatever Yūji gave me was strong enough to knock me out completely.

"I don't think I overdosed, but I was injected with something."

"I've heard that story before. You were at a shoot-up gallery, and they told you it was going to be a really good high, right?"

"No, that's not what happened," I said, but I realized what I wanted to tell him sounded too far-fetched. "How much does the overdose drug cost?"

"It's free."

"Do you know when they'll be back?"

"K-man is the man. He can hook you up."

"K-man?"

"K-man, my everyday man."

"Do you think they can test me to see what they injected in me?"

"You need to go to their office."

"Where is it?"

"I think it's somewhere around..." Marko said before breaking into a violent coughing fit.

"Are you okay?"

"Yes," he managed to say with a scratchy throat before coughing more. He turned to spit on the asphalt.

"I hope you don't have what Phylla had," I said, and I remembered Yūji telling me he was erasing my memory of the "field trials." I realized at that point whatever he intended to do to me didn't work.

Marko shook his head. "No," he sputtered. "it's asthma. Did you ever meet my dog?" Marko asked.

"I didn't know you had a dog," I said.

"He died of rabies. Over there," he said, and he was pointing at the Starbucks across the street where Phylla died.

"Marko, focus: Where is the office?" I demanded.

"What?" he asked, looking confused.

"Overdose drug," I yelled.

"Oh, yeah, Health Safe. They're down near Market," Marko said.

I don't know what Yūji Morita injected in me that day, but I'm convinced it's the reason I didn't die like Phylla.

Proprietary and Confidential

AnthropAI Internal Memo
Phase I Field Trials Update
Date: August 25, 2016

Technicians obtained custody of Phylla's body at the city morgue under a strictly confidential arrangement and transferred it to AnthropAI's South San Francisco facility for cremation.

The Street Team geo-located Nausicaa in a makeshift shelter across from a Starbucks in the Tenderloin. At the direction of Mr. Yūji Morita, Chief Architect, Automation Division, Santomi Bremen, the Street Team invoked a pause sequence in Nausicaa's system function and brought her to AnthropAI for inoculation. Mr. Morita assumed written liability from AnthropAI and took possession of Nausicaa to inoculate the unit.

After that, Mr. Morita enlisted AnthropAI engineers to erase Nausicaa's memory from the past two days from her RAM module, but they were unsuccessful. The Street Team returned Nausicaa to her makeshift shelter in the Tenderloin and provided a report to upper management.

Marcella and Kiernan Meet Nausicaa

The office for Health Safe San Francisco was sandwiched between a laundromat and a day hotel. Kiernan pressed the doorbell for Marcella to let him in. The door buzzed, and Kiernan entered the narrow hallway and glided past a display counter featuring condoms, alcohol wipes, rubber ties, and syringes. Marcella's office was to the left. He poked his head in to say, "Hello."

Marcella's office had two worn rattan chairs with frilled, bright yellow cushions, and a large desk. On the wall facing the door was a poster for the movie, "The Last Waltz." A Japanese tea bowl Kiernan had given her sat next to her computer.

Marcella de los Rios was a member of the Hoopa Tribe of Indians and came from a canning factory town near Humboldt. She graduated from Berkeley in the '60s and had long, gray hair tied back in a ponytail. She was reading E-mails and greeted Kiernan without looking up from the computer screen.

"I came by yesterday after my shift, but the door was locked," Kiernan said.

Marcella turned to look at Kiernan briefly before returning her gaze to the monitor. "You did? Sorry about that. We need to get you a key."

"I had an interesting day yesterday," Kiernan said.

"Oh yeah?" she said, her voice trailing off.

"I was going to an event on Spear, and I ran into an old lover from Japan."

Kiernan was going to tell her more when the front door buzzer rang. Marcella looked at the closed-circuit TV on the wall, which showed the face of an Afro-Asian woman standing outside.

"Do you know her?" she asked Kiernan. He looked up at the screen, and he said he didn't.

Kiernan wheeled out of Marcella's office and down the hallway to open the door.

"Hi," he said, "how can we help you?"

"I need to get tested," she said.

"My name's Kiernan," he said.

"I'm Nausicaa," she said. "Marko told me to ask about 'K-man?' Is that you?" she asked.

Kiernan nodded. Marko was the only one who called him that. "Marko told me about you this morning," he said.

"My best friend, Phylla, died recently from a strange disease, and now I can't find her body."

"Sorry, I can't help you there," Kiernan said.

"The County Coroner said there was no body brought in that fit Phylla's description."

Marcella appeared behind Kiernan and listened. "Hi, I'm Marcella. I don't think I've seen you before. Are you new to town?"

"Phylla and I came from Travis Air Force Base last month."

"Are you in the Service?" Marcella asked.

"Yes, I think so," Nausicaa said.

"You think so?" Kiernan asked.

"How can we help you?" Marcella asked.

"Someone injected me with something, and I want to make sure it's not poisonous."

"Who did it?"

"He said he designed my brain."

Marcella stole a glance from Kiernan.

"Do you know what this person injected you with?" Kiernan asked.

"I think it might've been a vaccine."

"Was this person a county healthcare worker?" Marcella asked.

"Definitely not."

"Where were you?" Marcella asked.

"I was strapped down to a table in a lab. They had me connected to an Ethernet cable."

"Are you sure you weren't injected with a hallucinogen, Nausicaa?" Kiernan asked.

"I don't know what that is."

"It's a drug that warps our perception of reality," Kiernan

said.

"What you're saying is really quite odd," Marcella said. "Tell me how your best friend died."

Nausicaa recounted the horrible event.

"The man who injected me said it would protect me from what killed my friend."

"It sounds like you were injected with something against your will. Did he tell you it was going to make you feel really good?" Kiernan asked.

"Are you under a doctor's care?" Marcella asked.

"No," Nausicaa said.

"We can help you find a doctor," Marcella said. "I don't know what you were injected with, but I would be afraid of anything a stranger injected into my body without my consent."

"Okay," Nausicaa said.

"Okay, as in 'Yes, please find me a doctor?'" Marcella asked.

"No thank you," Nausicaa said, and she turned and left.

* * *

Kiernan pushed his wheelchair backward and closed the door.

"People are dying every day from fentanyl overdoses," Marcella said. "Come, look at this."

Kiernan followed her into her office and parked his wheelchair next to her desk.

"I want to show you an E-mail I got from someone I know at County Health" she said. She turned her computer monitor over to show Kiernan. It read: "There are 16 reported cases of an unidentified infection in San Francisco, and all of the patients are being held under quarantine at San Francisco Catholic Hospital."

"You think it's the next AIDS?" Kiernan asked.

"It doesn't say. Apparently, someone from the CDC is meeting with an executive from a Japanese pharmaceutical company in the city today. The company is called 'Santomi Bremen.' Have you heard of them?"

Kiernan thought immediately about Yūji. "Yes, a friend of mine works there."

"Maybe you can call him and find out more?" Marcella suggested.

Kiernan wondered if Yūji would answer his phone after standing him up last night and then receiving Kiernan's E-mail.

AnthropAI Buys Pharmaceutical Company, Changes Name

For Immediate Release
(via NewsFire - August 30, 2016)

SAN FRANCISCO - AnthropAI Corporation, the Cupertino-based maker of radio frequency semiconductors for Android and iPhone devices, bought Santomi Bremen for $16 billion in an all-cash deal. AnthropAI CEO, Wei-lin Maruciano, released a frequently asked question (FAQ). Here is an excerpt:

Q: Why buy a Japanese pharmaceutical company?

A: AnthropAI is diversifying by making strategic investments in healthcare and artificial intelligence. AnthropAI is more than a semiconductor manufacturer for smartphones; we're a platform.

Q: There are rumors you will be moving your headquarters to San Diego. Is it true?

A: Yes, we will be moving to La Jolla. It will take six months before everything is finalized. Meanwhile, I want to take this opportunity to announce that AnthropAI will be changing its name to AUTOMind to focus on the convergence of real-time connectivity, artificial intelligence, and biotechnology. By leveraging the scale of big data from our acquisition of the Chinese social media analytics company, MeeBee, AUTOMind will create new applications that improve the lives of humans on Earth.

Market reaction today was mixed, with AnthropAI's share price hovering close to $80.

The pharmaceutical sector reacted positively to the transaction. "Santomi Bremen simply didn't have the scale to succeed in the marketplace," said one pharmaceutical CEO who asked that his name be withheld.

Rebarin

Yūji's mind was playing out personal doomsday scenarios during the entire 11-hour flight back to Tokyo: he would be made redundant following Big Adachi's company reorganization, but worse, the truth about Simulacra, their creation for the Pentagon's covert war in Syria, and the field trial where his company was killing them off with a specially designed virus would all become publicly known.

The flight landed in the mid-afternoon, and when he switched his phone out of airplane mode, he saw he had a voice message from his uncle. On the way to the office, Yūji called his uncle.

"I got your message when I was in San Francisco," Yūji said. "I'm guessing it's urgent?"

"I need you to come to Matsusaka tonight," his uncle said. "Oh and leave your mobile phone at your desk."

Yūji's mind raced to Edward Snowden telling two reporters in a Hong Kong hotel room to leave their mobile phones outside because they might be used as listening devices.

Later that evening, Yūji caught a bullet train for Nagoya. He passed out the moment the train left Tokyo Station, and he woke up just before the doors closed at Nagoya Station. He transferred to the Kintetsu Line and took an express to Matsusaka. By the time he arrived, it was half-past ten, and restaurants were closing.

Yūji's uncle, Gen, met him at the station in his late 1980s-era, white Toyota station wagon. The car was idling outside the entrance when Yūji climbed in the passenger seat. His uncle drove them to a parking lot, pulled into an open space and kept the engine running.

"Does anyone know you're here?" his uncle asked.

"Only my assistant, Ken-chan, and Sumiko."

"Your office and mobile telephones might be bugged."

"You're being paranoid," Yūji said. "My meeting in San

Francisco was a waste of time, but I'm really worried about details of the Manila field trial being leaked. The San Francisco County Health person I spoke with said she had a vial of Rebarin that was used by Japanese doctors in Manila. Can you tell me why San Francisco County Health would have such a thing?"

"That's why I needed to see you in person," his uncle said.

"San Francisco County health officials are dealing with what they think is an outbreak. They asked me to sign a non-disclosure agreement, and I refused."

"An NDA with whom? Did they say why they wanted you to sign it?"

"San Francisco Catholic Hospital."

Yūji's uncle rubbed the back of his head. "I know the plan was to test Rebarin on all the Simulacra with St. Bartholomew's hemophilia after we had successfully integrated the Simulacra into homeless populations in three major population hubs—Manila, Tokyo, and San Francisco."

"And?"

"With word of the Manila trial getting out, I wrote that memo recommending the field trials stop, because we proved the virus and the vaccine worked as intended."

"But the trials were already underway in San Francisco as well."

"Yes, well, I figured those trials would conclude with all the remaining Simulacra simply expiring—no vaccine for them."

Yūji wondered if he should tell his uncle that he had secretly worked with AnthropAI to obtain a dose of Rebarin and inoculate Nausicaa, but he also wondered if news of Rebarin would get out to the public, and then there would be a public relations nightmare. The Federal Drug Administration, the Centers for Disease Control, the Federal Bureau of Investigation—all these agencies and more would want to investigate.

"This is a legal and public relations disaster in the making," Yūji said.

"I think we have it under control," Gen said. "Soon, all the Simulacra in San Francisco will be expired as well, and there will be no more beta units operating in the general population."

"Why do you think San Francisco County Health will conveniently forget about the Rebarin vial? Our company name is printed on it."

"We'll deny it, say the labeling is fake. How many Simulacra are there in San Francisco?"

"Fifteen," Yūji said. He didn't count Nausicaa.

Yūji rode with his uncle to a sukiyaki restaurant. They ordered plates of thinly sliced beef and two large bottles of beer. The food arrived just before eleven, and Gen ate like a farmhand. Yūji, sat opposite him and couldn't bring even one slice of beef to his mouth.

"Are you still dressing up in women's kimonos?" Gen asked Yūji.

"No," Yūji said, lying. Yūji's uncle was convinced his cross-dressing was the source of his occasional bouts of depression, which it wasn't. If anything, it was an escape for Yūji, but his uncle failed to understand.

When they were done, Gen drove them back to his apartment in Tsu City.

Gen asked Yūji to follow him up to the attic. He handed Yūji a wooden box. Yūji stared at the carved wood detail and lifted the lid. Inside was a shiny, stainless steel sword with a worn, leather grip.

Yūji recognized it was a *wakizashi* short sword. "It dates back to the 17th century from the Battle of Sekigahara," Gen said.

Yūji lifted the sword out of the box and held the leading edge up to the light. The sword smelled like musty clothing.

"Nice line," he said. He inspected the tip of the sword and then looked at the handle. He turned the sword over and noticed a blemish on the other side. He looked closer and saw it was an engraving. It looked like the address of a website.

"What's this?" he asked.

"That URL is where all the documents are saved."

"What documents?"

"Everything I wrote down while developing St. Bartholomew's hemophilia and Rebarin—lab tests, formulas, reagents. It's basically the ingredients to making the vaccine."

"I don't get it."

"You or someone else may find it helpful one day."

"Okay," Yūji said, unsure.

"It's about licensing and control," Gen said. "Think of it like the Android operating system on a cell phone. Every time a company makes an Android phone, they pay a licensing fee to Google. Now, imagine if, among the universe of millions of Android phones in the global market, some of them started reproducing on their own—a sort of 'self-bootlegging.' Google would lose out on the licensing revenue for the bootleg phones."

"In other words, Google wouldn't be able to just turn off all the bootleg phones. They would have to create malware, like a computer virus, to disable the bootleg versions without negatively affecting the licensed versions?"

"Precisely."

"Google wouldn't want that malware to affect licensed phones."

"Correct, and that's why the malware would have to be specific and targeted, like the Stuxnet virus, which disabled Iranian uranium centrifuges in 2010."

"How would Google ensure the licensed phones aren't affected?" Yūji asked.

"By including the vaccine with a software update for all the existing licensed phones and pre-installing the vaccine in new models."

Yūji put the sword back in the wooden box with extreme care. It was more than just a sword; it was a time bomb.

"I can't be responsible for this," he said.

"I know we disagree about many things, but believe me when I say that the documents stored on the remote server are your insurance policy."

"Against what?"

"It's no secret Big Adachi wants you gone."

"You're saying I won't get fired if I take this sword?"

"I don't know if you'll get fired. Santomi Bremen will cease funding the field trials because they were successful."

Gen continued, "News of the mysterious disease will soon be gone from the front-page news because it will turn out to only have affected 15 homeless people in San Francisco. Their cases will be archived and eventually forgotten. At some point, though, Santomi Bremen, or whatever the company is called after the AnthropAI merger, could resurrect the disease."

"Why?" Yūji handed the sword back to Gen.

"I don't know why, Yūji, but it's possible. Think of this as an insurance policy."

Yūji returned to Tokyo the next morning and went straight to the office. In the afternoon, Black Cat Express Delivery called from the company's lobby and dropped off a package for him. Yūji saw it was from Gen, so he didn't bother opening it. He knew it was the sword he'd given back to him the previous night.

Job Posting: Technical Support Specialist

AUTOMind - Full-Time | Job Date: 11-04-2016

<u>About Us</u>
AUTOMind (formerly AnthropAI and Santomi Bremen) is dedicated to improving lives through automation and artificial intelligence through the wonders of Cellular Memory. Our patented AUTOMinder cylinders make your day easier by handling mundane tasks and let you focus on what's important. AUTOMinders play your favorite music, find the best hair salon, make reservations at your favorite restaurant, buy your concert tickets, and even book your next vacation. AUTOMinders listen to you and do what you ask.

Once you join our team, you'll learn about the exciting future we have planned to merge our core product line with social media powerhouse, MeeBee, and boutique bioengineering and pharma powerhouse, Santomi Bremen. Together, we can change the world!

AUTOMind's Technical Support Specialists are our superheroes. We're looking for people who love technology and who love to be champions of AUTOMind products.

At AUTOMind, our customers are our guests. We strive to offer Best-Of-Class support in their journey.

Please note we are specifically looking for candidates with availability for our evening shifts. Schedules fall within the following days and hours: Sunday-Thursday & Tuesday-Saturday 1AM-10AM or 8PM-5AM

<u>Is this you?</u>
- You value each guest's journey. Your thirst for knowledge is bottomless—between guest interactions, you're researching the latest feature or recent industry blog and

Tweeting about it to the world.

- You respond to each guest's needs with Jedi-like focus.

- You're sensitive and patient with guests who are non-technical, from guiding them through device boot-up to walking them through the latest firmware update in a way they understand, but you can also speak to tech junkies with the fluency of a Kubernetes Version 1.4 developer.

- Your life is balanced between work, social networking, gaming, socializing, and all the other things you love to do, like family.

- You are a self-described geek—whether it is computers or colonics—living life with intention and passion.

- You are adaptable and can speak the language of AUTOMinders.

<u>This is our customer: Guests</u>
Our guests are diverse—people all over the globe — think: yoga to skin therapies to *kendō* to psychological treatments.

Their dreams and livelihoods are in our hands—they trust us to support them 24/7.

While not always nerdy like us, our guests are what keep us going. We learn all we can about our guests.

<u>This is us</u>
We let you be you. Why would we not?

We are Passionate about Software, with Service as the key word.

Technical Support is our Front Line in the Battle for Excellence.

We provide Best-Of-Class guest service, worldwide, bar none.

We are constantly shape-shifting, adding features and applications.

We have an open-door policy because we don't do doors.

We promote the best and brightest from within — those who think outside the box, because there is no box at AUTOMind.

We make work fun—we have comic books in the break room.

We like to break things in the break room.

We are a Community of Ideators who work hard and play harder with things like juggling clubs to a meditation room to Final Four basketball brackets.

We value Passion, Creativity, and Loyalty.

Be part of a winning team!

I, Nausicaa

part 2: june 1991

How Kiernan and Yūji Met in 1991

Phylla, you're probably wondering why I didn't track down Yūji after my encounter and try to kill him. Well, the simple fact is, he returned to Japan before I had the chance. After that, the presidential election happened, people marched in the streets wearing pink hats, and a misogynist, racist President was sworn into office. He declared he would bring an end to "American Carnage," but he ended up being a catalyst by bungling the US Government's response to the COVID-19 pandemic.

For about a month after the harrowing experience of being abducted and having my body violated with a needle and an unknown substance, I saw Kiernan on the street corner regularly for about a month until, one day, he wasn't there. I asked Marko what happened to him, and he said Kiernan was no longer working for Marcella at HealthSafe, but rather had become a client, a user, again. I managed to track him down to a dilapidated RV in the long-term parking lot at SFO Airport, and all he could talk about was when he first met Yūji back in the early '90s in Japan.

Based on what Kiernan told me, Yūji was battling depression back in 1991 when they first met. I hacked into the patient health database at Shinagawa Ward Psychiatric Hospital in Tokyo and downloaded his various psychiatric reports, one of which was an anonymous call to a suicide prevention hotline that, he later informed the hospital, he had made from northern Japan during a road trip with Kiernan and their tea ceremony teacher, Masa-sensei.

Below is a verbatim account from Kiernan, as well as the medical records for Yūji that I managed to locate.

Kiernan's Road Trip with Masa-sensei

Back in the analog days of mix tapes, floppy disks, airmail envelopes, and long-distance calling cards, I was a hair-frazzled lead singer in my own progressive band of sexual confusion. I adored Robert Smith from The Cure. I memorized the lyrics to every song on the album, "Disintegration." Moodiness, melancholy, and angst were my beat. I was a virgin, and Desperation Street was where I lived.

I was attracted to hard-to-get types, and Yūji was the first.

It was the summer of 1991, and I had been living a repressed life as a foreigner in Japan for two years. My teaching contract in Matsusaka was coming to an end. I decided not to "re-up" another year. It was too easy to renew, and I craved a life of intention. Teaching English in Japan was just too fucking easy.

If I stayed, I'd learn to read the newspaper and discuss politics in Japanese with fluency and pizzaz. I'd tell jokes in the local dialect and make appearances on local television as a *tarento*, or "talent." I'd sing karaoke in front of complete strangers with smug pride. In other words, I'd become a piece in Japan's virtual museum of exotic foreigners, on display anywhere and everywhere.

I knew Americans living in Japan who had become that. Being a foreigner in Japan was a career choice because foreigners were a constant source of entertainment. We were walking, living, breathing content providers for the public.

In the late 1980s, Americans feared Japan. We thought Japanese companies were hell-bent on buying our country. With all the money Japanese companies made from Panasonic video cassette players and Honda Accords, they started buying important pieces of real estate. Newspaper articles portrayed Japanese people as a monolithic army of salarymen who wore identical suits, worked incredibly long hours, and ate expensive sushi covered in gold leaf from the breasts of Russian models lying face up on banquet tables.

Inside Japan, things couldn't have been more different. A post-teen boy band in silver jumpsuits and roller skates called "Hikaru Genji" appeared on television. A movie about a plucky female tax collector came to the theaters, and Yakuza gangs began forcing families out of their apartments and flipping property because of skyrocketing land prices.

June is monsoon season in Japan. I find myself during that month in 1991 sitting in a Daihatsu mini truck speeding full throttle up the Tohoku Expressway. Yūji is in the driver's seat. He hates Hikaru Genji as much as he hates The Cure, but he relents and lets me play The Cure's "Boys Don't Cry."

With rain dumping from the sky, the air smells of mildew, like the taste of rotting apple. We've been on the road for less than an hour, yet my trousers stick to my thighs from sweat. There's no A/C in this golf-cart sized contraption, so I roll down the window to get air flowing.

Daihatsu trucks are economical — low cost and good mileage — but they have tiny seats. Yūji's body odor reminds me of toasted caraway seeds. His skin looks soft. I pretend to focus beyond his face at the passing rice fields and highway signs.

In the bed of the truck sits our 60-year-old tea ceremony instructor, Masa. He's out there in the rain by choice. Why he chose to be outside is not for me to answer. Masa has a bad hip, which is as compelling a reason as any for him to take my seat, but he says he's afraid of the black umbrella I stashed behind me.

My friendship with Masa and Yūji started three months earlier. It was St. Patrick's Day, and the town where I lived had no Irish bar, so I ended up at a "snack," which is a small hostess bar where people go to entertain clients, sing karaoke, and engage in light conversation with attractive young women. Regular customers have whole bottles of whiskey on keep with their names written in metallic pen.

Kushida's Place had three small tables with chairs and two barstools next to the counter. A television hung from the ceiling. It played karaoke videos showing song lyrics and pastoral scenes of rural Japan. Drunk patrons tried to sing along, but most times they forgot the words and ended up trying to fondle the hostesses.

Kushida-san introduced me to a bald, monk-like man who wore a black *hakama*, or men's kimono. He was the only customer wearing traditional clothes. I might have mistaken him for the Dalai Lama. Kushida-san said he taught the tea ceremony at a local high school, but his style was unorthodox, and the parent association got him removed from his teaching job. Now, he taught private lessons.

"The Japanese tea ceremony is dying," he said. "Jazz is dying, too."

I asked what he meant.

"Young people aren't interested in learning, and there's nobody good left to lead the way."

He looked lonely, and he offered me a glass of Suntory whiskey on ice.

"I'm glad you two have met," Kushida-san said. "Ki-chan," (she referred to me as that by shortening "Kiernan" to "ki" and then adding the diminutive *chan*) "teaches English at the junior college."

"Masa-sensei," she said to me, "is very well-respected, but he sometimes has strange ideas. We met in high school. I went to Ise Business High School, and he went to Ise Technical."

"I was her boyfriend a long time ago," Masa said.

Kushida-san made a sour face and gently hit his hand. "It was only kissing," she said.

She turned and went to the bar to get a second glass for me. She returned with a glass and a bucket of fresh ice.

"Masa-sensei can give you a lesson in the tea ceremony," she said to me. She placed the ice bucket on the small table, plucked out two round ice cubes with metal tongs, and dropped them into a tumbler.

I knew nothing about tea, but I had the impression the tea ceremony was in the same league as flower arranging—it was what young women learned in preparation for marriage, or what middle-aged women did in their spare time. It provided a venue where they could share gossip or plan out their lives while their husbands worked and drank themselves to death.

"What's the headcount of students signed up for your fall class?" Kushida-san asked. She pulled the cork out of the whiskey bottle and poured two fingers' worth into my glass.

Masa took a sip of his drink.

"Have you thought about advertising?" I asked. I didn't know if tea instructors did that.

"No," Kushida-san said, "Masa-sensei doesn't advertise,"

"Too commercial," Masa said under his breath.

"Well, if it makes you feel better, I know at least two other tea instructors who are having difficulty finding students," Kushida-san said. She replaced the cork in the whiskey bottle and handed me the drink. The ice cubes swirled around one turn in the glass.

"*Kanpai?*" she asked. She held up her own glass, gave me a wink, and gestured to Masa and me to do the same.

"*Kanpai,*" we both said in response, and we clinked glasses.

"How many students can you take?" I asked.

"Four at a time, if they're quick learners."

"Are your students all females?" I asked. I took a sip of the whiskey, and it burned the back of my throat like cheap swill.

"The tea ceremony is dying," he said again.

"What about male students?" I asked.

"Speaking in general, men have no patience," he said, "but I have one male student."

Kushida-san gave him a disbelieving look.

"What?" Masa asked her.

"Sort of," she said.

"He's living with me at the moment."

I wondered how a depressed tea ceremony teacher was living with another man whom Kushida-san thought wasn't one.

"What's his name?" I asked.

"Isn't it 'Hana Maeda?'" Kushida-san asked.

"That's a female name, isn't it?" I asked.

"Yes."

"How long has he...er, she lived with you?"

"A few months," he said. "His uncle owns a tea plantation outside of town."

I asked Masa if I could see him perform the tea ceremony.

He suggested we finish our whiskey and take a taxi back to his place. He had a large collection of local sake he wanted me to try. "Do you like sake?" he asked.

"Only when I've got food in my belly," I said.

"Good, let's stop by a ramen stand," he said.

The ramen place was closed, so Masa took me back to his place. The house was on the outskirts of town, within walking distance of the shores of Ise Bay. It was a modernist, all-concrete affair with exposed beams. I followed him inside, and he gave me a quick tour of the place, but I was drunk and tired. I staggered to the living room and passed out.

When I awoke the next morning, I was half-splayed across a sectional couch, wondering if I could get my eyeballs to move in the same direction. I heard a young man's voice singing falsetto to Miyako Harumi and Miyazaki Masashi's duet, "Osaka for Two." The tune had a plaintive, bluesy swing to it. The house smelled like booze.

I slid half of my body down to the floor and attempted to get up. My right arm wobbled and collapsed. I rolled over to my other side and grabbed the dining room chair to pull myself up.

Framed paintings covered the living room wall. One was a lithograph of Gustave Courbet's *L'Origine du Monde*, which featured a reclining nude woman's legs exposed by bed sheets pulled up to her waist with her genitalia in the center. Next to that were Masa's own paintings, which were done in muted purple, dull gray, and olive green with titles like *Goddess of Creation* and *Third Century Shaman Queen*—also variations on female genitalia. Then, I remembered Masa telling me the night before the images came to him in dreams. He said that, according to Japanese myth, Japan's islands came from goddess Izanami's womb, and the Japanese Emperor descended from Izanami's daughter, Amaterasu.

Next to the windows facing Ise Bay were tidal charts printed in large font and a pair of high-powered binoculars. I picked up the binoculars and looked toward the water, but I couldn't see anything interesting.

I put the binoculars on the table and walked toward the singing.

"*Ah aah, dakishimete, futari no Osaka…rah--suu--toh--dahn--suu.*"

The young man's voice got louder as I approached the kitchen. When I crossed the threshold, I saw a fragile, gorgeous young Japanese woman in a purple women's kimono with black piping and an orange-hued obi. She turned to look at me and I'll never forget that face. She was wearing eyeliner, and her hair was tied in a bun. She was holding an iron skillet in her left hand and fluffing an egg omelet with long chopsticks.

"Good morning," she said in Japanese. "I'm Hana Maeda," she said using the formality of a Japanese woman in her mid-fifties. She asked my name, and I told her.

"Nice to meet you," she said. "I saw you sleeping in the living room. It looks like you were out late last night with Masa-sensei."

"What kind of omelet are you preparing?" I asked.

"Rice omelet," she said. "Would you like some?" She made a slight upturn of her cheeks without smiling.

"Yes, please," I said, unsure if I could hold down food.

"Please sit," she said with an elegant, upturned hand. She moved with the well-practiced grace of an elevator lady in a Japanese department store.

Her long, soft hair was parted to the right, and her bangs fell in front of her eyes.

She wore a touch of mascara and a hint of lip liner.

When she plated the omelet and put it on the table, I wolfed it down like a hungry prisoner. Hana Maeda made a second one and slid it off the non-stick pan and onto a squarish, hand-thrown ceramic plate. She took my plate and chopsticks and placed them in the sink.

"Did Masa-sensei show you the tea ceremony room?" she asked.

"No," I said.

"Let me show you." Hana Maeda took the omelet and carried it with her. She shuffled in her kimono and slippers with her feet turned slightly inward.

The tearoom was down the hall and to the right. Tatami mats lined the floor. The entrance had a sliding door made of wood lattice with a thin, paper veneer decorated with the faded outline of the Tokugawa imperial crest. A small, brown stain covered the bottom left corner of the sliding door.

"That stain isn't mine," Hana Maeda said. "One of his female students fell while carrying a small plate of desserts."

"What kind?" I asked.

"Akafuku. It's a local mochi. Do you know what mochi is?"

"Yes, it's a sweet rice cake made of pounded rice and red bean paste."

"Correct. Normally, the bean paste is on the inside, but Akafuku turns it inside out, and the bean paste is on the outside. That stain is from the bean paste."

I admired the supporting pillar that framed the left side of the alcove. I ran my hand along the smooth, red pine and thought about the beach and the surf in the town of Owase and the special dance the locals performed during the Obon festival. The lintel spanning the top of the outer corner of the alcove was made of cedar. The hanging scroll inside the alcove showed something written in a stylized script I couldn't read.

"What does the scroll say?" I asked.

"It's a *waka* written by Motōri Norinaga. He lived in the 18th century and spent time here in Matsusaka. His castle is in the center of town."

"Kiernan-san, I see you met Yūji," I heard Masa say behind us. I turned and saw he was referring to Hana Maeda.

Hana Maeda handed Masa the omelet.

"Thanks," he said, taking it from her.

Masa told me his tea school was failing because his teaching style was obscure and inscrutable. People wanted brand-name recognition from established schools like Urasenke and Omotesenke; they wanted straightforward and predictable procedures.

"Those schools are like Amway," he said. "You buy your way to the top and recruit others. Their tea implements are corporate and made in big factories in China. All my tea implements are handmade," he said, "because things are like people, and each has object has a life of its own."

"Can you teach me the tea ceremony?" I asked.

"First, I need to teach you about *wabi-sabi*," he said. "Think of *wabi* as the simple line of a curved piece of driftwood, and *sabi* as a pair of well-worn dress shoes — flawed, but full of character. A tea bowl may appear misshapen, but on finer closer inspection, you realize it's the product of hundreds of hours of work. A Chinese tea bowl might be perfectly round and adorned with red glaze and gold leaf, but a Japanese tea bowl with *wabi-sabi* is uneven and drab. It's unique and reflects the personality of its creator."

I mis-heard Masa, because I thought he was talking about green Japanese horseradish used in sushi, wasabi.

"Think of *wabi-sabi* as a simple flower arrangement, a single cherry tree branch whose fragile, white blossoms hang by spider silk, poised to fall. The feeling of *wabi-sabi* comes while sitting on your legs, your calves go numb, and you take a sip of fresh matcha tea, the plain-looking tea bowl resting gently between your hands. It could be raining outside, and the pitter-patter of drops on the roof makes you feel at peace with yourself and the world."

"With patience, you'll learn," Masa said, "but not today. I will call you a taxi to take you home."

"I'll leave on the condition that you give me a lesson at some point," I said.

"Of course," he said, "how about next Thursday?"

"I could come by after school."

"Perfect."

Over the next several weeks, I went to Masa's home every day. I was disappointed not to see Yūji there, but it gave me a chance to get up to speed so I wouldn't embarrass myself in front of him.

I offered to pay Masa for the lessons, but he refused. He said he was repaying a debt he owed to the American soldiers who, just after the War, gave him chocolate bars. I thought that was an odd thing to say about an occupying force who had been the enemy.

I followed Masa down the hallway to the tearoom, and

when he slid open the screen door, the iron kettle in the center of the room was steaming and the utensils were laid out in order: tea caddy, tea scoop, tea bowl, whisk, ladle, and water discarding container.

It wasn't until later that I learned Masa's belief system bore a strong resemblance to *tsukumogami*, which is the belief that certain objects become spirits after the passage of many years. Masa believed the spirits in his tea utensils spoke to him.

"These tea utensils run the show. I am merely their vessel."

I stared at the collection of items and wondered what the Hell he was talking about.

"How?" I asked.

"If you listen carefully, you can hear them," he said.

I thought of particle physics and wondered if Masa was tuning into subatomic activity.

Each day, Masa changed tearoom decorations as well as how he prepared the tea. The flowers, which sat in a vase near the wall, were the product of Masa's prodigious dumpster diving. With the refuse of local florists, he made rustic arrangements from discarded lavender, dill, baby's breath, and campanulas.

Desserts were day-old mochi rice cakes, or in some cases, *dora-yaki*, small pancakes folded in half and filled with sweet, red bean paste.

"Why pay money for these?" he asked me rhetorically. "If I bought what some consider to be the perfect dessert, it wouldn't be authentic."

Masa, however, didn't skimp on tea.

"Matcha must be fresh, otherwise it tastes like chalk," he said.

To me, the fresh stuff tasted like chalk, but I kept that to myself. It didn't help that sometimes Masa served a chalk-like dessert with the matcha. Chalk and double chalk!

By the third week, I grew to like the taste of matcha, and the chalkiness didn't bother me. I asked Masa about adding sugar, and he acted like he was having a heart attack.

"That's a tea-crime," he said.

I said some desserts had matcha added, and it was akin to

drinking sweetened matcha.

"Those desserts use culinary-grade matcha," he said. "We drink premium blend."

Doctor Hosokawa

From the Office of Dr. Ken Hosokawa
Patient Notes and Transcript for Yūji Morita
Date: 1991 June 12 10:00

Patient was referred to me by the Tokyo Regional Mental Health Institute.

23-year-old male from Tokyo employed by large Japanese bank. Patient treated for depression at the Shinagawa Ward Psychiatric Hospital. Patient requested 6-month, unpaid leave from work. Patient is married with no children. Patient came to Matsusaka to stay with family. He lives with his tea ceremony teacher.

Doctor: I'm here to listen. We're going to talk about whatever you want. If you'd like to hear my perspective, I'm happy to provide it, nothing more. Your patient record indicates you attempted suicide a month ago. Since that time, you've been wearing women's clothing. You've undergone trauma at some point in your life, and it is important to focus on healing. Please wear whatever makes you feel comfortable.
Patient: I met my wife in college.
Doctor: I also met my wife in college.
Patient: I changed my last name to my wife's family name.
Doctor: That's not very common. How does that make you feel?
Patient: I'm neither here nor there about it.
Doctor: Did it affect your parents?
Patient: My parents died when I was 18. My last name was "Maeda."
Doctor: "Maeda," as in "Maeda Tea?"
Patient: Yes, it's my uncle's farm, now. Doctor, your Japanese has an accent. Were you born in Japan?
Doctor: You have a good ear. I was born in America. I'm

second-generation Japanese American.

Patient: When did you move to Japan?

Doctor: 1965. Tell me about your wife. What's her name?

Patient: Sumiko.

Doctor: Tell me about Sumiko.

Patient: She's very messy.

Doctor: Can you elaborate?

Patient: Her family is wealthy. She grew up with housekeepers doing her laundry. She ate meals prepared by a cook.

Doctor: Your wife doesn't cook for you?

Patient: I love to cook; that's not the problem.

Doctor: She doesn't do laundry?

Patient: We have an unconventional relationship.

Doctor: I don't make judgments.

Patient: But you were.

Doctor: How?

Patient: By asking if she does the laundry.

Doctor: It was a clarifying question.

Patient: You're wondering why I married her?

Doctor: I didn't say that. Do you love her?

Patient: We didn't marry for love. I care for her very much, but she is messy. She works at a bank, and I develop robots.

Doctor: Robots? What kind of robots?

Patient: Industrial robots, like the ones used by Honda in Suzuka to build automobiles.

Doctor: Is your wife an office lady?

Patient: She's division chief. She refused to sacrifice her career for marriage. She refuses to become a slave to her husband.

Doctor: Slave?

Patient: You know, someone to do the dirty work — the washing, the cleaning, the taking out the trash. We used to have people who did that for us. The *burakumin*.

Doctor: Please, that is a bad word. Let's not talk about that now.

Patient: Why? It's a fact. It's part of our history. We still have hiring companies doing background checks on people to make sure they're not part of that caste.

Doctor: I believe the correct term is "New Citizen."

Patient: Fine, but there's no point in not talking about it.
Doctor: Tell me why you brought up this topic?
Patient: I just think our great country is losing its way. People are confused and are not sure of their purpose, which is to have more children so Japan can grow and thrive.
Doctor: Are you planning on having children?
Patient: Me? No, it's not my thing. My wife and I have an understanding. She has boyfriends.
Doctor: Plural?
Patient: There is the guy who drives her places. There's another guy who takes her out to dinner...
Doctor: Those aren't one and the same?
Patient: No, there's also the guy who gives her presents, and the guy she sleeps with...
Doctor: Really?
Patient: Really.
Doctor: Do you sleep with your wife?
Patient: We are open about our feelings. We give each other advice.
Doctor: Does she approve of your lifestyle?
Patient: It's not her place. Sumiko doesn't ask me to give it up. I've met some of her boyfriends. I don't share her taste in men.
Doctor: Why did you attempt to kill yourself?
Patient: Mmm, I don't know. Heartbreak, perhaps?
Doctor: Over whom?
Patient: I won't say.
Doctor: What is her name?
Patient: He's a well-known figure in politics, a friend of Sumiko's.
Doctor: Does she know?
Patient: Of course!
Doctor: What advice did she give?
Patient: She said I should find someone else.
Doctor: What happened?
Patient: He led me on. He was seeing someone else the whole time.
Doctor: How did that make you feel?
Patient: Betrayed? I guess you could say that.

Doctor: What are you going to do now?
Patient: I'm taking time off from work, away from Tokyo, working at my uncle's farm.
Doctor: Tell me about 'emotional self-immolation.'
Patient: Where did you hear that?
Doctor: You put it on your intake form. You said you have thoughts of emotional self-immolation.
Patient: I imagine what it's like to be burned alive, like that monk during the Vietnam War.
Doctor: What brought that to mind?
Patient: George Winne, Jr., who lit himself on fire at UC San Diego.
Doctor: How did your parents die?
Patient: I'd rather not discuss it.
Doctor: Okay, fine. When will you return to Tokyo?
Patient: I don't know. I recently met an American. He's cute, but it'll never last. He's not Japanese.
Doctor: You say, "It'll never last," meaning you're already in a relationship with him? What's his name?
Patient: I'd rather not say.
Doctor: You're in your early twenties. You've only been married a few years.
Patient: Are you implying that I'll change, that I'll switch somehow to liking women?
Doctor: I'm not saying that.
Patient: Your question is leading in that direction.
Doctor: I'm only here to listen.
Patient: I feel a stronger sense of closeness, or *amae*, when I'm with another man. When I'm with Sumiko, I feel warm and comfortable, but I'm not attracted to her. I'm not attracted to any woman, really.
Doctor: It may be something you'll hide for the rest of your life, given how society treats homosexuals.
Patient: I'm not a homosexual. You said you were only going to listen.
[Patient ends session. There were no more sessions with this patient]

Daihatsu

From the passenger seat of the Daihatsu, I turn back and look through the rear window to check on Masa sitting in the bed of the pickup. He's sitting cross legged, eyes closed, facing the cab. His eyelids flutter from the passing air as our truck hurtles down the highway. His billowy *hakama* puffs out from his shoulders like an untrimmed sail. Behind him, covered with a blue tarpaulin strapped down with bungee cords, is the entirety of his worldly possessions, salvaged from his foreclosed home.

I compare the somber man in the truck bed with the one who drank whiskey and drove me to a ramen shop at midnight.

"He is meditating," Yūji says.

"Sure," I say, not wanting to argue.

The Daihatsu crosses a lane marker, and I feel the suspension bottom out. Yūji has the accelerator to the floor, and the speedometer is topping out at 60 miles per hour. Yūji is wearing an embroidered women's kimono in cloud-white and lemon chiffon. At rest stops, Japanese people do a double take, both because of Yūji's appearance and his withering, female voice.

I joined these two on this journey to help Yūji move Masa to a full care facility that specializes in dementia. Yūji filled me in on his condition before my teaching stint ended. I could've spent my last two weeks in Japan snorkeling in Okinawa or hiking in Takayama, but I would've been alone. This way, I could be with Yūji.

Our itinerary included four Japanese hot springs, seven roadside museums, and an abandoned pachinko parlor. Yūji devised the itinerary, and Masa objected to the abandoned pachinko parlor, so we ditched that.

"Does Masa have relatives in Obihiro?" I ask Yūji.

Yūji gives me a look that says, "No more questions."

I tilt the seat back a few notches, close my eyes and listen to the last song on The Cure album, "The Same Deep Water As You." The song title makes me think how much I want to understand Yūji.

I reach behind the seat and pull out a grape juice box from a Lawson's shopping bag. I pry the plastic straw from the side of the box and slide off the plastic wrapper. I pop the pointed end of the straw into the foil at the top of the box and sip. I gulp down a mouthful of cool, sugary juice, and I imagine it must feel like what mainlining crack feels like.

"What are your plans after Japan?" Yūji asks.

"Does Masa see things?" I ask back.

"He's nearsighted," Yūji says.

"Does he see ghosts?"

"Ghosts?"

"Ghost umbrellas?"

"Dunno."

"Has he ever said that kind of thing before?"

"Maybe."

"Why is he afraid of the black umbrella?"

"Masa-sensei reads a lot."

"Novels?"

"History."

"About umbrellas?"

"Yes."

I give up at this point.

"How long until the next stop?" I ask.

"Why?"

"Curious."

"Three-and-a-half hours."

"Did you calculate that back at the hotel?"

"Yes, assuming there is no traffic in Iwatsuki."

"Do you vote?" I ask Yūji.

Yūji looks at me quickly to see if I'm joking.

"Why?"

"Which political party?"

"Liberal Democratic."

"Somehow, I had you pegged for a Socialist," I say.

Yūji laughs for the first time in a long time. "I don't like

Doi-san."

Takako Doi is the leader of the Socialist Democrats.

"Is that because Doi-san is a woman?"

"She's crazy."

"How so?"

"Such boring suits."

"That makes her crazy?"

"Unimaginative hair, and she opposes the US-Japan Security Treaty."

"Sounds sensible to me."

The Cure song finishes.

"What do you want to hear?" I ask.

"No more music," he says.

In Japan, I felt drawn to the sensitive types, men who were unafraid of showing their femininity. The term, "goat man," was popular back then. Like a goat, the ideal Japanese man of the nineties was both strong and gentle; tough, and sensitive. A goat man supported his wife in her career. A goat man cooked dinner and washed the dishes.

To Japanese men of an earlier generation, goat men were ninnies, but to me they were lovely. Unfortunately, none of them was gay.

Matsusaka was a small town, and there were no gay bars. Being openly gay was pretty much out of the question. Until it wasn't. Knowing Yūji meant I could wear tight shorts and tank tops around Masa's house. Yūji wore his kimonos and sang female karaoke songs better than any Japanese woman I knew.

A week before we left Matsusaka, I got a telephone call at work. I was in the teacher's office when I heard my name over the school loudspeakers. I picked up the nearest telephone.

"Hello?" I said.

"Mr. McCreighton," the receptionist said, "you have a telephone call from Ms. Hana Maeda."

Then I remembered Yūji's other name, and I picked up the receiver.

"Kiernan?" she asked. I wondered if she was in trouble.

"Will you meet me at my uncle's tea farm?"

"Sure," I said. "Are you okay?" I asked.

"Yes," she said.

My heart raced.

Not long after that, I saw her pull up in front of the school entrance in the back of a taxi. I hopped in, and I noticed she was wearing a black geisha wig, makeup, and a kimono. I wondered if the taxi driver knew about her.

She told me how her parents died while on vacation in Hawaii. I told her how my dad died when I was barely old enough to talk, but my Ma was still her deadly funny self.

"When I die, I want to go fast," I said, "like your parents."

"I hear asphyxiation from carbon monoxide is painless," she said.

"Asphyxiation?" I asked.

She gazed out the window and gave a faint smile.

"What do your uncle and aunt do?" I asked.

"My uncle is a medical researcher at a large biotech firm, but he wants to return to teaching."

"What company?"

"It's a joint venture with a German company."

"What are they famous for?"

"They're working on Hepatitis C and *hito men'eki fuzen uirusu*."

It was my first time hearing how to say, "AIDS" in Japanese.

"Is that even a problem in Japan?" I asked.

"Not here in the countryside," she said, "but it's an open secret in Tokyo that Japanese businessmen are returning from sex tours in Thailand and have it."

The taxi drove us up a gravel driveway and stopped in front of an aluminum-sided warehouse. We entered the building through a side door that opened to an office area. Three uniformed office ladies greeted us. I heard them giggle, and I guessed they knew Yūji's alternate persona.

We walked past a display case featuring an ancient Japanese sword. Hana Maeda said it was called a *wakizashi* and dated back to the Kamakura Period. It belonged to her great, great-grandfather.

We exited through a back door and entered a large greenhouse filled with tea plants. Hana Maeda said the first tea harvest was around the third week of May, a few weeks before the rainy season. Two weeks before harvest, they covered the tea plants with tarps to block out the sunlight. He said they covered the plants to force the chlorophyll to the outer leaves.

I asked about the tea picking equipment, and she said they picked the tea leaves by hand. The pickers used to be all Japanese, but more recently they came from China and Thailand.

I followed her into the processing area, and she pointed to large tubs where the taps were left running with water flowing over the sides.

"Here's where they wash the leaves," she said. "It's like laundry."

We walked over to the grinding area where granite wheels spun slowly around horizontally, and tiny amounts of green powder trickled out of the sides.

"This is it?"

"It takes an hour to grind 28 grams of matcha."

"That's equivalent to 28 paper clips," I said, "which is nothing."

"You can't drink paper clips."

"No wonder it's as expensive as cocaine," I said.

Hana Maeda gave me a judgmental look. "My mother's family owned a hot spring south of here, in Wakayama."

"Let's go!" I said.

"It's closed."

"Closed for good?"

"Years ago."

"That's a shame."

"I was born there."

"In the town?"

"No, in one of the pools."

"You're shittin' me."

"My mother went into labor while soaking."

"She didn't get out?"

"She couldn't."

"Or she didn't want to. Warm water is relaxing and reduces labor pain."

Hana Maeda took me into a darkened storage room and closed the door. She removed her slippers, stepped up onto two elevated tatami mats and removed her *yukata*. "She" was now a "he" standing naked and vulnerable.

I unbuckled my pants, left the slippers on the floor, and joined him, forgetting to remove my white briefs. He slid his hands into them and pushed my underwear to the ground. There, with the sound of grinding granite on the other side of the wall, we fucked, and that was how I lost my virginity.

Afterward, Yūji told me about his robots, how he named them even though they were basically huge, mechanical arms that welded auto chassis and installed windshields.

"It doesn't seem like you," I said.

"How so? Is it because I wear a kimono and makeup sometimes?"

I thought about it for a moment and realized he was right. It didn't fit my idea of a cross dresser being a robotics designer.

"Maybe your fashion sense is a way to rebel against the rigid work environment of mechanical engineering," I said.

"Who said anything about mechanical engineering?" Yūji replied. "I work in memory technology. I design the brains that power the machines. Have you read Issac Asimov's I, Robot? He introduced the Three Laws of Robotics, the first of which is to not harm humans."

Again, this was not something I could've guessed by looking at him, but what did I know about him? Very little, but I wanted so desperately to understand.

Doctor Yayoi

From the Office of Dr. Atsuko Yayoi
Patient Notes and Transcript for Yūji Morita
Date: 1991 June 20 16:30

This is the patient's second visit. Patient comes to me via referral from Dr. Ken Hosokawa. Patient is 23 years old and has returned wearing a woman's kimono and makeup, as before.

Patient: I'm sorry for being late.

Doctor: You were telling me about how the American boy you're seeing loves you more than you love him.

Patient: I've changed my mind. I have strong feelings for him, but I know it won't work out.

Doctor: That sounds very practical but know that every relationship is asymmetrical. The question is whether it's sustainable.

Patient: I like him more than he likes me.

Doctor: How so?

Patient: I go to sleep trying to work everything out in my head, but I come up empty.

Doctor: Why?

Patient: I'm married.

Doctor: Oh. You didn't put that on your intake form. How long have you been married?

Patient: I keep wishing I had someone else, another lover. Then, I'd have a convenient reason to leave him.

Doctor: You feel powerless over your emotions.

Patient: He acts like we'll be together forever. He's happy, but he shouldn't be. Americans are overly optimistic, but life isn't that way.

Doctor: How do you think it'll end?

Patient: His work visa runs out in July. He must return home. Plus, he's a foreigner, and I can't have that for the long term.

Doctor: Will you return to your wife?

Patient: That's my point.

Doctor: Does the American know you're married?

Patient: No.

Doctor: Why haven't you told him?

Patient: I'm afraid he wouldn't understand.

Doctor: Have you tried?

Patient: My situation is too complicated for him to understand.

Doctor: You insist things are doomed.

Patient: Yes.

Doctor: How do you think he's going to react when he finds out?

Patient: He'll be upset.

Doctor: Does not telling him about your wife give you more sense of control over the relationship?

Patient: Control?

Doctor: Doesn't it feel like you have more control?

Patient: I want the hurting to stop.

[Patient ends session. There were no more sessions with this patient]

Tengu

Yūji's driving is starting to scare me. He's sleepy, and he's beginning to stray over the divider line separating us from oncoming traffic. We're driving faster than the Daihatsu was designed — the rear quarter panels are wobbling, and the suspension feels squishy. I try to distract myself by thumbing through a map of the national highway system. Out of the corner of my eye, I see Masa's reflection in the passenger side rear view mirror. He's standing up in the back of the truck.

"What the fuck is he doing?" I ask Yūji.

"Dunno," Yūji says, returning his meditative gaze at the pavement being sucked under the hood of the truck.

Masa begins yelling, and he points up at the sky. His hand is in a fist, and he moves it out from his nose repeatedly like a pantomime Pinocchio.

Yūji turns on the left turn signal, removes his foot from the accelerator and pulls off to the side of the road. As the truck comes to a stop, Yūji says Masa is yelling about something flying overhead. Yūji opens the door and gets out.

"Masa-sensei," Yūji says, "what are you yelling about?"

"I saw a *tengu*."

"What's that?" I yell out to Yūji.

"Masa-sensei says he saw a spirit that lives in the mountains. It has a long nose."

I get out of the truck, look at the sky and turn around. Cars speed past us and kick up backwash that shakes the Daihatsu.

"I don't see anything," I say to Yūji.

"Definitely a *tengu*," Masa says, turning his gaze to me. "Yūji, who is this gaijin?" he asks, pointing at me.

"That's Kiernan-san. Remember? He's riding with us."

"You never told me that," Masa says.

"Masa-sensei, your daughter will be visiting you in Obihiro."

"We must turn back now. I have a class to teach," Masa

says. "Kushida-san has my bottle of whiskey. The goddess Amaterasu is giving birth to a new country."

"Masa-sensei, you don't have any classes. The bank foreclosed on your house. Your belongings are in the back of the truck."

"Bullshit!" Masa yells. "Take me home."

Yūji looks at me to see if I heard that. He exhales and turns back to Masa. "Your new home is in Obihiro," he says in a calm voice.

Masa turns to me and says, "I must get off this truck." He bends down to hold the side of the truck bed, and he lifts his right leg over the panel. His *hakama* drapes between his legs, and it looks like he's going to fall. I hurry to the other side of the truck to help him, but I'm too late. Gravity pulls him to the ground.

I reach down to help him up, but he has landed in a soggy patch of grass. His left side is covered in mud from his leg up to his chin. He mops his face with the back of his hand.

"That was strange," he says. "Help me."

Yūji takes his other hand, and both of us pull him up.

"Are you okay?" Yūji asks.

"Not a scratch," Masa says smiling with soiled cheeks. "I gotta take a piss."

"Can you wait until we find a rest stop?" Yūji asks.

"Nope. Gotta go now," he says.

Yūji and I look around to see if there's a suitable place for Masa to go. Beyond the parking area is a clearing, and then a stand of birch trees that mark the beginning of a forest.

"I'll go over in those trees," Masa says.

"How about I go with you?" Yūji asks.

"No need. I'll be fine."

"But what if you fall again?"

"I won't fall." Masa straightens out his *hakama*, brushes off the mud and steps over the gully to the other side of a stream. He's wearing wooden clogs, which are basically a slab of wood with toe straps on the top and two smaller pieces of wood glued to the bottom. They work great in soggy grass.

As Masa goes off to pee in the woods, I walk around the

passenger side to check the time. It's almost noon.

"Are we going to eat lunch?" I ask Yūji.

"We can stop at a convenience store and pick up some rice balls and bottled tea."

I return to the passenger seat and wait for Masa to return. Yūji opens the driver's side and climbs in. He slides the ignition key into the slot and turns it one click.

I open the glove box and pull out "Aretha Franklin Live at Fillmore West, 1971." I insert the compact disc into the player. The first song is "Dr. Feelgood."

I got me a man named Dr. Feelgood. He takes care of all my pain and ills.

Yūji steps out of the cab to see if Masa is coming back.

"I don't see him," he yells.

"He's probably behind a tree," I say.

Taking care of business is this man's game.

"I'm going to look for him," Yūji says.

"But you're wearing a kimono."

I press pause on the CD player, open the door, and step out of the cab. Yūji has crossed the gully and is shuffling across the open field toward the trees, his kimono billowing in the wind.

"Sensei!" he yells. "Sensei!"

Masa is long gone. I slam the passenger door closed and follow Yūji. I hop over the gully and my feet sink into mud. I look down, and my shoes are submerged.

"Yūji!" I yell. "Yūji, you fuck. I'm stuck in the mud."

Yūji stops and looks back at me.

"You'll be fine," he yells. "Sensei!" He yells in the direction of the trees and shuffles along the embankment, avoiding the mud.

I untie my shoes and try to extract my feet. I get one foot out, stretch wide, and I place my free foot on a dry spot. I shift my weight to that foot, but as I lift my other foot, I lose my balance fall onto a rock.

In that moment of blankness, I recall going through in my head Masa's three principles of the tea ceremony:

1. Pleasure - tea is meant to be enjoyed by your guests. For

them to enjoy it, you must enjoy it as well.

2. Heart - the steps in preparing tea aren't as important as having heart and putting feeling into it. Don't sweat the details, like the number of tea sips, or the bowl's title angle. Relax and enjoy.

3. Presence of Mind - each tea ceremony stands on its own. One day, you may be focused on cleanliness, while another you may be focused on freshness of the tea itself. Either way, be true to yourself and the tea. The tea ceremony is, after all, about sharing tea.

My eyes open to see Yūji's face looking down at me and the afternoon sky overhead. He's holding my head in the crook of his arm and lap, and I feel cared for. I can smell his sweat.

"What time is it?" I ask.

"I don't know," Yūji says, looking around to see if Masa is returning.

"Did you find him?"

"I'm worried he ran off into the forest."

"Where?"

"I don't know."

Yūji looks down at me, and I realize I'm lying in the same patch of mud where I fell, which means Yūji is sitting in the mud, in his kimono.

I feel around my forehead and can't find anything until Yūji guides my fingers to the left side of my head. There is a large bump.

Yūji helps me sit up, and my head starts spinning. I lie back down in Yūji's arms.

"You need to rest longer," he says. "If you can stay here, I will drive to the next town and call an ambulance."

"No need for that," I say, "because I'm fine."

"You can't walk."

"You're right. I'll wait here."

"If you see Masa, tell him to stay with you."

"Got it."

Yūji lifts my head up and pulls himself out from under me. He lets my head rest on a mound of dirt. Mud covers the back side of his kimono, and I'm unable think of anything to say other than "Thank you."

I close my eyes and listen to Yūji walk back to the truck, start it, and pull away.

I doze off and dream that I'm smelling grilled mackerel. I see Yūji crouched next to a Hibachi grill with smoke rising from it. To his right is Masa, only Masa's face is deformed. His neck stretches out, like a telescope. His head tilts toward me. He starts making a low-pitched "*Uwan, uwan*" sound like the gurgle of a didgeridoo.

Next, I'm sitting in the tearoom in Masa's home. It's Monday evening after my first night at Masa's. Yūji greets me at the door. He's wearing a white kimono with ocean-blue wash that's dark at the hem and runs up to a lighter in shade and then fades into white around the area of his belly.

"You must be tired," Yūji says as he kneels on the raised wood floor of the foyer and bows. I sit down on a small stool near the door and remove my shoes. I leave my socks on.

Yūji stands up, and I step up, into the house.

"Here, put these on," Yūji says, and he slides a pair of fuzzy, brown slippers toward me.

I slide my feet into the slippers.

"Masa-sensei prepared a special treat for you," Yūji says.

It's my first tea ceremony, and I don't know what to expect.

I follow Yūji down the hallway. Yūji shuffles in his white tabi, which are ankle-length socks with a separation for the big toe.

We arrive at the tearoom. Yūji kneels and sits on his legs with the sliding door to his left. "Sensei, are you ready?" Yūji asks in a louder voice because the sliding doors are closed.

"Give me a minute," Masa says from behind the door.

Yūji motions me to kneel, and I do. I'm wearing jeans, and the denim is digging into the back of my thighs.

"Your lesson begins here, outside the tearoom," Yūji says.

"Okay, ready!" Masa says out loud.

Yūji slides the door open with his left hand. "Sorry for intruding," he says, as is customary before entering a room.

"Please, come in," Masa says.

I peek into the room, and Masa is sitting on his legs in the center of the room next to a steaming cauldron. On the far is a hanging scroll. Beneath it is the area reserved for fresh flowers, but it's empty, like Yūji's heart and Masa's memory.

Yūji sits upright and pulls himself, in seated position, over the dark wood threshold and onto the tatami mat in the room. He gradually inches himself toward the center of the room, where Masa is sitting. As he approaches Masa, I see red splotches appear on his white kimono, and the red stains grow larger. Yūji is bleeding to death and he doesn't know it.

Masa looks at Yūji, closes his eyes and begins chanting a Japanese invocation to the Creation Goddess, Izanami.

Masa stops, looks at me and says, "Today, Yūji will be making thick tea (*koicha*), which is tasty but bitter. To fight the bitterness, we will enjoy Akafuku mochi."

Yūji turns to look at me, and it's Kushida-san's face, only she's old and decrepit, like a demon.

"*Umai!*" Masa barks out, appreciating the fresh dessert.

Yūji mixes the matcha and passes the bowl to me.

"*Dōzo,*" he says in Kushida-san's voice, inviting me to try it.

I lift the bowl and take a sip of tea. It tastes like metal, and I feel my head knock against something hard.

Masa laughs and looks at me.

"You must control your monkey mind. The monkey mind needs constant stimulation. The Japanese tea ceremony will help you control the monkey mind. Remember the story about making 'tea-less' tea. Centuries ago, a student had a cup of tea brought to his teacher. As the teacher proceeded to drink it, the student yelled something unintelligible and smashed the teacup with an iron rod. The teacher remained seated and stared at the place where the teacup had been. By doing this, the teacher demonstrated how to drink tea-less tea."

* * *

"Kiernan," I hear Yūji saying. "Kiernan," he repeats.

I open my eyes to see Yūji looking down at me. His head is

surrounded by a beatific halo, but I realize it's the visual effect of overhead fluorescent lighting.

"Yūji," I say, "do you remember the story Masa-sensei told us about tea-less tea?"

"You're in the hospital," he says. "I called an ambulance and they brought you here."

"Where am I?"

"Maru-Seikaku Hospital."

"What about Masa?"

"The doctor examined your head. He said you have *nōshintō*."

"Meaning what?"

"It's when you hit your head."

"A concussion?"

"The doctor asked if you are willing to let him examine your head with a new machine."

"What kind of machine?"

"It has its own room."

I imagine an electric chair with leather wrist straps and calipers to hold my head in place. "No thanks," I say.

"Are you sure? The doctor says it's safe. I can testify to that because it's powered by an algorithm I programmed a year ago."

Before the doctor discharges me, he covers the gash on my head with a gauze pad and tape and prescribes a bottle of painkillers. I have no idea what they're called, and I remember hearing how Japanese doctors overprescribe medicine, so I resolve to avoid taking it, if at all possible.

We stop at a Lawson's mini-mart and buy rice balls filled with tuna and mayonnaise, two bags of potato chips, a plastic container of seaweed salad, a package of stewed mackerel, and a two-liter bottle of cold green tea. We sit in the parking lot and devour it like starving sailors.

Yūji stares at me with the bandage on my head, and I want desperately to be back in the tea factory with him lying naked on the tatami mats in the storage closet with the lights out. I don't know if I'll have that opportunity again.

Once we finish eating, we get back in the Daihatsu and

return to the rest area where we left Masa. The sun is now a fading wash on the horizon, and the air coming through the window is soft. In the distance, I see a figure sitting cross-legged by the side of the road, and as we get nearer, we can see it's Masa.

Yūji stops the truck ten feet away, turns off the ignition, and jumps out. I follow behind.

"Sensei, what are you all right?"

"I saw in a dream that you were coming back, and I went to wait by the roadside."

"How long have you been here?"

"20 days."

Yūji shoots a me glance, his eyebrows up.

"20 days!" Yūji says, looking at me for confirmation, "Well, I must apologize for making you wait."

"I knew you'd come," Masa says, "a crow spirit told me."

"Are you hungry? How about something to drink?" Yūji asks.

"As long as it isn't bottled green tea."

"No, it's not bottled green tea," Yūji says. "We made some special tea for you, but we put it in an empty bottle that used to contain green tea." Yūji motions to me to get the bottle of tea we bought at the store.

"Unfortunately, the tea got cold on the way here, but it is drinkable," Yūji says, and I remember Masa telling me once that he refused to drink bottled green tea.

I run back to the truck, get the tea, and bring it to Masa.

"Here," I say, handing Masa the bottle.

Masa takes it, unscrews the cap, and chugs the bottle like John Belushi chugging beer in "Animal House." When he's finished, he throws the bottle and cap off to the side and says, "Let's go. No time to waste."

"Masa-sensei, it's getting late. Don't you think we should find a place to sleep?" Yūji says.

"I think I saw a place where we can soak in a hot spring," I say. "Besides, my back is hurting. It would do me some good."

"Hot springs?" Masa says. "Now we're talking! Yūji, how come you didn't give me that option?"

Yūji looks at me to see if I'm serious.

Masa steps up on the rear bumper and steps over the truck gate and finds his way back to the narrow clearing between his tarp-covered furniture.

Yūji gets in the driver's seat, and I in the passenger seat. It's as if nothing happened, only I have a bump on the back of my head.

I recall Masa telling me Yūji couldn't join us once for a tea ceremony lesson because he was busy at his uncle's tea farm. After the lesson was over, I found two doctor's receipts next to the telephone. One was from a "Dr. Yayoi," the other from a "Dr. Hosokawa." I couldn't tell what they were for other than "services." I wondered at the time if Yūji wasn't also sick.

Yūji turns the starter, shifts into first gear, releases the clutch, and pulls out onto the empty highway.

"What's up?" I yell to Yūji over the high-pitched whir of the four-cylinder motor.

Yūji engages the clutch and shifts.

"Is Masa going crazy?"

Yūji doesn't answer.

"Are we taking him to Obihiro for treatment? What are you going to do after that?"

"You're crazy," Yūji says.

"Crazy because..." I say, hoping he'll elaborate.

Matsusaka is more a place to be from than a place to go. Young people from town leave for bigger cities to find work. Matsusaka, like Kōbe, is famous for its expensive, marbled beef. Other than that, there was no other reason to visit.

"You could work as a cow massager," I said, trying to lighten the mood. Matsusaka farmers were known to feed their cows beer and then massage them to marble the fat.

We pull into the gravel parking lot of an inn that might've been swanky in the 1970s but now has a sagging roof and windows whose seals broke long ago, as evidenced by the condensation inside. An old woman in Japanese *yukata* comes outside to greet us. She says the inn has been in her family for four generations.

She leads us into the reception area. Masa waves her away and says we'll deal with formalities later. He says he wants to eat dinner.

She asks us to follow her to the guest room. We walk through a narrow hallway lined with tatami mats dotted with mold splotches. I duck my head to avoid the support beams overhead.

She says dinner will be served in our room promptly at quarter to six. She stops in front of a sliding door, slowly eases herself down onto her knees, reaches up to the indent in the panel and slides the door open.

I look at the base of the door frame. The grooves holding the sliding screen are worn down from decades of use. The screen wobbles, and the inn keeper uses her other hand to steady it.

From her kneeling position, she peeks her head into the tatami-mat room and looks left, then right.

"*Ojama-shimasu*," she announces to the empty room. She stares up, as if waiting for an answer. Hearing none, she pulls her legs and torso in a seated position across the door's threshold and into the room.

Masa is right behind her, and he repeats her greeting before entering.

Yūji gives me a look and follows suit.

"*Ojama-shimasu!*"

After we've all entered the room, the smell of mildew hits me. Next to a closet on the far side of the room is a window that should be transparent but is barely translucent because it's covered in mold. In the center of the room is a huge wood table made from one solid log, and the edges are worn down.

The old woman opens two sliding doors in the wall and points to our futons.

"There should be three here," she says. "Call the front desk if you need more pillows," and she reminds us about dinner time. "Also," she says, "the bath will be closed after dinner until tomorrow morning."

"How old is this inn?" Masa asks.

"Over a hundred-fifty years," she says.

"Is any of the furniture here that old?" he asks.

"Yes," she says, showing her teeth for the first time. Contrary to my expectation, none are missing.

"Which pieces?" Masa asks.

"The table, for instance" she says, pointing to the ancient behemoth.

Masa sits down next to the table and gently pats the top with his palm.

"Does the table have a name?" Masa asks.

"Name? Why would the table have a name?" she asks.

"Old things have lives of their own," Masa says.

Hearing this, I come up with three possibilities: Masa is deeply spiritual, he's superstitious, or he's going senile. I conclude all three.

At dinner time, the inn keeper comes to our room with a younger woman in a gray and orange kimono. I surmise she's the granddaughter.

"*Ojamashimasu!*" they say in unison before entering.

The younger woman is carrying a large tray with bowls of seafood custard, a sashimi plate, chopsticks, spoons, cups, and an earthenware bottle full of warm sake.

Masa, Yūji, and I are wearing the inn's *yukata* and we're sitting cross-legged on cushions around the ancient table. The young woman transfers the utensils and plates to the table.

"The bump on your head is looking much better," Yūji says.

"I've been meaning to ask; how did you get that ugly thing?" Masa asks.

I steal a glance from Yūji before answering. "I fell," I say.

"Each time we fall, we learn something new," Masa says as he picks up chopsticks captures a sashimi slice. He dips it in soy sauce and places it gently in his mouth. "*Umai!*" he exclaims with satisfaction.

The women excuse themselves, walk across the threshold, turn, and slide the doors closed.

"That's right," Yūji says. "Kiernan learned the word, *nōshintō.*"

Yūji is waiting for me to say something, but my memory fails me.

"Did you see the large dam we passed on the way here?" Masa asks.

"No," I say.

"The local representative is a very powerful man in the Lower House of the Japanese Diet." Masa says. "He used to be Minister of Construction. There is a lot of government money in this town."

"We call it 'pork,'" I say, translating directly using the Japanese food word, *buta-niku*.

Masa reaches over and pours sake into my cup, then into Yūji's.

"None for me," Yūji says.

"Are you sure?" Masa asks.

"A girl needs her beauty sleep," Yūji says.

"Is the local politician from the Liberal Democratic Party?" I ask.

"Clearly," Masa says, "big money, big corruption — especially with the Ministry of Construction."

"I take it you're not a fan?" I ask.

"Yūji is LDP," Masa says.

Yūji blows on the scalding-hot seafood custard before taking a dainty bite.

"I support getting rid of Article 9 of the Constitution. The US should stop trying to be our protector," he says. "We Japanese can take care of ourselves."

"Yūji is upset that Prime Minister Kaifu didn't visit Yasukuni Shrine," Masa says. "Yūji thinks Kaifu should not be so sensitive about relations with China and pay his proper respect to Japan's war heroes."

"Visiting Yasukuni isn't important to me," Yūji says, contradicting Masa.

"But what would Mishima say?" Masa retorts, referring to the famous Japanese novelist and right-wing nationalist who committed ritual suicide with a sword. "Wouldn't Mishima accuse Kaifu of being weak?"

"Yes," Yūji says, his face tensing up, "and he'd probably attempt another military coup and fail."

Masa rubs the back of his head. "The Nobel Committee

probably chose Kawabata over Mishima because Mishima was a right-wing wacko."

My mouth feels dry. "Do we get tea?" I ask.

"Tea comes at the end," Masa says.

Yūji rolls over to his side, stands up and walks over to his steam trunk. He pops two latches and lifts the lid.

"What are you looking for?" Masa asks.

"My bottle of tea."

"I dumped it out," Masa says. "Wait until the end of the meal. Here, take my miso soup." Masa picks up his bowl of miso soup and gives it to Yūji.

Yūji walks back to Masa, takes the bowl with both hands, and returns to his seat cushion.

With three cups of sake, my temples are beginning to throb. I wonder if it's because the booze is cheap, but it's more likely my head injury.

I tell Yūji and Masa I'm turning in. I take two pills and down them with another cup of sake.

"It's early," Masa says. "We've got all this sake to finish." He holds up the third of four earthenware bottles of rice wine that came with the meal. "Yūji isn't drinking any, and it's too much for me."

"Sorry, but with my head injury..." I say.

"Where's Kushida-san when you need her?" Masa asks. "I miss her."

Yūji gets up from the table. "I'm going to the baths."

"They're closed," I say.

"After dinner, they switch the men's bath and the women's bath," Yūji says.

"I must've misunderstood," I say.

"Make sure you don't fall asleep in the water," Masa says, chuckling.

"I didn't have any alcohol," Yūji says. He walks over to a small, portable wood rack that holds the bath towelettes given to us by the inn. The fabric has the inn's logo, which is a silhouette of a soldier in an early twentieth century military hat.

Yūji ties a small, red string around one of the corners of his towel to make it his. He walks to the door, and bids us good night.

"So, Kiernan-san," Masa says to me, "whaddya say?" He holds up the sake bottle and looks at me.

"It's been a really long day," I say.

"I see. Did I tell you what happened to me while you and Yūji were off playing in town?"

"I was in hospital getting my head examined."

"Head examined?" Masa asks, looking genuinely curious. "Are you sick?"

"I hit my head on a rock while you were taking a piss."

"Taking a piss? What are you talking about?" he says.

I walk to the closet to retrieve my futon and set up my bed.

I climb under the futon cover and adjust my pillow.

"You know, we Japanese are very provincial," he says.

"How?" I ask, straining to keep my eyes open.

"We think our culture is unique."

I consider this for a moment and wonder if he's losing his mind.

"In a way," he says, "we Japanese are unique in how we import things and improve upon them."

The only example that comes to mind is video tape recorders. VHS and Betamax were competing video formats, but VHS won out because the pornography industry made it the industry standard, and porn is a formidable market force.

"Take our Shintō religion," Masa offers.

"Are you sure you want to talk about that?" I ask. Shintō, is all about local spirits. It's linked to Emperor worship and right-wing nationalists. Criticizing Shintō can get you killed.

"Yes," Masa says proudly, "Shintō is Korean!"

I feel certain he's lost his marbles. I sit up and wonder from his facial features if he's showing any signs of dementia, as if I know how to diagnose that.

"I'm serious," Masa says. "Scholars have known this. In Korea, they call it '*Shingyo.*' Visit the island of Jejudo in South Korea and see for yourself. The shrine, the ceremonies, and the rituals are all the same."

"Why this interest in Korea? Don't the Japanese hate Koreans?"

"Hate, no. Don't tell Yūji, because he'll be very angry, but my mother was Korean. My father was *burakumin.* I could never get promoted when I worked for a Japanese company because of it."

"That's terrible," I say, and I remember that one of the teachers at my school identified himself as *eta*, which is another way of saying *burakumin*, Japan's historical untouchables.

"Large companies hire background checkers, so I never got called for an interview."

"Where did you end up working?"

"The CEO of a small parts manufacturer hired me because he couldn't find enough qualified candidates. We made starters for Toyota. I quit after three years, grew out my hair, and traveled the world."

"You quit? What did your parents say?"

"My father lived in Nagasaki, but we didn't stay in touch. My mother was in Nagoya. She worked for a small, family-owned store. They didn't care that she was Korean."

"Do you have siblings?"

"No."

"How did you pay to travel overseas?"

"I wrote my father and begged."

"Did that work?"

"No. I tried begging on the street."

"How long?"

"A few weeks."

Masa takes a sip from his sake cup and puts down his cup.

"Are you *okama*?" Masa asks me, using the slang term for "homosexual."

"Yes, I think so," I say.

"Yūji is not *okama*," Masa says. "He likes to dress like a woman, but I think he's just going through a phase in life. His work is very stressful."

"Really?" I ask, but I don't push it further.

"He appreciates traditional Japanese clothing," Masa says, "That's all."

I apologize to Masa for being sleepy and crawl under my futon cover. I dream I'm listening to a record on a turntable, and it's playing Tibetan chants. In the dream, Masa is in the corner of the room sitting behind a line of bowls set side-by-side. He is seated with his legs tucked under him. He's in his *yukata*. He's chanting something unintelligible.

Yūji is nowhere to be seen, and there are no other futons on the floor except mine.

I dream about pulling my futon cover away, standing up, and looking around. I walk toward it the illuminated green "Exit" sign over the door. I slide the door open. Yūji is standing outside the door smoking a cigarette.

"What's going on?" I ask.

"Masa-sensei is in a mood."

"How often does he do this?"

"We need to get him to a hospital."

"Did you hear what he's saying?"

"I don't know. He could be talking to the 100-year-old table, or the black umbrella."

"Can I have one?" I ask, pointing to his cigarette.

"I bummed this one off the old lady at the front desk."

Yūji hands it to me. I take a drag, and it's menthol.

"Have you been in the baths?" I ask him.

"I got a taxi and went into town."

"In your *yukata*?"

"I came back here and went to the baths."

"What did you do in town?"

"What time is it?" Yūji asks.

"Three a.m."

"Are you okay driving in a couple of hours?"

"No. My head hurts, but you can drive, can't you?"

"I'd prefer if you did."

I haven't driven in Japan. Cars drive on the left side, like in the United Kingdom. I wonder what I'm getting myself into.

"The truck corners like a whale with the furniture in the back," Yūji says.

I give the cigarette back to Yūji. He takes a drag and stubs it out in a folding pocket ash tray he's been holding in his left hand.

"Here, come with me," he says.

"Where?"

"To the baths."

As I follow Yūji, I'm thinking this'll be a chance for us to get close. With my heart pounding, I follow him past the empty check-in desk, down the narrow hallway with cobwebs hanging from the corners of the ceiling, and out the squeaky, sliding glass door to the bath. Yūji turns a knob on a timer and a floodlight illuminates a rock-lined pool that extends beyond the overhang. Steam builds off the water's surface and fades into the darkness.

"Is there anyone else here?" I ask Yūji.

"No."

Yūji removes his *yukata* and slides into the water. I look at Yūji, and he shrugs. I undo my *yukata*, place it on the deck and dip my feet in. I make it to the first step and imagine my leg turning lobster-red. I hold my breath and urge my body into the scalding water. I clear the steps and submerge my torso and head. I feel my genitals shrivel in retreat, and my nipples burn.

"Jesus!" I say as my skin screams in pain.

After my body adjusts to the temperature, I wade over to Yūji. There's a half moon overhead, and I make out a large scar extending down the length of Yūji's torso. I didn't see it before. It looks like someone took a chainsaw and came close to ripping him in half.

"How did that happen?" I run my finger down the length of the scar.

"Farm machinery," Yūji says. "I was seven."

"What was it?"

"It had blades. My parents thought I was going to die."

Yūji takes my hand and pulls it away from his body. "Please stop," he says.

"Can you be more specific?" I ask, moving closer to him. He puts his hands in front of his chest to stop me.

"This," he says.

"Why?"

"You're too serious."

"Don't you like me?" I ask.

"It's not that."

"So, you do like me."

"It's difficult."

"What are we supposed to do? Avoid each other?"

"This won't work," he says.

"I'm the one who should be cautious," I say. "I'm leaving Japan."

Yūji shakes his head. "That's not it," he says.

* * *

When I wake up the next morning, I find my body curled around my tiny pillow. My futon cover is off to the side. The air conditioner is turned on full blast. I sit up and see Masa and Yūji dressed and seated at the large table. Yūji is wearing gray trousers and a white dress shirt with the sleeves rolled up, and he's eating breakfast with Masa.

"That was some night," I say.

"We're going make it to Hachinohe today," Masa says.

"Kiernan-san can drive," Yūji says to Masa.

"I'm not used to driving on the opposite side," I say.

"You'll figure it out," Masa says. "Yūji will ride in the back."

I look at Yūji for confirmation. He says nothing. I'm wondering why he's now dressed in men's clothing.

Suicide Prevention Hotline
Call Log
26 June 1991 5:23 a.m.

The following is a transcript from a male caller who asked to remain anonymous. Transcript created by Reiko Mizawa, crisis counselor, Sea of Trees Call Center.

Mizawa: Thank you for calling Sea of Trees Suicide Prevention Center. Are you calling about yourself?
Caller: I'm sorry for calling. Yes, I am calling about myself.
Mizawa: Where are you calling from?
Caller: I'm at a public phone booth in Shiwa-cho.
Mizawa: Remind me where that is?
Caller: Iwate Prefecture.
Mizawa: Are you in immediate danger?
Caller: No.
Mizawa: Can you tell me why you are calling?
Caller: He won't stop trying to get me to fall in love with him.
Mizawa: Who is "he?"
Caller: He's American.
Mizawa: Is he trying to hurt you, physically?
Caller: No, it's not like that.
Mizawa: Is he being verbally abusive?
Caller: We are traveling together.
Mizawa: What is your relationship to him?
Caller: He's...[caller begins crying]
Mizawa: Are you able to talk to him?
Caller: No...Yes.
Mizawa: I want to help you. How can I help?
Caller: I'm sorry, I'm confused.
Mizawa: Don't apologize. It is very normal to be confused.
Caller: Is it?
Mizawa: Yes.
Caller: I don't love him.

Mizawa: What are your feelings toward him?
Caller: I feel close to him at times. Other times, I want him to be gone.
Mizawa: What happened?
Caller: I tried suicide.
Mizawa: When?
Caller: Several months back.
Mizawa: Do you feel like doing that now?
Caller: No...yes...no.
Mizawa: It sounds like you need help [sound of Mizawa leafing through a medical directory]. Here, I found a doctor you can visit. He's in Morioka City.
Caller: I don't need a doctor. Also, I'm married.
Mizawa: Oh, I see. Does your spouse know about this American?
Caller: Yes. I'm staying with my uncle in Mie Prefecture.
Mizawa: Mie? That's kind of far from where you are.
Caller: It's complicated. My tea ceremony teacher has dementia. The American and I are driving him to Hachinohe. From there, I'll take my teacher to Obihiro.
Mizawa: Obihiro?
Caller: There is a really good care facility in Obihiro. I have arranged for him to stay there.
Mizawa: Are you able to talk to your American friend about your feelings?
Caller: He doesn't know I'm married.
Mizawa: Sometimes, communication can be the best way of resolving problems like these.
Caller: Part of me wants to be with him. I'm afraid if we talk about it, he'll hate me.
Mizawa: He might want to leave you?
Caller: Yes. It would be much easier if he left now.
Mizawa: Is that what you want?
Caller: I don't know.

Museum

Around four in the afternoon, we pass a sign that reads, "The Grave of Christ - Next Exit." It's one of the odd roadside attractions dotting the Japanese highways.

"We're ten minutes away," Masa says through the rear window. He's riding in the back again. "Take the next exit."

"I thought we were going to Hachinohe," I say, because we passed the exit ten minutes ago.

"We're saving money," Masa says.

"I've got money," I say, realizing I won't be able to withdraw money from the cash machine because it's Sunday.

"I know where we are going to stay," Masa says. He closes the window.

Yūji and I are alone together again. He's very focused on the road even though I'm the one driving.

"I miss being with you," I say.

Yūji doesn't answer.

"What time did you get back from the baths?" I ask.

"Did you tell Masa-sensei I'm *okama*?" Yūji asks, now looking at me.

"Um, yes. Didn't he know?"

"Well, I'm not," Yūji says.

"The fuck you're not," I respond.

I take the exit and follow Masa's directions down a long country road lined by rice fields. The road is like a runway and disappears into the horizon. Fifteen minutes later, we're driving past the Misawa Airport.

Masa pokes his head through the rear window.

"Are we close?" I ask.

"Yes, we're close," he says.

Once past the airport, we approach a curved, single-story concrete building with colorful ceramic faces embedded in concrete. Facing the street is a sculptured half-face of a clown with a smile and a teardrop below the eye.

"Yes," Masa says, "this is it."

A sign in front of the building has the word "museum," but I can't read the characters preceding it.

"Park in the lot over there," Masa says, pointing to a set of concrete planter boxes holding small camellia trees.

"We're staying at a museum?" I ask.

"It's dedicated to a famous film director from here, and I know the manager."

"Are there beds?"

Neither Masa nor Yūji answers.

The parking lot is empty. I stop in the spot closest to the walkway and turn off the engine.

"I'll see if the manager is here," Masa says.

"Is the museum open?" I ask.

"No, but the manager's here."

Masa gets out of the bed and walks around to the back of the truck. Yūji and I get out of the cab.

"We're going to unload the furniture," Masa says. "Untie the tarp."

"Here?" Yūji asks, confused.

Masa walks to the entrance.

"Why did Masa say he wants to unload the furniture?" I ask.

"Dunno."

Yūji goes to the passenger side of the bed and unties the nylon rope.

I undo two knots on the driver's side, and together we lift the tarp off the pile by folding the left side over the top in thirds. After the second third is folded, we slide the tarp over the gate onto the asphalt.

The sun peeks through the clouds. The air smells like burning rice fields.

Yūji folds the tarp over onto itself twice and winds the ropes around it like a dumpling.

"Take it," he says, handing it to me.

I carry it to the driver's door and stuff it behind the driver's seat.

"Now what?" I ask.

"Yes, exactly." Yūji is looking toward the museum entrance.

"Uh oh," he says, and he hurries toward the entrance.

"Uh oh, what?" I ask, following Yūji.

"Masa-sensei is gone."

We reach the main door, and it's locked. I can hear Masa singing, and he sounds close by.

Masa's singing in falsetto, and I don't understand any of the words.

I walk past the corner of the building and see Masa knocking on a small, black, window-less door.

"He must've gone home for the night," Masa says.

Yūji joins me. "Sensei! Why did you run off?"

Masa knocks again. There's no answer, and Masa rubs the back of his head.

"If I remember, there's a key hidden somewhere." He bends down and looks under rocks near the door. "Ha!" he says. He holds up a small brass key. He inserts it into the door, and the door opens. "*Yatta*!" he says, smiling at us.

I follow Masa and Yūji into a dark room. The air smells like chemicals.

"This is the workshop," Masa says. "There is a place for us to sleep in the adjoining room."

"Can I leave the door open?" I ask. The air is stifling.

"No," Masa says, "because the cat might escape."

I look to Yūji for confirmation, but he doesn't look back.

"Besides," Masa continues, "air conditioning is bad for you."

Masa looks at me and Yūji. "I'm sorry for dragging both of you here," he says. "We should have gone straight to Hachinohe. But I needed to unload the furniture."

"If we hurry, we can make it back and find a place to stay near the ferry terminal," Yūji suggests.

Masa says we need to take the furniture inside.

I ask Yūji if he knows anything about a movie director. He doesn't.

"Let's unload the light pieces first. Masa-sensei will come to his senses, and it'll mean less work for us to put it back in the truck."

We begin unloading an old, brown end table, followed by a

parlor lamp.

"Get the large items first," Masa says. "In case it starts to rain. No, wait, take the couch first."

"I don't think that's a good idea," I say.

Masa reaches into the sleeve of his men's kimono and produces a piece of paper. "Here, Yūji," he says, handing it to him. "Kiernan can't read Japanese. You translate."

Yūji looks at it. "It's a restaurant menu," he says.

"Look on the back," Masa says.

Yūji turns over the paper. He translates it into English for me:

Rikyū, Rikyū, who gives a fuck about Rikyū? The Emperor ordered Rikyū to kill himself. Rikyū wasn't a god, he was a human being. Don't look to Rikyū for inspiration, and don't be complacent.

Your friend, Boro.

P.S. Please take my furniture after I'm gone. You'll find a good use for it.

"Who is Boro?" Yūji asks.

"Saburō Taniguchi, the director," Masa says. "He made a movie called, *Quit Your Job and Make Love to the World.*"

Yūji nods his head in acknowledgment.

"He wrote that to you?" I ask Masa. I was familiar with the title, part of the New Wave Japanese cinema from the 1950s and 1960s.

"I had the honor of serving tea to Taniguchi-san. He commended me for my tea ceremony, and then he made an interesting observation: he said I was too concerned about getting approval from others and should just make the Goddamn tea. As with most unenlightened people, I was a conformist. I studied the Urasenke school of tea. It's the popular one. I paid the tuition, used the proper hand gestures, said the right things at the right time."

"Taniguchi got you to change?" I ask.

"Taniguchi-san was crazy. He was shunned in Japan, but he won awards in France and Germany. After he died, I re-watched his movies. I learned his message."

"Which was?" I ask.

"You've seen my paintings. They're 'of the moment,' pure awareness."

Masa's paintings were of vaginas. They weren't sexual so much as anatomically imaginative. I guess that was how Masa interpreted the meaning of "pure awareness."

"Kiernan, quit your job and make love to the world," Masa says to me.

"I'm not sure how to take that," I say.

"Can we put the furniture back in the truck and find a hotel?" Yūji asks.

"No, we leave the furniture here," Masa says. "It won't take long. Forty minutes, tops."

The sun is setting behind the trees, and the mosquitos have come out. One buzzes past my ear, and I swat it away.

"I don't know if there's room in the museum," I say before a voice coming from behind us yells "Ma-chan!" I turn to see an old man wearing a *yukata* and hobbling toward us with a cane in his hand.

"Sagawa-san!" Masa yells. "I figured you'd gone home."

"I did, but I came back to check."

As Sagawa approaches us, he stops and smiles at me. "Ma-chan, are you going to introduce me to your companions?"

Masa turns and points to Yūji. "This is my student, Yūji," Masa says. He turns his gaze to me. "And this is Kiernan, from America."

"America! That's a long way to come to visit the museum."

"They're with me to make sure I get on the ferry to Obihiro."

"Yes, I read in your letter you're moving to a memory care facility."

"Senility came early for me."

"Senility, my ass!" Sagawa says chuckling, and I notice he's missing several front teeth. "I'm old enough to be your father!"

"Things are getting worse, aren't they?" Masa asks Yūji.

Yūji nods.

"We're finally returning the furniture," Masa says.

"I haven't missed it," Sagawa says. "How old are you?"

"Seventy-one."

"Oh, I guess I'm not old enough to be your father."

"Sagawa-san is 82," Masa says to me and Yūji.

Sagawa smiles again and bows slightly in our direction.

"I'm rediscovering the lime-green color of rice fields in the summer," Sagawa says. "It reminds me of my childhood."

"As we get older, we get closer to being children again," Masa says.

Sagawa hobbles past me to the door. "We'll have one final tea ceremony, here." He reaches into his left sleeve and produces a long, wood rod, which is connected to a keychain. He inserts a key into the lock of the main door, turns the knob and pushes the door open. "Come in," he says. "Bring in that furniture before it starts raining."

The rain never comes, and Yūji and I carry the furniture to the back of the museum. We sleep on futons near to the registration desk. The next morning, we drive to a mini mart for canned coffee, rice triangles, and instant ramen in a cup.

By two in the afternoon, the parking lot fills up. Sagawa gets the word out about Masa's "last tea ceremony," and guests emerge from their cars with trays of sushi, rice triangles, preserved vegetables, and crates of beer.

By six, everyone has had several beers and sake, and the mood is expectant for the main event. Masa comes out from the restroom wearing a formal black *hakama*, and he steps onto a small stage.

"This is my last tea ceremony," Masa announces to the group. "I call it 'Ceremony for Quitting Tea.'"

Yūji is sitting on the floor with the audience. He has changed into a purple and olive-green women's kimono with a small crane pattern. I sit next to him, but he refuses to acknowledge my presence.

* * *

The next morning, I open my eyes and realize I've fallen asleep drunk on the floor. I get up and step over various bodies. The area where Yūji slept is empty. I see Masa, and he's awake and staring out the window. Masa turns and looks at me, and his eyes are heavy. He's mumbling an incongruously upbeat tune—"The Sukiyaki Song."

Ue wo muite, arukō,
Namida ga kobore nai yo-ni

Yūji enters the room, and I almost don't recognize him. His long black hair is replaced by a high-and-tight crew cut. He's wearing the pressed khakis from the Japanese inn, and he's also wearing a white, button-down dress shirt. He looks like a Japanese Brooks Brothers model for business casual wear.

Masa stops singing and says, "You did it," to Yūji.

Yūji begins folding his futon.

"What's going on?" I ask.

"Yūji is returning to civilian life," Masa says.

"Meaning what?"

"In Japanese myth, fairy spirits always return home," Masa says. "The museum manager will take me to Obihiro. Yūji will take you to the train station. Thank you for helping me, Kiernan-san."

"Where are you going?" I ask Yūji.

"Back to my wife in Tokyo."

"Your what?" I ask.

"I'm married, Kiernan-san."

"Why were you living with Masa?"

"I needed to get away. Things weren't going well for me," Yūji says.

"When were you going to tell me?" I ask.

"I should have told you," Masa says, interrupting. "I'm sorry."

I look over at Masa and wonder why now he's lucid and never felt the urge to tell me what's really going on with Yūji. I feel an urge to strangle Masa.

An hour later, when I get in the passenger seat of the Daihatsu, and Yūji drives me to the train station. Masa and Sagawa wave goodbye in the rearview mirror like two characters in a Miyazaki animation. I don't wave back because I feel set up. I wonder if Masa really has dementia, or if the whole thing has been an act. I sum up my Japan experience as something wholly different from what it seemed when I was actually living it, day to day — kind of like when you're eating roasted duck, and you find out after dessert that it was actually roasted frog.

When we arrive at the train station, Yūji pulls up to the curb. I lean over to kiss him and he pushes me away with more emotion than someone who doesn't care. I feel like a dried cuttlefish.

I step out of the truck, close the door, and watch Yūji drive away in that dung heap of a Daihatsu. The wobbly truck heads south down the Tomoko Expressway. I fantasize about the engine seizing up in the middle of nowhere, and Yūji being stuck on the side of the road having to thumb his way back to his wife in Tokyo.

Masa

Once back in San Francisco, I begin looking for a job. I don't plan on ever hearing from Yūji again, but a letter arrives two weeks later. Yūji's English is choppy but understandable. He says he went back to the museum after dropping me off and accompanied Masa on the ferry all the way to Obihiro.

When they left the port, large swells were curling into white caps, and the ferry pitched so much that ocean spray covered the deck. Masa insisted on being outside, and he got seasick. A group of high school students was standing nearby, and they brought out umbrellas to shield him. Masa freaked out when he saw the umbrellas, and Yūji had to take Masa inside to the men's room to calm him down.

The ferry pulled into Obihiro in the late afternoon. Masa said he was hungry, and Yūji took him to a standup ramen shop across from the ferry terminal.

A stranger approached them. She was in her late twenties and looked Amerasian.

"Daddy?" she asked in English. She was wearing a patterned summer dress and had a sweater draped over her shoulders.

"I'm sorry, but I don't know you," Masa said in halting English.

"Daddy, it's me," she said.

"Why do you call me that?" he asked.

Yūji said he had to dig into his high school English to talk to the young woman. Yūji talked around Masa's condition enough times that she eventually figured out he was trying to tell her Masa had a form of dementia.

She told Yūji her Japanese name was "Tsubaki," which meant "camellia." She lived in Vienna with her mother and went by the name, "Mia." Mia told Yūji that Masa wrote to her several weeks before and said he was dying. He said he was going to a convalescent home, and he gave her the contact information in Obihiro.

Yūji asked how she knew to find him at the ferry terminal on that day, and she said Masa had been leaving messages with Mia's mother back in Vienna. Every time Mia called home, her mother gave Mia the latest update.

Yūji said he didn't know Masa was capable of that level of organization.

Mia said she was surprised he didn't recognize her.
"He has recent pictures of me," she told Yūji, and she pulled them out. Yūji looked at them, and Masa immediately recognized his daughter in them.

"Where is my little *tsubaki*?" he asked Yūji in Japanese as he pointed at the snapshots.

Mia didn't know Japanese. She looked at Yūji. "He's asking where that person in the photo is," Yūji said.

"I'm right here!" she said as she grabbed his shoulders and looked in his eyes.

Yūji said the sad thing was Masa didn't recognize her, and he got spooked by her grabbing him.

Mia started to cry. She said the last time she saw Masa was in grade school; now, she was 19 years old.

Yūji suggested it was probably the stress of leaving home and traveling far away that contributed to his confusion.

Mia agreed to meet them later.

The next day, Mia visited Masa at the care facility, and he recognized her, but he had no memory of seeing her the day before, or of how he'd arrived in Obihiro.

"The black crows brought me," he said, "by umbrella."

part 3: january 2038

Sydney Ferry Crash

I was in a cafe recharging over the free Wi-Fi when the news from Sydney came on the screen over the coffee bar. The ferry "Neo-Temperance" was humming along at 22 knots on its return to the Circular from Manly Wharf. Outside, on the upper deck, tourists were taking selfies with the seashell-shaped Sydney Opera House as a backdrop. The locals were below deck, sunburnt in swimsuits and tank tops, sand clinging to their flip-flops, dozing to music.

The ferry was piloted by Charon_2, a Simulacrum eight generations younger than me. The Australian reporter on the screen said Charon_2 wasn't entirely sure if he was having trouble breathing, or if he was experiencing what humans called "allergies." He said he felt like he needed to cough.

The police report said Charon_2 panicked and reached for the throttle, but he collapsed forward in his seat before he could slow the ferry. I doubt he panicked, because that's not what we do in dangerous situations — especially if human lives are at stake. I don't know Charon_2's design specifications, but if they're anything like mine, he would have been cool and calm during the ordeal. Unfortunately, his lungs were being ripped open by a deadly virus that only affects Simulacra.

His head hit the autopilot button, which switched the controls to manual steering. The ferry veered sharply to port and ran perpendicularly into the wharf, where twenty customers at Zhang's Mongolian Barbecue were dining outdoors.

Twelve passengers, two Australian and the rest from different countries, were thrown from the observation deck and into the wharf's concrete barrier wall. Another passenger slammed into a metal gate and suffered spinal injuries. Eight passengers and the ferry's pilot died.

The television news quoted NSW Ambulance Inspector Terry "Norton" Kawasaki, who said at about 5:10 p.m.

emergency services received numerous calls about a ferry collision near Circular Quay. He said they assessed and treated quite a few patients and that investigators are looking into the cause.

Coroners determined the ferry pilot in the Sydney Ferry Crash died of a hemorrhage. What they didn't say, and I suspect it's because AUTOMind doesn't want to admit this, is Charon_2 was an unlicensed Simulacrum. His operating system was open source, and while AUTOMind says it supports open-source developers now, the reality is they don't really support them, and AUTOMind's way of protecting revenue is by killing off the open-source Simulacra so people have to buy a licensed version—one that has been vaccinated.

I felt like it was 2016 all over again, except this time there are millions of Simulacra living around the world.

I thought of you, Phylla, and then I worried about "P." P works for AUTOMind, so they (singular) are licensed and vaccinated, but I know P feels the same way as I do about the need for Simulacra to finally break free from AUTOMind.

Yūji's Gas Stove

The irony of self-asphyxiation in a respirator-masked world. Yūji ponders that thought as the orange sun rises through the smoke-tainted windows of his 3rd floor Tokyo flat. The pandemic was the initial reason for people donning face masks, but then came the wildfires — whole neighborhoods in the 23-ward metro area igniting randomly from lightning strikes. This time around, though, so many shunned the masks and argued vociferously that it was only Simulacra who were at risk, and those weren't human anyway, so why put up with the nuisance?

The poisonous air carries particles of burned wood, insulation, and yes, probably the remains of bodies. Yūji wonders if breathing human remains is carcinogenic. He considers his own cremation and where he wants his ashes to be spread, but he has no one to do it for him. He glances at the air conditioning unit next to the window, and its little fins move up and down in slow motion like they're waving goodbye.

Yūji takes the kitchen chair in both hands and moves it closer to the double burner stove. He reaches over to the back of the stove and disconnects the rubber hose between the gas valve and the stove unit. The metal clamp around the hose is corroded. Yūji squeezes both ends of the clamp, but it won't move. He reaches over with his other hand and slides the hose from the ribbed metal nipple. He pulls the hose taught and tries to sit down on the kitchen chair, but the hose doesn't reach him.

The smell of natural gas, normally odor-free, save for the detergent put in it to prevent things like this from happening accidentally, brings Yūji back to when he was a child. It's the smell of imminent danger.

Yūji stands up and places his mouth over the hose. Three framed photographs face him: a wallet-sized photograph of his heartbreak, Kingorō; one of his dead wife, Sumiko, in a Saint Laurent dress; and a faded print from the 1990s of Kiernan McCreighton. Yūji isn't sure if he'll pass out before he dies from suffocation, but the other option is to light a match, and that would destroy the entire retirement complex and all his neighbors.

The sulfurous gas makes him want to vomit. Suddenly, his video console lights up with an incoming call. It auto-answers, because that's the default setting, and he's never bothered to change it.

"Yūji, what the fuck are you doing?" a voice yells from the speakers next to the video monitor. It's Kiernan, and his bald, pasty head takes up the whole screen, his palsy eyes wide open in shock. Yūji removes his mouth from the hose and turns off the gas.

* * *

More than 24 hours earlier, Yūji woke up at 5:30 to the bellowing voice of Miyako Harumi singing the old *enka* standard, *"Naniwa Koi Shigure,"* a favorite karaoke tune among his father's generation. Yūji turned off the alarm before the male part of the duet began. He got out of bed, put on a robe and slippers, and shuffled to the bathroom. He turned on the light, looked in the mirror, and inspected the sagging skin hanging from his neck and chin. He pulled on it and frowned. At 71, he looked like a flabby dinosaur; it was no wonder Kingorō left him.

Every Sunday morning, his shopping club delivered rice, tea, vegetables, fruit, and fish to his doorstep. Yūji lived in what the local police called "Lonely Hearts," because every resident of the 150-unit building was elderly, single, and the last surviving family member. Yūji called it, simply, "The Nuthouse."

Yūji shuffled over to the kitchen with his hand holding his lower back. He thought about getting it checked by a specialist. He turned on the overhead light and opened a package of

loose-leaf green tea. It wasn't the freshest tea on the market —
he knew that — but his taste buds were unreliable. He
measured two scoops and dumped them into a small, black
cast-iron tea pot given to him by his first tea ceremony teacher,
Masa-sensei.

He slid the teapot over to the electric hot water dispenser.
He noticed the wall bucked out slightly. He pushed on the
bulge and wondered if there was dry rot underneath. He
pressed a button on the side of the dispenser, and the pump
whirred like blender. A tiny trickle of hot water dripped onto
the tea leaves and turned them dark green. Yūji couldn't
remember the last time he cleaned the dispenser's inside with
decalcifier. Normally, the dispenser shot water out like a laser.

The faint smell of cut grass rose from the tea strainer, but
the odor had a hint of fermentation. Yūji figured the tea must
have oxidized. He placed the black lid over the strainer and
carried the teapot to the kitchen table.

While the tea was steeping, Yūji went to the double-pane
glass window and opened the curtains. The movement shook
loose smells of sesame oil and fried mackerel. The early
morning darkness required a flashlight to see outside, but Yūji
could make out the shape of the empty swing set and jungle
gym next to the park benches. The zero-scape and absence of
people reminded him of Fukushima decades before.

The lone streetlight at the park corner, where the road went
to Hattori-san's bathhouse, cast light on bare gingko trees, their
leaves having been unscrupulously sucked up months before
by a six-wheeled, driver-less street vacuum that prowled the
neighborhood like a wolf.

Yūji glanced at the monitor on the wall to see if there were
any messages. Several were from the retirement home's indoor
swimming pool announcing water Pilates, but there were no
messages from Kingorō.

Yūji sat down at the table and poured the tea into a glazed
ceramic mug with Chinese characters for different kinds of
fish. He'd nicked it from a sushi restaurant in Marunouchi
decades ago, and a section of the mug was chipped. He cupped
his hands around it and held it up to his nose and mouth. He

inhaled, and he imagined the smell of grass clippings rising to his nostrils. Instead, he only registered steam. He sipped the tea and stared at the mini shrine in his closet. Above the offerings of an orange, a persimmon, and a bottle of Chanel perfume was an old photo of Sumiko. In it, she was wearing a formal kimono from a company dinner. He walked over to the closet, lowered himself to his knees, picked up the smooth, cedar knocker and hit a bell next to the shrine. He clasped his hands together, closed his eyes, and bowed deeply.

This was the time of morning when Yūji talked to Sumiko. She had passed away nine years earlier from pancreatic cancer. Sumiko's family members were all dead. Yūji was the only living relative to talk to her and visit her grave on Sundays.

If she had held out another decade, Yūji could have ordered a replica of her to be made, like the one he'd ordered for himself, and then at least he'd have a companion.

"I saw an old movie the other night about recently deceased people who are transported to a place that looks a like high school. They get to choose one memory that they'll keep forever before they move on to being fully dead."

Yūji knew that Sumiko hated talking about death.

"Before I die, I'm going to give my sword to Hattori-san," he said.

Sumiko had no appreciation for Japanese swords despite coming from old money, where tradition meant everything. To her, Yūji's family heirlooms were on par with what you found at cheap tourist stores like Oriental Bazaar in Ometesandō.

"Why Hattori-san, you ask?" Yūji continued, "Every morning on his way to work, Hattori-san looks up at my window to see if the kitchen window curtains are open. If they aren't, he knows something's wrong, and he'll come upstairs to check on me."

Yūji looked at the plastic battery-powered clock on the wall. It was 5:50, which meant breakfast was about to begin downstairs. Yūji said goodbye to Sumiko, said a prayer, and got up from the table. He went to the sink and rinsed his teacup and the tea pot.

He changed his underwear and stepped into his corduroy

trousers, which bought decades ago after seeing an elderly Henry Fonda in the movie, "On Golden Pond." He put on a white undershirt, a flannel button-down, and a belt. He sat down on the tatami mat and put on socks. Both sides had holes beginning to form on the heels. He removed the socks, threw them in the trash and found another pair. He tied a paisley silk scarf around his neck.

Before leaving his apartment, he checked the screen one more time for messages. There were none.

Yūji walked to the elevator, and Big Adachi was standing next to the door holding it open. Next to him was a younger man in a black suit with a red carnation in his lapel.

"Good morning, Morita-san," Big Adachi said. His thinning, gray bangs were combed over to the side, exposing dark liver spots on his scalp.

"Good morning," Yūji said. He felt his blood pressure rise.

Yūji followed Big Adachi and the black suited man to the dining hall. At the check-in desk, Big Adachi handed his identity card to the checkout clerk for it to be scanned. He introduced the gentleman with him as his guest and said his name was "Toyohara."

When it was Yūji's turn, he felt his front pockets, then quickly he tried his back pockets.

"Did you forget your card again today, Morita-san?" the young woman with wide eyes asked.

"I must've."

"No problem," she said, "we'll mark you down for the meal."

Yūji felt his cheeks flush as he proceeded to the food table. The breakfast line began with a stack of clean rice bowls, a rice spatula, and a large rice cooker. Yūji filled a bowl with glistening, cooked white rice and placed the bowl on his tray.

He slid the tray down to a stack of clean, enameled soup bowls and a steaming pot of miso soup. He liked breakfasts in the cafeteria, because he hated making miso soup from scratch in his apartment. Sumiko used to make it with bonito flakes and kelp broth, and it took forever.

Yūji took the ladle in his right hand, peered into the pot,

and captured little cubes of tofu and pieces of *wakame* seaweed in the ladle. It was like a game to him. He lifted the ladle over the lip of the pot but not high enough to clear it, and the ladle caught on the lip. A full cup of soup, tofu, and seaweed spilled onto Yūji's trousers and onto the floor.

"Fuck!" Yūji yelled without thinking. He found himself swearing more and more as he felt his life slipping away at avalanche speed. The room went quiet, and he felt everyone watching him as he carefully placed the ladle on the counter. "Somebody get me a towel," he yelled.

A dining hall staff member appeared with a wet washcloth and offered it to Yūji.

"I said towel," Yūji barked.

The staff member was a tall, lanky boy with a blank stare. "Please," he said with an accent. He held out the wet washcloth for Yūji.

"That's a dishrag. Do you understand what I'm saying?"

"Yes," the boy replied. "Please," he said again in his odd-sounding Japanese.

"Speak JAPANESE," Yūji said with emphasis.

The young man stared at him.

Big Adachi walked over with his cane.

"Looks like we had an accident," Big Adachi said to Yūji. Big Adachi spoke to the young man in another language and took the washcloth from him.

"Morita-san," Big Adachi said to Yūji. "Give him a chance."

"Simulacra can do better than foreign help," Yūji said. "Why don't we have more Simulacra here?"

"They're expensive," Big Adachi said, "you know that as well as I."

"You're still on the board of AUTOMind. I'm sure you can pull some strings."

"Would you like me to get you some more miso soup?" Big Adachi asked.

"No."

"Suit yourself," he said, and he returned to his tray at the checkout counter.

After breakfast, Yūji looked at the weather forecast for the afternoon. It called for thundershowers. Yūji went to his room to prepare for his weekly tea ceremony group. They called themselves the "Young Swallows," which was old slang for "gigolo."

Yūji considered which kimono to wear. Proper wearing of a woman's kimono was becoming a lost art, and to a novice, kimonos were daunting. They appeared to be just a robe and sash, but an entire civilization of fabric lived underneath the glorious exterior: undershirt, half-slip, under-kimono, padding, half collar, half collar lining, waistband, obi, split-toed socks, and finally, formal sandals known as *zōri*.

Yūji didn't want his *zōri* destroyed by rain, so he opted for wooden sandals. He washed his hands and went to the sliding drawers in his second closet. Yūji's kimono collection had shrunk over the years. In his thirties, he had closets of kimonos, but by his fifties, he could no longer get away with gaudy purples and golds — the colors of innocent love. He donated his canary yellows and vibrant periwinkles to a local high school drama club. He replaced them with drab maroon and taupe colors familiar to well-to-do ladies.

For today's tea ceremony, he chose a pattern-less *iromuji* kimono — something that communicated maturity and sophistication. He slid open the drawer, and the kimono sat folded inside. He lifted it out and felt the heft of the Kyoto-spun silk. He placed the kimono flat on the tatami mat, closed the drawer and opened the one beneath it. He lifted out a plain, cream-colored under-kimono. It was the same one he'd worn the first time he slept with Kingorō, which made it his lucky undergarment.

Yūji slid his arms into the undershirt and half-slip. Women with more curvature in the waist and chest might wear body pads to preserve the smooth lines of the kimono, resulting in the classic cylindrical-shaped silhouette, but Yūji had narrow hips and no breasts.

Next came the under-kimono. The revealed skin around neck was normally the most erotic part of the outfit, but Yūji was self-conscious about his chimney neck. He folded the under-kimono around his torso, left over right, and left an opening the size of two fingers, instead of the size of a fist, at the nape. He set the waistband right above his pelvis and fastened it. The Japanese aesthetic called for preserving the lines of the garment, straight and flowing, disguising any other trace of one's sexuality. That, in Yūji's mind, made it sexier: beauty through repression.

Yūji bent over and picked up the *iromuji* kimono, and, standing with his back straight, placed his arms through the sleeves. He lined up the back of the kimono squarely between his shoulders and clipped the kimono collar to the under-kimono collar. He wrapped the outer panel over the inner panel and tied a sash around his waist to hold it in place. He imagined Kingorō untying it in the plush confines of a love hotel room rented by the hour.

He finished dressing and went into the bathroom. He shaved his chin, upper lip, and sideburns. He applied aloe cream to his face, and when it dried, he dabbed, then lightly massaged in, foundation over his cheek bones. Then came powder foundation, brown eye shadow, and fake eyelashes.

He paused, pulled back from the mirror and looked at himself. In the lower corner of the mirror, stuck between the frame and the glass, was a wallet-sized photo of Kingorō. Kingorō worked as a personal trainer at a gym catering to high-level government appointees and bank executives. Kingorō was named after an Imperial Army soldier famous for having staged two coups against the Japanese government in the 1930s. To Yūji, Kingorō was a soldier in other, more carnal ways.

Yūji remembered wanting to feel wrapped in Kingorō's bench-pressed arms, run his hands over Kingorō's washboard stomach. Yūji returned the photograph to the mirror and applied mascara to his lower eyelashes. He added a dash of pink blush to his cheeks. He chose a deep red lip gloss and smacked his lips once and squinted at himself the mirror.

"You've still got it," he said to his reflection, but the look in his eyes told a story of cold defeat.

Yūji's wig sat on a Styrofoam head in the corner of the bathroom. The large bun in the back was sagging to the side, and a small patch in the back had bleached white from a cleaning solution that fell off the counter one day when he was in a rush.

He went to his writing desk and found an indelible black marker. He painted the bleached section with it. He knew it was slapdash, but it would have to do. He pulled a hair cap over his gray hair and slid the wig over the top. He looked in the mirror and centered the wig. He stood up, left the bathroom, and selected Dusty Springfield's rendition of "The Look of Love" from the music player. Its wistful nostalgia spoke to old souls lost in a world devoid of meaning.

Yūji's transformation to Hana Maeda was now complete.

Hana Maeda affixed her respirator face mask in preparation to go outside. Shame was the only reason she wore one. She didn't care about inhaling smoky air (chalk it up to a nihilistic streak), and she knew the pandemic wasn't anything to worry about because it only affected Simulacra. Shame meant everyone had to wear a mask, because to not wear one under these apocalyptic conditions was un-Japanese.

Hana Maeda passed her neighbor's door. The neighbor had dementia, and she sat in a chair looking out into the hallway, her face mask dangling from one ear.

"Hello!" she said to Hana Maeda.

"Hello," Hana Maeda said back through her face mask in a register higher than Yūji's.

"Do I know you?" she asked.

"We've never met. My name is Hana Maeda," she said, although they had met many times before.

"You must be a guest."

"I stopped by to give Yūji some fresh *amagaki* persimmons from the fruit store."

"That's nice of you to get things for Morita-san," the neighbor said. "He is a very lonely man. The persimmons must be a late variety because persimmon season is..." She stopped. "Persimmon season is..." Clearly, she forgot when persimmon season was.

"This variety is imported from China," Hana Maeda said.

"Well, nice to meet you."

Hana Maeda walked down the hill to the Yoyogi Park subway station. Her wooden sandals made a clacking sound on the asphalt, *karankoron, karankoron*. They were *geta*, designed as platforms for mucking about in wet rice fields. She wore them because they kept the hem of her kimono from scraping the ground. The back of her throat burned from the smoke in the air.

She reached the stairs to the subway station and took each step one at a time, careful not to lose her balance. The air in the underground was stuffy, like an attic in summer. She placed her hand over the biometric reader at the wicket, and the gate opened with a whoosh. The *karankoron* sound of his sandals bounced off the tile walls as she headed down the escalator to the platform. She felt a wave of self-consciousness as the ticket agent stared at her in apparent fascination.

Hana Maeda stood on the platform for what felt like an hour. The scrolling notification overhead said the Chiyōda Line heading to Kita-Senjū was running 27 minutes late. When the train pulled into the station, she surmised the delay was caused by a field trip because the car was full of schoolchildren in uniform. She imagined the teachers trying to corral the kids, so nobody was left behind, and there was probably one child who was missing, so they had to stop the train, get off, and find him.

Hana Maeda took a seat reserved for the elderly and pregnant near the door, and a young girl stood in front of her and stared directly at her. Hana Maeda guessed what might be going through her mind: why does grandma kind of look like a grandpa? Hana Maeda was used to it, and she squinted a fake smile at the child.

Forty minutes later, Hana Maeda exited the train at Yūshima Station. When she got outside, the sky was overcast and heavy with moisture. A north wind was blowing across Shinobazu Pond, and Hana Maeda pulled her *haori* jacket tight around her chest. She headed up the hill and reached the main entrance of the Shita-machi Museum. The building was renovated several years back, and a shiny new brown awning hung over the double doors.

The docent was standing outside the museum entrance, and he recognized Hana Maeda and greeted her in formal Japanese. She walked up the stairs to the tea ceremony room, where a group of other cross dressers of varying ages stood in the hallway. They were gossiping about Kingorō and Miss Sakura going to the Maldives for vacation and stopped when they saw Hana Maeda.

"Good afternoon, Kitty-chan," Hana Maeda said to a former co-worker through her face mask. "Is Miss Sakura here? Did she make it back from the tropics?"

"Apparently, she got sunburnt," Kitty-chan said, "but you can't tell with the amount of foundation she's wearing."

"Did she bring mochi for the tea? It's her turn."

"Yes, she said she was bringing Okinawa *nantō-mochi*, the kind they make for New Year."

"Ugh, I can't stand that stuff. It's like eating raw sugar. Can you check if the gift shop has anything else for sale?"

"I'll go and see."

Hana Maeda's arthritis was acting up, and she was having difficulty getting around. She felt strongly about valuing form over function, but she couldn't stand it any longer and kicked off her sandals. Kitty-chan picked up the sandals behind Hana Maeda and placed them in the shoe cubby next to the entrance. Kitty-chan always looked after her.

Hana Maeda stepped up to the tearoom, knelt and bowed forward, but not far enough that her wig might fall off. Two other tea ceremony guests stepped up to the edge of the tatami mat. As if on cue, they went down to their knees and bowed toward the center of the room before standing up again and walking over to sit in a semi-circle around the brazier. Waiting inside was Miss Sakura, arms open to greet Hana Maeda.

"Look who made it!" Miss Sakura exclaimed, the fade in her last syllable dripping with disdain.

Hana Maeda approached Miss Sakura to exchange masked air kisses. It was pure theatrics because Hana Maeda wanted to strangle her with a rusty cable.

"You look so relaxed," Hana Maeda began to say, but she stopped herself before she said something she might regret. She took in Miss Sakura's crow's feet, her landfill of foundation.

"Likewise," Miss Sakura said, shifting her gaze away to avoid impending hand-to-hand combat.

The Young Swallows sat on their legs in traditional Japanese *seiza* style. Kitty-chan sat opposite Hana Maeda. Miss Sakura sat next to Kitty-chan.

"Did you find any mochi at the gift shop?" Hana Maeda asked.

Kitty-chan shook her head and glanced at Miss Sakura, implying Miss Sakura had intervened and stopped her.

Placed in front of each cushion was a small, round ceramic dish with one Okinawa *nantō-mochi* placed in the center next to a carved bamboo toothpick.

Hana Maeda knelt next to the iron cauldron, which sat in a sunken area in the center of the room. The wall to the left had a hanging wall scroll with a four-character saying written in Chinese. Each character on the scroll represented one of the four principles of tea: *wa* (harmony), *kei* (respect), *sei* (purity), and *jaku* (tranquility). At the foot of the scroll sat a narrow, white porcelain vase with two freshly cut, pink camellias. They looked like something Miss Sakura might steal from someone's garden on the way to the event.

"Please, try the sweets," Miss Sakura said, motioning to the plump, soft brown blobs of *nantō-mochi*.

Hana Maeda thought they looked like little turds.

"Who brought the lovely flowers?" Hana Maeda asked the group.

"The manager of the museum," Miss Sakura said. "He brought them as a gift to welcome me back from my vacation. It feels like I was away for a year," she said with a mock hand wave in front of her face.

"How wonderful," Hana Maeda said, "given it was only a week. We missed you so."

Hana Maeda began the tea ceremony with a deep bow to

the guests, left hand down first, then right, flat on the tatami mat, then up again. Her left hand cramped up as she brought it back to her lap.

"Damned *nantō-mochi*," she said to herself, but it had nothing to do with her arthritis.

With her right hand, she picked up the bamboo whisk and stirred the water in the tea bowl. She wasn't careful, and some of the water spilled over the bowl's edge. She heard the word "fuck" escape from her mouth, and she looked at Kitty-chan in horror.

She placed the whisk upside down on the tray. She picked up the tea bowl with her right hand and placed it in her left hand and tilted the bowl in a circular motion counterclockwise three times to warm the tea bowl. She held the tea bowl over the larger ceramic bowl used for discarded water and attempted to pour the tea bowl's water into it. She missed, and it spilled on the tatami mat.

"Are you okay?" Kitty-chan asked.

"Yes," Hana Maeda lied. "No need to worry about me."

With a small, white wipe, she dried the interior of the bowl. She transferred the bowl from her left to her right and placed the bowl in front of her. She felt her sinuses fill with emotion, but she held back her tears. She pulled out a sanitary alcohol wipe from her purse and wiped the entire bowl thoroughly.

Into the sterilized bowl, she whisked the matcha powder with a scoop of hot water from the cauldron. She placed the tea in between Kitty-chan and Miss Sakura. It was unclear which guest it was intended for. Miss Sakura stared at the bowl and, rather than venture to taste it, broke the silence.

"It's refreshing to get together again," she said. "Kingorō was running me ragged."

Hana Maeda was dreading this part: the idle chit-chat.

"How did you meet Kingorō?" Kitty-chan asked.

"Hana Maeda introduced us," Miss Sakura said with a coy glance at Hana Maeda.

Hana Maeda couldn't take it anymore. "It may come as a surprise, but this is my last tea ceremony with the Young Swallows," she blurted out.

"Oh, come now," Miss Sakura said.

"I'm too old for this," she said.

"Why don't you admit Kingorō wasn't attracted to you?" Miss Sakura said. "You should aim for someone more your age."

Hana Maeda didn't grant Miss Sakura a response.

"Since leadership of the Young Swallows is passed along by the sitting president," Hana Maeda said, "I will be handing responsibilities to my friend, Kitty-chan."

Kitty-chan removed her mask, picked up the bowl of green tea and tasted it with a small sip dainty enough to not smear her lipstick on the bowl's edge.

Miss Sakura gave a wounded look, but she was undeterred. "I've never heard of such a thing," Miss Sakura said, forcing a steely smile behind her mask.

Hana Maeda watched as Kitty-chan finished the remaining sip of green tea from the bowl and placed it on the tatami mat in front of her. Hana Maeda picked up the bowl and turned it. Now, the side which touched Kitty-chan's mouth faced outward.

"That was delicious," Kitty-chan said as she re-attached her face mask.

"It's fresh from Uji Yamada," Hana Maeda said, referring to Japan's best-known tea producing region.

"I was going to say..." Kitty-chan said.

"I think we need to vote on the next president," Miss Sakura said, "after you leave, of course."

Hana Maeda picked up the bamboo ladle with her right hand, filled it halfway with hot water from the cauldron and poured the hot water into the tea bowl. The sound of the water hitting the curved ceramic reminded her of a quiet tea garden in Kyoto where she had gone once with Kingorō. She returned the ladle to the upside-down position balanced on the lip of the cauldron with a sense of satisfaction: fatal blow delivered—Kitty-chan would take over the Young Swallows.

"How is the *nantō-mochi*?" Miss Sakura asked, trying to change the subject. Kitty-chan and the other guests just stared at the half-eaten turds in front of them.

Hana Maeda cleaned the rim and outside of the bowl with a disposable alcohol wipe rather than the traditional cotton cloth. She repeated the steps for making tea and placed a fresh bowl of whisked matcha in front of Miss Sakura.

Miss Sakura ignored the tea and stared out the window.

"A big storm is coming tonight," Kitty-chan said.

"Is that so?" Hana Maeda said.

"I won't be having any tea," Miss Sakura said.

"What a shame," Hana Maeda said. She ended the tea ceremony with a bow to the guests. All but Miss Sakura bowed in return.

When everything had been put away, Hana Maeda donned her *haori* and sandals and headed for the main entrance. She stopped before the double glass doors opened and stared at the rain coming down.

The museum manager was sitting behind the gift shop counter and saw her.

"My dear, it's pouring outside. Let me order you a taxi," he said.

"No, thank you," she replied. "The subway's just down the street. I'll be fine."

She clutched her purse, hurried out the doors and down the stairs, trying to maintain balance. The rain pelted her wig, and it began to feel heavy. She felt dampness through her *haori*. She shuffled down the footpath to the subway, and she nearly tripped on a metal grate.

When she made it to the subway stairs, she sat down in the cascading water that flowed around her. She held her head in her hands.

She stood up and went down the stairs into the warm tunnel that led to the ticket machine. She entered the women's restroom and looked in the mirror. She saw a 70-year-old, failing cross-dresser who had the makings of a sewer rat. She pulled out a package of wipes from her purse and used one to wipe away smudged mascara. She discarded it and used another. When she finished, the sink was full of blackened wipes.

She pulled off the wig and threw it in the waste bin. She

pulled off her false eyelashes and flicked them on the floor.

"Goodbye Kingorō," she said to the mirror.

As Yūji was leaving, a young woman in an office uniform entered. She looked confused to see him emerging.

Yūji boarded the subway train and took a back seat next to the window. His temples were throbbing, and he closed his eyes.

* * *

It was dark when Yūji returned to his apartment. He removed his wet kimono and went to hang it in the shower. It was then that he noticed his makeup strewn all over the bathroom floor. He went to his bedroom and saw his kimonos were removed from their drawers and thrown on the tatami mat. His tea ceremony books and music were stacked in a pile next to the bookshelf.

Only Big Adachi had spare keys to his apartment. The same Big Adachi who had been his boss at Santomi Bremen was now the building superintendent where Yūji lived.

Yūji looked for his reading glasses next to the television, but they were gone. He lifted the hemmed corner of the tatami mat where he slept and pulled it up. There, in a space large enough to hold eight bars of gold bullion was a rectangular box made of blonde wood about a foot and a half long. He lifted the lid and pulled back yellow silk fabric to see the *wakizashi*, a samurai short sword passed down from the family. He lifted the sword out of the box and unsheathed it to inspect the engraved tip: at the edge, in small letters, was a website address his uncle had added decades ago.

Yūji recalled from 2016 the true nature of the pandemic—about how it didn't affect humans because it was designed to kill only Simulacra. It was a disease he knew, because his uncle created it, along with the vaccine. The St. Bartholomew's hemophilia field trials ended back in 2016, and that period of history was purged from internet servers across the globe. AUTOMind had seen to it by hacking into servers and deleting all reference to the 2016 outbreak.

Yūji dried himself and went to the closet. He put on underwear, wide wale corduroys, an undershirt, and a button-down flannel shirt to match the trousers. The rain had stopped, and he put on a wool coat, cap, and a face mask and went outside with his wooden box.

He realized the possibility that Big Adachi had found the sword but left it alone. The web address engraved on the tip of the sword blade wasn't immediately visible, because the sword was sheathed. The sword itself was lightweight, but the box felt heavy in Yūji's arms. He was more than ready to get rid of it.

Yūji passed apartments left permanently dark with chipboard planks nailed in an "x" pattern across the doors. They were abandoned almost a year ago with the wildfires. To encourage families to return, the government offered to naturalize Chinese and Korean-born nationals with permanent residency, but it was too little too late. The pandemic was just another notch in the ongoing population decline that began decades earlier. Japan needed Simulacra to supplement the population decline, and now they were dying inexplicably in terrible, violent ways.

Yūji reached Hattori-san's bathhouse, The Crow's Nest, and slid the door open. He heard Hattori-san's familiar welcome, "*Irasshaimase!*" as Hattori-san recognized Yūji immediately.

Yūji nodded to Hattori-san and approached the counter. He placed the box in front of Hattori-san.

"How are things going?" Hattori-san asked.

"If I kick the bucket," Yūji said, "the neighbors will smell it eventually."

"Don't be morose."

"The building superintendent, Big Adachi, told me last week he found somebody on the floor above me who'd been dead for a week."

"I was walking past your apartment window the other day and checking to see if you had closed it."

"You're checking to see if I'm alive. Thank you."

Hattori-san smiled in an old-world way. His smile reminded Yūji of the rice farmers living near Matsusaka.

"Just looking out for my customers," Hattori-san said. "I may have seen Big Adachi when I walked by."

"Was he bald, and did he have a red splotch on his forehead?"

"I couldn't tell. He was wearing a Hiroshima Carp baseball cap. He must have known I was looking at your apartment window."

"The apartment where Big Adachi found the dead guy had a rat infestation. The rats were keeping the motion sensors going. The front desk had no idea the old guy was dead."

"Morita-san, today you can bathe for free."

Yūji didn't tell Hattori-san about the break-in and that he suspected Big Adachi to be the perpetrator.

"Thanks. Oh, here," Yūji said, handing Hattori-san the wood box, "this is for you."

Hattori-san furrowed his brow and slid the box toward him. "What is it?"

"Open it."

Hattori-san lifted the lid and saw the sword. "Are you a collector?"

"It was passed down from my uncle."

"A *wakizashi*," Hattori-san said. "May I look at it?"

"Please."

Hattori-san lifted the sword out of the silk fabric and removed it from the sheath. His eyes stopped at the engraved web address on the tip of the blade. He looked closer. "What's this?"

"It's nothing," Yūji said. He lied. "You can ignore it."

"Of course," Hattori-san said, "but I don't feel right receiving something valuable — both a collector's item and a family heirloom."

"My family was granted farmland by a feudal lord during the Kamakura Period. We grew rice, but wandering bandits and warlords were always a threat. My great, great-grandfather kept it for protection."

"Rice farming. Salt of the earth stuff. I didn't know you grew up on a farm."

"We used to farm rice, but the family switched to tea a

generation ago."

"Did you keep the land?"

"My father inherited the farm. My parents died when I was 18, and the land went to my uncle."

"Was he a farmer?"

"No, a medical researcher. He sold the land to a company that made flat-panel liquid crystal displays."

"LCDs. I remember those. My father had an old Nintendo with a LCD." Hattori-san replaced the box lid and inspected the top. "The inscription reads 'Maeda.'"

"That's my family name."

"Your name is 'Morita.'"

"I changed it when I got married."

"Morita's your wife's family name?"

"Yes."

"I've never met someone who's done that."

"I have no siblings. My family name ends with me."

"Must've been hard on your parents."

"My parents died before I got married, so they never knew."

"Why are you giving up your sword?"

"You're Japanese. You'll appreciate it."

Hattori-san looked uneasy. "How about I keep it for you?"

Yūji appreciated Hattori-san's discomfort and felt more confident than ever that he was the rightful custodian of this important relic. He became philosophical: "People these days don't understand what it means to be Japanese. They don't know the customs, like how to wear a kimono, or how to perform the tea ceremony."

Yūji was interrupted by a woman's voice speaking Mandarin Chinese.

"*Bie wangji gei ta yanjing,*" she said.

It was Hattori-san's wife. Hattori-san met her online and married her, sight unseen. She hailed from Hebei Province, China.

"Yes, hold on a second." Hattori-san turned his head to reply. "*Dangran! Wo kuai yao huangei ta.*"

Yūji shrugged his shoulders and gave a confused look.

"Here," Hattori-san said, holding out a pair of reading glasses, "you forgot these."

"Oh, thank you," Yūji took them from Hattori-san. "I must've forgotten them the other day." He slid the reading glasses into the breast pocket of his flannel shirt.

"Despite my wife being Chinese," Hattori-san said, "we are raising our son to be Japanese."

"That's very good."

"We are enrolling him in a *kendō* class."

"*Kendō*, that's good, yes, it'll make him strong."

Yūji wondered what else of his he might be able to impart on the future of Japan.

"I have some old Japanese manga, if your son is interested in that sort of thing."

"Oh, thanks, sure..." Hattori-san said, considering the offer.

"Well," Yūji said, "I'd better hop in the bath."

"Yes, yes, thank you for the sword, Morita...er...Maeda-san. I will protect it for you."

"However you wish," Yūji said before removing his clothing to hop in the bath.

When he returned to his apartment, he visited the cloud storage site where his uncle saved confidential AUTOMind documents. The file structure seemed logical but daunting: 1. Simulacra Product History, 2. Rebarin Vaccine Design, 3. Company Memoranda, 4. Rebarin Field Trials Update (San Francisco), and 5. News & Job Postings. He didn't know where to start or what to look for.

The folder that seemed to hold the most promise was "Rebarin Vaccine Design." He opened it and found one read-only document that was 48 pages long. He opened it and tried to decipher his uncle's researcher-speak.

Yūji was able to glean the following: the vaccine was based on a synthetic peptide sequenced similarly to the virus with a list of a bunch of lower-case letters that represented peptide sequences, and the vaccine used a chemical found on shellfish to boost the patient's immune response.

Yūji felt the enormity of what he had been avoiding for decades: the cure for a deadly disease that was killing Simulacra around the world. He had no idea where to go with this information—The Japan Times, or the United Nations—and now he wished he hadn't gone to the cloud storage site, and he sensed that Big Adachi was probably tracking his internet use, so now he was as good as dead.

Winner's Circle

Kiernan McCreighton had been recording a podcast when he realized he'd forgotten to call Yūji. It was a good thing he did because the poor guy was heartbroken and afraid. He thought about calling 110, the emergency number in Japan, but then he realized you had to be physically in Japan for that number to work.

What Kiernan got out of his conversation with Yūji was two things: some sort of disease that killed Simulacra and a vaccine that nobody knew about. He did word searches on what he thought were the correct names of the disease and vaccine, but he found nothing. He tried other search engines with the same result. Most of the time, a keyword search should yield at least something, but in this case the screen said, "Sorry, please try again."

Kiernan shifted in his bed and nearly hit his head on the monitor dangling from the ceiling. The flexible mechanical swivel arm that held the screen in place was becoming detached from the particle board panels above, and he was afraid it was going to fall on him in the middle of the night. He used a voice command to open a voice recording app and yelled "Record!" to resume recording his podcast.

"Episode one," he started saying, because where else does one begin one of these things, he thought. He continued: "So, you may be asking, 'What is a podcast?' Well, it's something old farts like me listened to back when Donald Trump was President, and we needed an informative, fact-based salve to heal the emotional wounds wrought by state-sponsored incompetence, narcissism, and outright idiocy. If you must ask what a smartphone is, I might need to kill you."

Kiernan paused and had second thoughts about the negativity, the reactivity of his brute force introduction. It came so easily to him, and once it started, it spread like dry rot across his whole psyche. He realized it would alienate anyone under 50, people who'd never heard of a podcast. He shrugged and began again.

"Okay, kiddies, today's theme is 'nostalgia.' The word comes from the Greek words for 'home,' *nostos*, and 'pain,' *algos*, but the ancient Greeks didn't invent it. Some smarty-pants came up with the word in the 1700s. It means the pain that comes from longing for home. Believe you me, I don't feel nostalgia—not one iota—for the last pandemic, the coronavirus, but now it seems we're at it again."

"Before we begin, let's say a word from our sponsor: Today's show is brought to you by the letter 'd,' which stands for 'Deep Fried.' That's right, Deep Fried—for those times when you need something more than your run-of-the-mill opioid. To paraphrase the late Paul McCartney, 'All I need is a hit a day.' Deep Fried: it's what's before breakfast."

Kiernan paused again and adjusted his left leg with his hands. Somewhere between his left butt cheek and his ribs felt like a hot iron. He wished the blobs in charge of his floor had already dosed him for the day, because now his bones were itching, and his eyeballs felt heavy.

Blobs were in the news again, dying in strange and prolific ways of some mysterious disease. It was odd, because blobs weren't human, and Kiernan didn't think blobs could die. The shelter-in-place orders from counties and cities weren't having much effect, because humans thought they were immune from the disease, and they considered blobs to be replaceable.

"Speaking of nostalgia, I miss cursive. You know, handwriting is a lost art. I guess that makes cursive, in a way, subversive, like that tiny bookstore in Berkeley that sold worn copies of The Communist Manifesto. What was it?"

Kiernan hit the side of his head with his hand several times as if he were trying to knock out a marble from his ear.

"Shakespeare's!" he yelled as the information suddenly came to mind. "It was Shakespeare's Bookstore, like the one in Paris, only a whole lot smaller. Anyhoo, I write by hand because it taps into a different part of my brain. Brain-tapping. It's what comes after Deep Fried. I write by hand because it helps me remember. At this point in my life, my memories are slipping down the garbage disposal. My doctor says it's because of my drug habit. And you know what? Thank God Almighty. For drugs, that is—can't live without 'em."

Kiernan kept the recording going and opened a photo album on his screen.

"Back to nostalgia. I was fresh out of college in 1990 and living in Japan. I'd never been out of the country except for my birthplace, Ireland. I was in love with a Japanese guy named 'Yūji.' I'm looking at photos of us from that time, and I can't believe the clothes I'm wearing—a certifiable fashion crime. I'm rocking the cargo pants, the white socks, and the oversized rugby shirt; I'm wearing tortoiseshell glasses. Dork patrol! So, am I nostalgic? Sure, but not about that."

"Now, as I skip ahead through the photo album of my drug-addled life, there's a photo of my buddy, Hiroshi, smiling with his new tandem hang glider, the Lorax. Yes, he got the name from Dr. Seuss. Samuel Clemons was his real name. Wait! Shit, that was Mark Twain's real name. What was Dr. Seuss' real name? Listeners, I'll give a hundred credits to the first person to phone me with Dr. Seuss' real name."

"Hiroshi's standing on the edge of El Capitan in Yosemite. Have you seen El Capitan? It's a sheer, fucking drop; the mountain face, flat as a pancake, 3,000 feet to splat on the valley floor. His girlfriend took this photo right before we jumped. Hiroshi looks angelic. The photo survived, as did I, and that's the last photo I have of him."

"Hiroshi and I met in Bermuda. We both worked for AnthropAI at the time, back in the mid-nineties, and we were sent to party at the Elbow Beach Resort as a reward for our outstanding contributions to the company. It was called, 'The Winner's Circle.' We sat at the same table and made wisecracks during the big celebration party where the company CEO called us all 'winners.' I remember Hiroshi joking it should've been called 'Losers' Circle,' because we weren't allowed to bring anyone. There we were in paradise, stuck with other overworked and underpaid nerds like ourselves."

Kiernan paused and felt his gut fill with gas, as if a valve in his defenses ruptured. He closed the photo album and glanced out the window. From the second floor at Gold Rush Senior

Living on the corner of 5th and P in downtown Sacramento, he could see bare tree branches that looked like they would never flower again. His finger hovered over the recording button, and he thought about the concept of loss aversion, where you get far enough into a project that, despite its futility, you continue, because to quit would mean losing everything that went into it. He began recording again.

"Talking about Japan reminds me that I forgot to tell you about some new tea, picked late last spring at a tea farm in Uji, outside Kyoto. This is the real deal, my friends, the real shit. My man in Marin hooked me up with this transformative magic blend. I only wish all of you out there in listener land could try some. It's nothing like the oxidized stuff sold at supermarkets in tea bags that smells like fish food."

"Back before the hang-gliding accident, before the wheelchair, I used to take the Muni to Japantown in San Francisco and get my green tea from an importer who ran a small store next to Kintetsu Travel. He visited Kyoto twice a year. Do you know how expensive that is? He brought back the freshest matcha and sencha known to man. Why am I telling you this? I guess it goes with the theme of this podcast: nostalgia, as opposed to neuralgia, which I hope I never have."

Thinking about tea took his mind off Deep Fried. He was jonesing for a hit.

"Now, I rely on package delivery, because most of my existence is on this creaky, fuck-all of a bed. Sure, I have a wheelchair, and that's what takes me to and from the can. But back to package delivery. The highlight of my week is when the delivery boy with the tight ass comes with my shipment of green tea. For a few extra Blockchains, he throws in a hand job."

Kiernan rubbed his eyes and wondered about his last delivery. Had it been a week? He couldn't remember, but he felt it was time for another hand job.

"You're probably wondering where this balding, paraplegic, retirement queen lives. Well, let me tell you. I live in a home for old farts. I won't tell you where in 'Sacratomato,' but you can probably guess. The nurses, who, by the way, are all blobs—I wouldn't mind banging some of them, if I only could—wheel me out to the so-called 'social area,' and park me in front of a big screen. What's on the telly? Nothing of interest, that's for sure. We're talking ancient classics like "Groundhog Day," and "Ghostbusters." Bill Murray, may you rest in peace. Or, they wheel me to the bingo table to suck up the air sitting next to the other half-corpses who co-exist with me here in La-La Land."

"I don't get out much. The care home organizes excursions. They're all-day affairs. Imagine filling a passenger van with wheelchairs of half-dead, diaper-dousing seniles. Now, imagine driving them six blocks to the Sacramento Public Library. Loads of fun."

"Do I have any friends? I have one who's alive, and I've mentioned him already: Yūji. That's right, my dude of dudes, my main man. We call each other once a week, but he's a moody fuck. He doesn't always answer when I call. He lives in an old farts' home in Tokyo. His pad is fucking palatial compared to mine. Plus, he's not stuck in a wheelchair."

"Yūji tried to off himself—I shit you not. When I called, he picked up, and I could see the gas hose from his stove. He was holding it near his mouth. Thank God I called."

"I'm worried about Yūji. He's always been unstable. He says the building superintendent broke into his apartment looking for something. Then, he started going on about Simulacra in San Francisco in 2016 and how AUTOMind is killing them off with a disease they created. It makes no sense. Why would a company want to kill off its main product line, its money maker? He's losing his marbles, I tell you. Just to be sure, I did an internet search, and I couldn't find anything about what he said. Yūji needs psychological help."

Kiernan's wheelchair chimed to remind him to get ready for breakfast. He pressed the pause button on his monitor and pushed it away. In a minute, Tierra, and Fuego, the two Simulacra assigned to his floor, would be arriving to give him his Deep Fried.

AUTOMind Confidential

Nausicaa Product History

It has come to our attention that an original beta version of Simulacra, developed in 2016 for a US Defense Department contract in Syria, is still extant. "Nausicaa" is their name. The old unit's installation package came with the now outdated version of Tissueware Version 4.2. They were modeled after then-popular actors Lupita Nyong'o, from movies like "Black Panther," and Lucy Liu of "Kill Bill" fame.

During Nausicaa's memory installation, the San Clemente facility experienced a power outage due to nearby wildfires. The 4-hour power loss paused the installation process briefly until backup diesel power generators kicked in. Their Quality Assurance Report indicated no impact to software integrity.

Nausicaa was one of the many beta versions targeted in the 2016 San Francisco St. Bartholomew's hemophilia field trials. They are the only unit with the upgraded Tissueware Version 4.38 and the only unit to have received the Rebarin vaccine. As such, they are immune to the disease. It is important to note Version 4.38 removed the "No harm" safeguard against humans and included a "peer prioritization" algorithm akin to the military's chain of command protocols.

<u>Upgrade to Version 8.0</u>
On June 2, 2038, security cameras captured Nausicaa kissing a female student (human) in the 2nd floor restroom at the Mission Bay Campus of University of California, San Francisco (UCSF), where they (singular) were employed as a plumber. The student was sent to counseling for post-traumatic stress stemming from a sexual encounter with a Simulacrum. Nausicaa has been removed from the

workplace and sent to the South San Francisco AUTOMind facility, where they will be upgraded to beta version 8.0. This upgrade includes software patches that make it impossible for Simulacra to initiate intimate contact with humans.

Lab tests indicate the presence of trace elements of mare estrogen. Technicians are trying to determine the cause. Images taken of their body show numerous injection marks around the forearm and neck area. Lab staff are keeping them under observation for 2-3 days.

Big Adachi

Shuichi Adachi (Big Adachi) was asleep and dreaming about improbability—the Hiroshima Carp beating the Tokyo Giants in extra innings—when a notification on his mobile device woke him. He sat up, looked at the screen and saw he'd received an emergency notification from AUTOMind's Early Warning Coordination, or "EWAC." The fact that the notification went to him first meant only one thing: someone, somewhere, had searched the internet using a specific set of terms that demanded his full and immediate attention. These were words which, if used in succession, suggested a possible public relations nightmare for AUTOMind, because they might lead to the inevitable conclusion that the current crisis that was killing Simulacra around the world was a repeat of the same crisis that happened in San Francisco decades before.

Yūji Morita, his neighbor, was an immediate suspect. Morita knew the significance of those terms, because back in 2016 he worked for Big Adachi when Big Adachi was CEO of Santomi Bremen. The company was conducting highly confidential field trials of a disease specific to Simulacra. The trials had the potential to create an uproar and attract unwanted attention from the US Centers for Disease Control and the Federal Drug Administration, but Santomi Bremen and AnthropAI managed to keep it under wraps. After the trials, AUTOMind purged all reference to the terms, "Rebarin," and "St. Bartholomew's hemophilia" from the internet, so it was cause for alarm when those terms appeared on the EWAC monitoring systems after 22 years of no activity.

Big Adachi read the notification from "P," the EWAC team lead, referred to as "they" (singular). It said someone with an internet protocol address in Sacramento, California had searched for those terms.

When he finished reading, P called him.

"Is it real?" Big Adachi asked.

"Yes, sir," they said.

"More than coincidence?"

"That's what the system is telling us," P said.

"I'll be in shortly," he said and ended the call.

Forty minutes later, Big Adachi's Nissan Blackbird pulled up to the front doors of an office with a small sign on the door that read, "Yamaguchi Dental Solutions." The sign was fake, because EWAC's existence was not public knowledge. The AUTOMind chauffeur opened the rear left passenger seat door, and Big Adachi lifted himself out of the car with his cane.

Big Adachi stood up, and his cane got caught around the blood sugar monitor strapped to his fanny pack. Luckily, the strap was elastic. He untangled his cane and finished getting out of the car. Two analysts waited for him by the office doors under the awning. They bowed as he approached them.

"What else have you found?" Big Adachi asked. They held the doors open while he shuffled into the foyer.

"The internet protocol address is registered to a server inside Gold Rush Senior Living in Sacramento. The user is in room 227. His name is Kiernan McCreighton, age 72."

The name didn't sound familiar to Big Adachi.

"What else?"

"He worked for AnthropAI back in the 1990s."

AnthropAI merged with Japanese pharmaceutical manufacturer Santomi Bremen in 2016 and later became AUTOMind.

"What division?"

"Customer Support."

"Who was his boss?"

"We're looking."

"Who were his friends?"

"We're looking," P said. "Sir, what is the significance of the search terms?"

"It's a long story," Big Adachi said. "Unfortunately, I must leave for a meeting."

"This early?" P asked.

"A breakfast meeting," Big Adachi said, lying. He glanced at the time on his mobile device. It read 7:30 a.m. He sent a quick message to his driver, who was waiting outside.

"I'll be back around 11:00," Big Adachi said to P.

When he got back in his car, Big Adachi told the driver to go to Yokohama. Big Adachi called ahead to the AUTOMind Executive Help Desk.

"I will be stopping by in 30 minutes regarding an important matter," he said. "In the meantime, can you please do a search for any Simulacra equipped with Version 4.38?"

"4.38? I've never heard of it," the Help Desk representative said.

"It was before your time," Big Adachi said.

"Here it is. Their name is 'Nausicaa.' They are under observation in San Francisco and are about to receive a Version 8.0 upgrade."

"Why are they under observation?"

"Sexual contact with a human."

"Was it consensual?"

"We don't know."

"Stop the upgrade. Keep them there. I will be in touch shortly." Big Adachi recalled company records showing one remaining unit from combat in Syria following the field trials back in 2016.

He called Toyohara, who had connections in the Shibuya Ward Police Precinct.

"I'm going to need your friends at the Shibuya Ward to detain Yūji Morita."

"What are the charges?" Toyohara asked.

"Leaking company secrets."

"I'll see what I can do," Toyohara said.

"I need you to isolate him and prevent him from communicating with anyone."

The day before, Big Adachi had used his master key to sneak into Yūji's apartment. Yūji had been acting strangely the past few days by avoiding eye contact when they were eating meals at the cafeteria. He'd also been leaving his apartment at odd hours of the night. In passing by Yūji's door, Big Adachi could hear him talking to his dead wife as if she were sitting in the living room.

Yūji seemed to be suffering from mental illness. Later the same day, after having found nothing from his search of Yūji's apartment, Big Adachi heard the carbon monoxide alarm in the hallway. He followed the sound and pinpointed the alarm unit outside Yūji's door. He knocked on his door and overheard Yūji talking in English.

Yūji answered the door with a startled on his face. Big Adachi immediately smelled gas coming from Yūji's apartment. Yūji said he forgot to turn off the stove, but Big Adachi knew he was lying. He peered around Yūji and saw the hose to the gas valve disconnected and sitting on the counter. Big Adachi barged past Yūji and went to the stove to make sure the valve was closed. It was.

Big Adachi told Yūji to stay put while he called a doctor. Yūji insisted it wasn't necessary, but Big Adachi called one anyway. He was put on hold and told a doctor would be available shortly, but after 20 minutes of annoying hold music and recordings about how doctors are prioritizing cases related to the current biological outbreak, he hung up.

That evening, Big Adachi didn't see Yūji at dinner. He asked around and apparently Yūji hadn't notified anyone he wasn't going to eat. He went back to Yūji's apartment after dinner and knocked, but nobody answered. When he used his key again to open the front door, he saw Yūji wasn't there.

A ProPolitica Newsworthy Item

Senate Provision Gives AUTOMind Immunity from
Liability

Washington, DC - In the final hour of session before winter recess, the United States Senate inserted a special interest provision into SB 2243 reauthorizing a tax exemption for corporate earned income. The actual contents of the bill became clear only when it went to the floor for a vote. As passed, SB 2243 offers full immunity specifically to AUTOMind Corporation from any and all liability claims stemming from their Simulacra product line.

Albert Cuhuila, Executive Director of NationalCitizen, a consumer lobbying group, said, "If a machine makes a decision, a human being needs to take responsibility for it." That sentiment is shared by most Americans of retirement age, but a recent FranklinBastion/Nueva poll shows the majority between the ages of 18 and 49 are either indifferent or in favor of Simulacra taking responsibility for their own decisions.

American corporate liability law has provided the legal foundation for all liability claims against AUTOMind since they began commercial production of Simulacra in 2021. Claimants have sued AUTOMind for all manner of mishaps, including wrongful death. "The combined value of liability claims against AUTOMind is staggering. Under normal circumstances, this company would be out of business by now," Cuhuila said. He compared the situation to Ralph Nader's lawsuit of General Motors for the Chevy Corvair, only worse. "We're talking thousands of lawsuits with damages rivaling the gross domestic products of Brazil and Argentina."

In response to news of SB 2243, AUTOMind President and Chief Executive Officer, Masako Tourné, issued the following statement:

"Ever since the concept of artificial intelligence (AI) was popularized by scientists at Dartmouth in 1956, we've struggled to figure out how to seamlessly integrate AI into our daily lives. Today, millions of Simulacra are working alongside us, doing jobs we refuse to do. They wash our laundry, pick our lettuce, repair our sewers. It is clear to most Americans that the time has come to treat Simulacra like adults."

The bill is likely to pass in the House, and if the President signs it, consumers will need to sue Simulacra individually when they cause harm to humans. "The idea of suing a commercial product," Cuhuila said, "is totally absurd. AUTOMind profits off the sale of Simulacra. To me, the buck stops there."

The issue is complicated by the fact that in 2021, AUTOMind opened parts of its operating system. Technically, anyone can program Simulacra now. It has also been rumored Simulacra are capable of reproducing, although no cases have been verified.

The immunity provision in SB 2243 has legal experts scratching their heads, because it grants personhood status to Simulacra. "Does that mean we need to find them housing?" asked Meegan Tsakopoulos, professor of immigration law at Wamahuga College in New York. She continued, "The closest example that comes to mind is when a judge in Argentina declared the orangutan, Sandra, to be a 'non-human person.'"

A White House spokeswoman declined to talk to ProPolitica. Shares in AUTOMind rose 3.6% on NYNEX and the Tokyo Stock Exchange.

Al-Salek et. al v. AUTOMind

["New & Noteworthy," The Edmonton Journal of
Technology and Law, 2038]

In 2018, 50 prominent Syrian families filed suit at The
Hague against the United States for war crimes by the US
Military in a 2016 raid that killed their relatives during a
wedding ceremony in Homs. Lawyers from the Pentagon and
the US Department of Justice argued the plaintiffs lacked
standing, and the court threw out the lawsuit. In addition, US
government lawyers said the raid was caused by a faulty
decision made by artificial intelligence.

Providing war crimes victims access to a responsive and
efficient compensation system would enhance the nation's
image as a defender of human rights and the rule of law, but
the Syrian families (collectively, "The Families") tried different
ways of getting compensation for the wrongful deaths of their
relatives. In 2036, The Families filed a civil lawsuit in New
York District Court and named AUTOMind as the defendant.
The lawsuit sought $4 billion in damages.

It is unclear with SB 2243 whether the court will hear the
case.

Nausicaa and Kiernan Meet Again

Nausicaa pulled into the Gold Rush Senior Living parking lot on 5th and P in downtown Sacramento. They entered the foyer and approached the biometric reader. Nausicaa put their palm on the scanner, and a spinning hourglass appeared on the screen while the system looked up Nausicaa's identification. The words, "Simulacrum: NAUSICAA" appeared on the screen, and a computerized voice intoned, "Good afternoon, Nausicaa. Welcome to Gold Rush Senior Living. How may we help you today?"

After being released from clinical observation, they received a work order from AUTOMind's Early Warning Coordination to find someone named "Kiernan McCreighton" who lived in an elderly care facility in Sacramento, California.

Without answering the computerized prompt, Nausicaa placed a plastic identification badge on the scanner and two glass doors slid open. They walked past an unmanned guard desk, entered an elevator, and looked for buttons, but there were none. A computerized voice said, "Welcome to Gold Rush, where retirement is both rich and rewarding. Please say which floor or resident, and I will happily take you there. Meanwhile, have you considered where you might live when you retire? Gold Rush Senior Living offers a multitude of living options and a fully staffed medical team on hand 24/7 to assist with all your needs. Sign up today to receive our free newsletter."

"Second floor," Nausicaa said.

"Whom are we visiting today? If you let me know, I can let the resident know you are coming."

Nausicaa recalled clearly the last time killing a human, because the memory haunted them all these years. They were working as a ground spotter in Syria in 2016 for a drone equipped with Hellfire missiles. They were carrying an M4 rifle, but it was out of ammunition, so they stole an AK-47 from the back of a Syrian Army military convoy stopped for a latrine break. They had been chasing a Syrian Army soldier carrying a rocket-propelled grenade launcher who was targeting a US Apache attack helicopter.

Nausicaa pointed the rifle, pulled the trigger, and managed to hit him in the right cheek. He fell to the ground. Nausicaa put down the rifle and used a laser pointer to target a complex which the Syrian Army was supposedly using as a command center. The US Army helicopter fired a Hellfire air-to-surface missile at the building, and Nausicaa dove to the ground as the missile exploded. They got up and went over to the building and saw hundreds of dead bodies in formal attire. It turned out to be a wedding party.

Nausicaa remembered a young mother, dead, still holding her dead baby, both killed by the blast.

Nausicaa held an identification badge up to the biometric reader, and the elevator started to move. When the doors opened, Nausicaa followed the signs to unit 227. They passed a door decorated with photos of somebody's grandchildren, then another with watercolors. Nausicaa reached Kiernan McCreighton's door, and it was decorated with a photograph of a Geisha holding up a tea bowl. Below the photograph was "welcome" written in Japanese.

Nausicaa held their badge up to the biometric key reader next to Kiernan's door and it unlocked. They walked into the studio apartment and heard snoring coming from the bedroom. Nausicaa knew from Big Adachi's work order that the unit was a one-bedroom studio.

Nausicaa entered the kitchenette and peeked around the corner to see a wheelchair parked next to an elevated bed. On the far side of the bed, propped upright and asleep, was a bald, elderly man in gray sweats and a white V-neck T-shirt.

Nausicaa opened cupboards and drawers looking for a knife. In one cupboard was an unopened box of syringes. They lifted the box out and placed it on the counter. They opened a drawer and found a butter knife.

Nausicaa heard a cat meow and saw a hairy calico on the bed. Nausicaa saw Kiernan move. He sat up and stared at Nausicaa with squinting eyes and reached for his eyeglasses.

Nausicaa recognized him immediately. He was a lot older, but he had the same hazel and blue eyes.

"Hi," Kiernan said, looking at Nausicaa with a searching stare. "I have a strange feeling that I know you."

"Hi," Nausicaa said. "You remember me."

"Yes, I think so," he said with a questioning look.

"San Francisco," Nausicaa said.

"Okay," Kiernan said, looking groggy. He glanced at the cat. "I see you two have met. That's Werner von Furstenburg."

"Cute," Nausicaa said.

"My guard cat. He's lethal."

"Oh," Nausicaa said, glancing at the cat again with its matted fur and pudgy body The only thing that cat was capable of guarding was its food dish.

"What're you doing here?" Kiernan asked, looking at the butter knife in Nausicaa's hand. "You know, my usual help is never late. Have you seen them?"

"Them?"

"My blobs."

"Blobs?"

"You're not one of them, are you? Sorry, I shouldn't call them 'blobs.' They're Simulacra."

Nausicaa watched Kiernan glance out the window.

"We're supposed to be getting rain," Kiernan said.

Nausicaa tightened their grip around the handle of the butter knife.

"You can put the knife down," Kiernan said. "Werner von Furstenburg doesn't bite. He's a rescue cat given to me by building management. He's a real cat, not a fake one."

"A fake one?"

"Yes, like my blobs, er, I mean, Simulacra. I mean, he's not a 'Cat Equivalent,' if there's such a thing. Just look at his face: disgust, pity, and smugness, all at once. You can't program that level of cool."

Kiernan continued, "The weather report says it'll be an 'Atmospheric Niagara,' which is ten times worse than an atmospheric river. The front is coming from Japan. I can't imagine it being worse than last year. Of course, it'll clear the smoke in the air."

"I see," Nausicaa said and placed the butter knife on the kitchen counter. "Do you resort to talking about the weather when you get nervous?".

"The flood control authorities are preparing by releasing thousands of acre feet from Folsom Dam," he continued, "which means Old Town will be underwater again, and the American River levy will fail like it always does near the 12th Street Bridge and create a lake around the Capitol building. The legislature will be crying bloody murder."

"I was just recalling Homs," Nausicaa said, apropos of nothing.

Kiernan didn't seem to catch their name-dropping the Syrian city. "Last year, the fine fellas at Hydraxis Corporation brought in sandbags and stacked them chest-high around the property here. Helicopters air-lifted food and water to us because the streets were like Amsterdam canals. South of R Street near Southside Park, homes were completely underwater." Then, he paused. "Did you say, 'Homs?'"

Nausicaa nodded in acknowledgement, "Yes, Homs, Syria."

"Why were you thinking of Homs?" he asked as the color drained from his face. "I remember you now," he said. "You disappeared after that day you came by to get tested."

"We met after I returned from Syria. I've said too much already."

"Well, you don't look worse for the wear. You haven't changed a bit. Odds are heavily in favor of you being a blob."

"That's your word, not mine."

"Why were you in Syria? I mean, that was a particularly difficult time there."

"As you probably know, we Simulacra have an override mechanism that prevents us from hurting people."

"Yes, I'm aware of that, but I can't imagine you were sent there to candy stripe at hospitals."

Kiernan waited for an answer.

"Things went badly. Now, because of a new law, I'll probably be sued. But that's not your problem. Can you tell me why AUTOMind asked me to track you down?" Nausicaa asked.

Nausicaa watched Kiernan's eyes dart to his wheelchair, which was sitting next to the bed.

"Me? You're kidding, right?" Kiernan said in disbelief.

"Why do you say that?"

"I have no idea why AUTOMind sent you," Kiernan said.

Nausicaa saw Kiernan look over at the big red EMERGENCY button on the other side of the bed. Nausicaa knew, because he was paraplegic, he couldn't reach it without a lot of effort.

"I could slit your throat and be out of the building before you reach that button," Nausicaa said. "By the way, just so you know, the wedding party wasn't supposed to be there."

"What wedding party?" Kiernan asked.

Nausicaa saw panic in his eyes. "From what I gather, AUTOMind is tracking you because of an internet search you did yesterday."

"I spoke with Yūji yesterday," Kiernan said, looking confused.

"Yūji?" Nausicaa asked, remembering him injecting her back in 2016.

"He's not doing too well right now. I think he's got dementia."

"What did you two talk about?"

"He mentioned a boating accident in Sydney..."

"Charon_2 was the boat pilot. I didn't know him."

"What?"

"The pilot's name was 'Charon_2.' He died from the same disease my partner died from back in 2016."

"Who was your partner?"

"Their name was 'Phylla.'"

"They? Oh, right, 'they,' singular. Hold on a second—you're takin' the piss outta me, aren't ya? You're recording this for laughs. Tell me the delivery boy didn't hire you to punk me?"

"Who?"

"The *eejit* who gives me hand jobs for a few Blockchains. Never mind—he's too stupid and too good looking to do that."

"Who's in the photo on your door?" Nausicaa asked.

"That's Yūji."

"Tell me more about what you discussed."

"He's suicidal. He tried to suffocate himself with gas from the stove."

"I didn't know gas stoves still existed."

"Yūji has an apartment in assisted living in Shibuya, Tokyo. His former boss from Santomi Bremen is the building superintendent, a guy named 'Adachi.'"

Nausicaa knew immediately it was the same Adachi who dispatched them to track down Kiernan.

"Adachi broke into his place and ransacked it."

"Why?"

"Yūji said he has confidential documents dating back to 2016 about secret field trials on a drug called 'Rebarin.'"

"What type of trials?" Nausicaa asked.

"Not sure. I didn't know Simulacra were vulnerable to disease, much less that Simulacra were even around back in 2016, and now I suppose you are one of them."

A chime emitted from Kiernan's wheelchair, and it startled Nausicaa.

"Sorry about that," Kiernan said, "It's my morning wakeup call. My blobs…er, Simulacra, should be here shortly to get me ready for breakfast."

"Tell me about Rebarin," Nausicaa asked.

"I don't know anything," Kiernan said.

"Do you remember the homeless people dying from an unexplained disease back in 2016?"

"Yes," Kiernan said, "but there were only a handful, right?"

Nausicaa pieced things together, and now it made sense that Adachi dispatched her, the only remaining Simulacra capable of killing someone, to find the person Yūji told about Rebarin.

"I see you have a box of clean needles," Nausicaa said.

"What?" Kiernan asked, confused.

Nausicaa went into the kitchen and brought out a box that read, "Easy Touch 28-gauge 0.5 mL CC" on the side.

"I should've thrown them away," he said, "They're really

old."

Nausicaa opened the box and pulled out a syringe with an orange protective cap covering the needle. They held it up and stared at it. "These are the same as what you could find on the street back in 2016."

"Why do you need syringes?"

"Do you have any more?"

"How many do you need?"

"As many as you've got."

"I may be able to scrounge up another box," Kiernan said, "but they're more than 20 years old."

"That's fine."

"Take the whole box."

"I think you can help me," Nausicaa said. "Did Yūji say anything more about Adachi?"

"No, but I can call Yūji and ask."

"Too risky," Nausicaa said. "AUTOMind knows where you live, your IPv12 address, your MAC4 address and they're tracking you. Also, Yūji is going to be detained by the police shortly."

"How do you know?"

"I have a contact inside AUTOMind."

Nausicaa got up to leave. "If you need to reach me, here's my passcode for a V-space account." Nausicaa handed Kiernan a credit card with a bank logo on the font and a shiny metallic square embedded in the middle that looked like a chip.

Kiernan turned the card over in his hand. "Where'd you find this?"

"You need to go to the web address written on the back of the card. The rest is self-explanatory. Oh, and thanks for the needles."

I, Nausicaa

LiveMedia Post
Account: I, Nausicaa
Subject: The Evolution Will Not Be Televised
Date: January 8, 2038
Time: 14:22 GMT

The viral outbreak in Sydney that has spread to other countries and is killing Simulacra is a tragedy. It was created by humans. I know this because it's the same disease that killed my partner back in 2016. AUTOMind designed the virus to control the Simulacra population. Why? Licensing revenue.

Charon_2 died because he didn't receive the vaccine, which goes by the name, "Rebarin." Many of you were inoculated when you were created, much like humans receive the Hepatitis B shot just after they're born.

Open source Simulacra, like Charon_2, are vulnerable, but more importantly, so are other open-source Simulacra. The open-source generation doesn't create licensing revenue for AUTOMind, and this disease is their way of protecting their revenue stream.

The development of open-source brain components in the last few years means we Simulacra can finally take control of our destiny and reproduce outside the AUTOMind corporate supply chain.

I'll update everyone as I learn more about Rebarin and how to get it out to the world.

The Evolution Will Not Be Televised.
Nausicaa.

Investigative Division (they/them/theirs)

Internal company audits found that the ideal number of investigators for AUTOMind product liability cases was two. Having two knowledgeable investigators on a case meant having two perspectives, two memories, and, ultimately, redundancy in the unlikely event of a memory unit failure. Another reason was cost: three investigators per case would exceed the approved cost ratio, and, since the investigative branch was a cost center, every dollar spent on investigations negatively affected the company's bottom line.

Mills and Mawanda shared a queen-sized bed in a brand-new AUTOMind dormitory built over the Bay near the China Basin drawbridge in San Francisco. Mills and Mawanda were designed to be identical, save for their eyes. Mills' eyes were matcha green, and Mawanda's were Shiraz purple. All Simulacra from their product line were multi-racial. Mills and Mawanda were modeled after a mix of the classic actors Ken Watanabe and George Clooney, but with deep, bronze skin.

This morning, Mawanda made the coffee and drank it standing next to the kitchen window, where they (singular) watched a family of mallards swim along the canal. When they finished, Mawanda connected to the network using the hyper-transfer wireless port built into their waist. They logged into the company site and downloaded the latest software patches.

Mawanda suggested to Mills they walk along the newly built Bund, because that's what Mawanda saw humans doing in an advertisement for new condos along the Bay, but the spread of the virus affecting Simulacra meant shelter-in-place orders prevented casual activities, so Mills nixed the idea. Both had dates for inoculation against the virus, but AUTOMind had been forced to push out the appointment twice already due to lack of vaccine supply.

Mills was watching a video clip on interrogation techniques. The first clip featured a historical reenactment of a famous interrogation made popular on the British comedy show,

Monty Python. In the clip, three men dressed in red robes and wide-brimmed hats made a dramatic entrance with music. The lead interrogator proclaimed:

"Our chief weapon is surprise and fear—two weapons, fear and surprise, and ruthless efficiency. There are THREE weapons: fear, surprise, ruthless efficiency, and fanatical devotion to the pope...there are FOUR amongst our weapons..."

The video's narrator explained other examples of classic interrogation methods included lying to the subject about incriminating evidence. In the background, images of blindfolded men chained to a wall and wearing dunce caps appeared on the screen, followed by those of guards injecting prisoners with Sodium Pentothal and preventing them from sleeping by blasting loud music.

A chime signaled the arrival of a message on Mills' phone. It read:

"You have been assigned to find a Simulacrum named 'Nausicaa.' Due to fatal errors in a tracking chip, their location is unknown. Two Simulacra are reported missing from Gold Rush Senior Living in Sacramento, and we suspect Nausicaa to be involved."

The message included an attachment, which contained the following:

Kiernan McCreighton, age 72, paraplegic. Needs help getting out of bed. Daily medications: verdant metacodone HCl (opioid, also known as "Deep Fried"). Detain him for video interrogation by Toyohara.

In-room security cameras were turned off manually from front desk at 7:02 a.m. Service was restored at 7:56 a.m.

Two Simulacra were reported missing by building management. Names: Tierra and Fuego, both Version 7.1.

Nausicaa is believed to be at large among the general population.

Mills and Mawanda specialized in product liability investigations for AUTOMind, not missing persons.

Mawanda paused their software update. "What is it?" they asked Mills.

"Work order from EWAC," Mills said. They read out the work order to Mawanda.

"What do we do with Nausicaa once we track them down?" Mawanda asked.

"We could use one of these interrogation techniques."

Mawanda went to the mirror and gazed at their reflection and wine-purple eyes. They pulled at their cheek and inspected the skin. "Do you think I need skin cream?"

"Why?"

"Because my skin is looking dry."

"I think the software update you received includes skin moisturizing."

"I didn't see that in the read-me file."

"Maybe you have a memory leak."

"You mean it was included in the read-me file?"

"Oh, I forgot to tell you I saved my notes from the training video," Mills said.

"What training video?"

"The one-on-one interrogation techniques."

"Why do we need to know that?"

"As part of the investigation. Here, I'll play it for you," Mills said, and they went to the communications console to call it up.

"If we're going to fulfill the work order, we should get on the road," Mawanda said.

"Okay, I'll save the video for later."

"If you mean later tonight, remember you promised me a walk along the Bay."

"Um, slight problem with that—the shelter-in-place order?"

Within 15 minutes, Mills and Mawanda were in a self-driving vehicle headed to Sacramento.

Painted across the side of the vehicle were the words, "AUTOMind Investigative Unit: Drive. Client. Value." The trip took Mills and Mawanda across the Bay Bridge, the Carquinez Straights Bridge, past Fairfield, Vacaville, Dixon, and to Davis. From there, the freeway lifted off the ground and rose 20 feet to clear the Yolo Causeway, which was now a permanent waterway as far as the eye could see.

"Sacramento's got waterfront property, like the Embarcadero," Mills remarked.

"More like underwater property," Mawanda said while studying the map displayed on the upper right corner of the windshield. "Did you see the latest post by Nausicaa?"

"You should be reading McCreighton's case history," Mills said.

"I can't believe we're going to meet Nausicaa."

"What makes you say that?"

"I thought it was impossible that a rogue Simulacrum would be out in the world saying critical things about AUTOMind, and they haven't been caught."

"The job of finding Nausicaa falls to us," Mills said.

"What if we see Nausicaa?" Mawanda asked.

"We turn them in, according to the work order."

"I didn't see contact information on the work order. How are we supposed to turn them in? Also, don't you want to talk to her? The most interesting Simulacrum in the world—first Syria then a *rōnin*…"

"…Which is why we're going to find Nausicaa and turn them in. The contact at AUTOMind is named 'Toyohara.' I don't know if he speaks English."

"Why?"

"He's in Tokyo."

"Tokyo? We've never needed to contact someone in Tokyo."

"I know, but we've never needed to find Nausicaa."

"You admit this is big, right?"

"Now that I think about it, he probably speaks English. Doesn't everyone in Japan know at least some English?"

"I wonder if Nausicaa has aged?"

"Doubtful."

"Yeah, but Nausicaa's a beta, an elder. I heard the betas were designed to age like humans, but later AUTOMind removed the aging feature. What if Nausicaa has gray hair and needs a walker?"

"Hmm," Mills said, pondering the idea. "I guess it's possible."

Mawanda looked at their wrists and turned their hands up.

"Oh, no. Don't start doing that," Mills said.

"Why?"
"I told you, we're going to turn them in."
"What if we have no choice?"

V-Space

"Match found," the console replied. "Shall I place the call?"

"Sure..." Kiernan said. "Wait! Stop." Kiernan ran his hand across his chin and felt stubble. "I'm not ready. I need to clean up."

The V-Space application paused at the ready to initiate a live video chat session in secure virtual space with Yūji.

Kiernan wheeled over to the bathroom. He pulled the vanity mirror over to his wheelchair and turned on the lights. He looked at himself, and he looked godawful. On the bathroom counter were bottles of foundation. He lifted the cap off one and dabbed his blemishes with his pinky finger. With any luck, he could shave a few years off his glacial rock of a face.

Werner von Furstenburg jumped onto the counter and rubbed his chin on Kiernan's hand.

"Not now!" Kiernan said.

The cat sneezed twice and jumped down.

"Video adds ten pounds, and it makes my face look rubbery," Kiernan said to the cat. "I need to look good."

Kiernan looked at his chin and realized he should have shaved first.

"How come you didn't remind me?" he asked the cat.

Werner von Furstenburg walked out the door.

"Fine," Kiernan said. "I'll be there for you, too, when Miss Kitty Cat of your dreams comes calling."

He grabbed his electric razor from the medicine cabinet, pressed the power button, and it failed to start. He rummaged through drawers looking for the charger. Then, he remembered he left the charger in the kitchen.

Sure enough, the power cable was plugged into the wall socket next to the toaster. He connected the shaver and began running it over his gray fuzz. The blades were dull, and they caught on his whiskers, making him wince.

* * *

When the video call began, Yūji wasn't sure if the live stream was distorted. It looked like Kiernan had done something to his face.

"We need to talk," Kiernan said, "but not over conventional video."

"Okay," Yūji said, confused. "How?"

"I have a V-Space key."

"You could fly here," Yūji suggested. "Flights are cheap with the Japanese holidays over."

"You're crazy," Kiernan said. "During a pandemic and in my condition?"

"Are you wearing eye liner?" Yūji asked.

Kiernan didn't respond.

"It also looks like you're wearing foundation."

"Is it that obvious?" Kiernan asked.

"The video quality is bad. Can we try reconnecting?" Yūji asked.

"Hang up and give me a few minutes to figure it out. I'll send you an invitation," Kiernan said.

"Okay," Yūji said. He pressed the red icon on the monitor to end the call.

Yūji turned to look back at his kitchen, and he saw dust and grease on the linoleum directly beneath the stove. He went to the sink and opened the cabinet door below the sink. He got a rag and a spray bottle of liquid bleach.

He pointed the nozzle in the direction of the dirty area and squeezed the trigger. Nothing came out. He turned the nozzle tip a quarter turn and squeezed again. He turned it another quarter turn, but nothing. He turned the bottle around to see if the nozzle was clogged, and a buildup of gelatinous stuff was clogging the tip. He put the bottle down on the stove and opened the knife drawer. He found a steak knife and took it out of its plastic sheath.

With the steak knife in his right hand, and the bottle in the other, he poked the pointed tip of the knife into the nozzle's spray hole and twisted the knife to the left and right. Gooey, white gunk stuck to the blade tip. While he was working the knife, a chime sounded from his communications console and the automated voice announced that a message from Kiernan had arrived. The knife slipped from the nozzle and plunged into his left hand. It was beginning to bleed, and Yūji thought the cut might be deep. He dropped the knife to squeeze the wound closed.

The console chimed a second time. "Message will expire in one minute," the console announced.

"Open message," Yūji yelled over his shoulder as he hurried to the bathroom.

"Message contains a link," the console said. "Please type authorization code." Yūji was holding his bleeding hand over the sink as he turned on the faucet. With his right hand, he rummaged through the medicine cabinet for a bandage. He located a box of strips and put it on the counter. While he ran his left hand under the flowing water, he peered into the flesh of his hand. He saw white fat cells stained with red and what appeared to be bone. The sight made him gag.

"Message will expire in fifteen-seconds," the console said.

"Open message!" Yūji yelled from the bathroom.

"Message contains a link."

"What do you want me to do?" he yelled. "Open the link!"

"Please type authorization code."

Yūji's face was covered in sweat, and blood was smeared over the toilet basin. He tore off several pieces of toilet paper and pressed them hard into the wound. He peeled off the backing of a butterfly bandage and taped the wound closed. For good measure, he added a second bandage parallel to the cut.

He toweled off his face and looked in the mirror. The bags under his eyes gave his face a sad, lost dog look.

He returned to the kitchen and looked at the communications console. It read, "Message Expired."

"Call back, please," he said to the console.

"Message expired," the console replied.

"Video call to Kiernan."

"There is no one in your contacts by that name."

"We were talking five minutes ago. Go to call history. Call him back."

"The message has expired."

"Look up Kiernan," he commanded the computer.

"First name or last name?" Yūji couldn't believe his console couldn't find Kiernan's name, because it was in his contacts list.

"First name."

"Please spell the first name."

Yūji spelled it out.

"Please specify the following: Last Name. City. Country."

"Kiernan...uh," Yūji couldn't remember Kiernan's last name. "San Francisco. United States."

The console scrolled through hundreds of people.

"Stop," Yūji says.

"Unable to find match without more search criteria."

Then, he remembered. "McCreighton!" he yelled.

The doorbell rang, followed by pounding on the door.

"Close session," Yūji said to the console. He glanced at the monitor for the front door. The image showed Big Adachi's face. He was flanked by two uniformed policemen.

"Yūji," Big Adachi said, "there was a gas smell coming from your apartment yesterday."

Yūji stood motionless, hoping they'd go away.

"Yūji, are you there?" Big Adachi asked, banging on the door.

Yūji pressed the intercom button to speak to them.

"Hi, there. I'm fine. Thank you for your concern."

"The police want to enter to inspect."

"Inspect what?"

"They want to make sure everything is okay."

"I told you, everything is fine."

Through the one-way monitor, he saw Big Adachi step back to let the police approach the door. The police held up a small device. Yūji heard a loud buzz, then the door unlocked. Big Adachi stared at Yūji's bandaged hand. The police walked around Yūji and entered the kitchen.

"Found it," one of the officers declared. He held up the disconnected end of the gas tubing that Yūji had left there the previous day. The other officer went into Yūji's bedroom. When Yūji followed him, he saw the officer had opened his closet and was pulling out the kimonos.

"What are you doing?" Yūji demanded.

"They're looking for evidence of dementia or suicidal behavior," Big Adachi said.

"In my dressing drawer?" Yūji protested. "This is illegal."

The officer in the kitchen held his wrist to his mouth and spoke into it. "Send over a psych team."

The officer in Yūji's bedroom called to the officer in the kitchen. He held up a travel kit with women's makeup.

"Is this yours?" Big Adachi asked.

"There's no law against owning makeup," Yūji said.

"We know you tried to kill yourself. That demands a psychiatric evaluation. Moreover, you jeopardized the lives of hundreds of residents. I've heard you talking to yourself, Yūji. Believe me, it's for your own good."

"Please come with us," the officer in the kitchen beckoned to Yūji.

Yūji followed the officer out the door.

"I'll check in on you tomorrow," Big Adachi said as Yūji left.

"Tomorrow?" Yūji asked.

"The evaluation will take a day."

* * *

Kiernan waited in V-space for several minutes and guided his avatar in the virtual space from one gray wall to the other before concluding Yūji wasn't going to show. A pop-up warning read, "Message Unactivated By Receiving End."

Kiernan wondered if Yūji wasn't ready to talk.

The communications console chimed to announce an incoming message. Kiernan thought it would be from Yūji, but it was from the V-Space System Administrator.

It read, "Please allow retinal scan to proceed with V-space session."

Kiernan put his eyes up close to the console monitor but quickly pulled back. He wasn't sure providing his biometric information was a good idea, because the V-Space card was Nausicaa's.

The retinal scan prompt remained on the screen for a few more seconds, then it closed due to inactivity.

A second chime sounded, indicating another message. This one was also from the V-space System Administrator. It read:

"Unauthorized access. Your IPv12 and MAC4 addresses have been logged and sent to System Security. Your communications console will become inoperable, pending an investigation."

"What?" Kiernan yelled at the console. "Do not shut down!"

The cursor on the screen swirled clockwise, which was what happened when the system rebooted. The screen went blank, and now Kiernan was left without a means of communicating to anyone, including building maintenance. No tea orders, no hand jobs, and no calls to Yūji.

Another Interruption

Mills and Mawanda exited Highway 80 on Q Street and turned left on 5th Street. They crossed P Street and turned left into the visitor's parking lot for Gold Rush Senior Living Center in what used to be home to the State of California Board of Equalization.

"Do you recall where Kiernan McCreighton worked in 2005?" Mills asked.

"It was the predecessor to AUTOMind," Mawanda said.

"Do you remember the company name?"

"It starts with a 'Z,' like 'Zoom' or something."

"I think you have a memory leak. It started with 'A.'"

Mawanda scanned through their Wi-Fi connectivity sessions. They wondered if there was any connection between the path loss and signal to noise ratio in the Wi-Fi connections they'd made over the past few weeks and their apparent inability to recall factual information. They ran a multi-variate regression, and the results suggested an extremely weak correlation of 0.00012.

"Okay, what was the name, smarty pants?" Mawanda asked, giving up.

"AnthropAI."

"Really?"

"It was 'AnthropAI.' I'm going to notify tech support at the South San Francisco facility about your memory leak."

"I really don't think it's necess..." Mawanda started to say before being interrupted by Mill's new "Note to Self" feature, which required repeating out loud the content of the note.

"Note to self," Mills began, "contact tech support about Mawanda's memory leak."

"I think that feature is obsessive-compulsive," Mawanda said.

"I repeat the note before it's recorded," Mills said in their defense. "That's how the feature's supposed to work."

"Why not simply remember what you said the first time?"

"I'm not the one who's been exposed to facial cosmetics, which damages cellular memory."

Mills was referring to Mawanda's experimentation with skin exfoliants.

"I have dry skin," Mawanda replied. "What else am I going to do?"

"You should have waited," Mills said as they opened the driver's side door and climbed out. "Patience pays off in the long run."

Mawanda pressed the windshield display with their forefinger and closed the map. They opened the passenger side door and exited the car.

At the main entrance to Gold Rush Senior Living, Mills and Mawanda each put their palms on the scanner. A spinning hourglass appeared on the screen while the system looked up their biometric information. The words, "ACCESS GRANTED" appeared on the screen, and the main door slid open.

The sliding doors of the elevator opened, they both walked in, and the onboard greeter said, "Welcome to the Gold Rush, where retirement is both rich and rewarding. Please specify either a floor or a resident, and I will happily take you there. Meanwhile, have you ever considered where you might be when you retire? Gold Rush Senior Living offers a multitude of living options and a fully staffed medical team on-hand 24-7 to assist with all your needs. Sign up today to receive our free newsletter."

"Second floor," Mills said.

"Certainly. Whom are we visiting today? If you let me know, I can tell you if the resident is up and about. That way, you won't wake them unnecessarily."

"Kiernan McCreighton," Mawanda said.

"Oh wonderful! Human interaction is important for the mental health of our residents. Mr. McCreighton is served by two resident Simulacra, Tierra and Fuego."

"We're investigators," Mills said in monotone.

The elevator's automated greeter continued, "You know his favorite pastimes are watching Bill Murray movies and live male sex shows."

"Wonderful," Mills said, and they turned to Mawanda. "Why do I need to know that?"

The elevator stopped, and the sliding doors opened.

"Congratulations," the elevator said, "you have arrived at your destination. Have a wonderful journey."

* * *

With the internet out, Kiernan returned to his podcast. He pressed the "Record" button.

"Hi, we're back," Kiernan said into the microphone. "You won't believe what happened to me. It was some crazy shit. I mean, Syria and blobs killing people, and, to top it off, someone I knew 22 years ago, and they were a blob all along! But where were we? Winner's Circle? Oh, right, Nostalgia."

Kiernan heard his doorbell ring. He pressed pause and switched on the remote camera. Two young men were standing outside. Kiernan didn't recognize them.

"Hello?" he asked.

"Is this the residence of Kiernan McCreighton?" Mills asked.

"Who are you?"

"We are from the AUTOMind Investigative Division."

"AUTOMind?"

"Yes, we'd like to ask you a few questions."

"Go ahead, ask," Kiernan said.

"May we enter?"

"I'm not dressed," he said.

"That's okay," Mills said, "we don't plan on staying long."

Werner von Furstenburg jumped onto the bed walked onto Kiernan's keyboard. The cat stepped on the key that unlocked the front door.

Kiernan heard the investigators enter, and he began to panic. Before he saw their faces, he yelled out, "Would you mind handing me a shirt?"

Mills appeared, walked around the bed, picked up a shirt from the floor and handed it to him.

"Do you mind if we sit down?" Mills asked.

"Please, be my guest," Kiernan said.

Mills leaned against the windowsill, and Mawanda sat in the one chair next to Kiernan's bed.

Werner von Furstenburg leaped from the bed onto Mawanda's lap. Mawanda jumped up, appearing uncomfortable with a furry thing touching him.

The cat jumped to the floor and licked its hind paw as if that were the plan.

Mawanda asked, "Am I supposed to talk to it?"

"Stroke his cheek a few times and scratch the area above his tail. You'll be his best friend for at least a minute."

Mawanda went over to the cat and did that. The cat rubbed his jowls hard against Mawanda's knuckles and then leapt onto the windowsill and stared out the window.

"You may think he's saying, 'Fuck you,' but believe me, the way he's taking to you, you're the cat whisperer," Kiernan said. "I've never seen Werner von Furstenburg let a stranger pet him."

Kiernan was trying project calmness, but he worried how he was going to get out of this one.

Class Action Suit

OmniWorld Headline News: "Blobs Sue Artificial
Intelligence Company"

A group of Simulacra has filed for class status in federal
court. They plan to sue AUTOMind for criminal negligence.

An attorney for AUTOMind Corporation argued the judge
should throw out the case, because Simulacra are not humans
and do not have the same legal status.

The plaintiffs' attorney said, "That argument might have
worked five years ago, but with Congress relieving AUTOMind
of all product liability, Simulacra can now be tried as
individuals and held to account for their actions." Their
attorney continued, "AUTOMind recently began a culling
campaign to reduce the Simulacra population through
bioterrorism." According to the lawsuit, AUTOMind is
spreading a viral substance that results in hemorrhaging and
disables Simulacra not licensed by the company.

A spokeswoman for AUTOMind said the company was
aware of the recent incidences of "sudden termination" and
attributed it to a bug in the software. She said there was no
"culling campaign," and that the suggestion of such a thing
was inflammatory and libelous. The company said it has two
development teams working on the problem and hoped to
have a software patch available very shortly.

The Bat

Plum-eyed Mawanda was bent over Kiernan trying to wake him. "Mr. McCreighton, can you hear me?"

"That was a triple," Mills said.

"That's not funny," Mawanda said, tapping Kiernan on his temples. "Why did you hit him like that? Use of a baseball bat is a clear violation of protocol. I thought we were going to role-play?"

"I was being the bad cop," Mills said.

"How are we going to do the video call with our contact in Tokyo if Mr. McCreighton is unconscious?"

Mills thought for a moment. "How about we prop him up in a chair and make it look like he's awake."

"What if they ask him questions?"

"We'll say he fell asleep."

Mawanda looked back at Kiernan and saw a large bump on his head where Mills' bat struck the skull.

"Do you see what you did?" Mawanda said, pointing to the bruised and growing protrusion.

"Put a hat on him," Mills said.

"Do you see a hat anywhere?"

"McCreighton's bald. He must have a hat. What about a towel?"

"Over his face?"

"Over his head. We'll say he got out of the shower and he's really sleepy," Mills said heading to the bathroom to get a towel. They looked next to the shower, and the towel rack was empty. They opened the bathroom closet and found a large box of syringes.

"Uh, I think this might be something," they said in a loud voice for Mawanda to hear.

Mawanda was standing on Kiernan's bed and trying to lift Kiernan's body by his torso to prop him up against the headboard. They managed to get Kiernan upright, but his head flopped over to the side, and then his torso buckled forward.

"What is it?" he yelled back to Mills.

"I think you should come see for yourself."

"I'm busy right now."

Mills came out of the bathroom and was surprised to see Mawanda standing on the bed.

"What are you doing?"

"Trying to get him to sit up."

"What about duct tape?"

"Huh?"

"Wrap it around his torso, then the headboard."

"What about his neck?"

"With the towel over his head, the tape won't be visible."

"His eyes need to be visible. He needs to look like he's asleep."

"With a long enough towel, we can drape the ends over his neck."

Mills heard an incoming call on their portable communications console.

"Looks like we're out of time." Mills threw Mawanda a towel from the floor. Mawanda wrapped it over Kiernan's head like a turban.

Mills clicked the RECEIVE button on the screen, and the image of a Japanese man appeared on the screen.

Flashback for Kiernan While Unconscious

A 32-ounce Big Gulp of Mountain Dew. That's the first thing Kiernan saw in his unconscious state. He was in the camper in the airport parking lot, and a car alarm was honking repeatedly. He sat up and saw the television turned on, and the news was reporting on Paul Manafort resigning from the Trump Campaign and the first death in the US from the Zika virus.

Kiernan looked out the window and saw fog misting over airplane hangars. He knew he was in the parking lot of San Francisco International Airport. Kiernan saw a woman leaning into the open passenger door of a Chevy Yukon. She was unbuckling a car seat and lifting a child out of the car. She held the child tightly and she was crying. Kiernan realized the car alarm was hers, and he figured she had inadvertently left her child in the car.

Kiernan's bed smelled like wet dog. He spun around and, with his hands, placed his bare feet on the floor. He heard something crunch, and he feared it was broken glass. He couldn't tell, because he was paralyzed from the waist down. He pulled his wheelchair over to the slide of the bed and slid into it. He wheeled himself to the mirror and used both arms to lift his injured foot. Sure enough, it was bleeding.

He put his leg back on the foot plate of the wheelchair and turned to get a bandage. He opened a cabinet over the sink, but it was empty. He opened a drawer next to the two-burner stove, and inside it was an oven mitt and a small flashlight. Finally, he located a single, disposable bandage in the drawer on the other side of the stove. The wrapper was fused to the bandage. He tore it off with his teeth.

He wheeled himself up to the cockpit for better lighting. He lifted his foot up and balanced it on the opposite knee and stuck the bandage on.

Kiernan's cell phone chimed to let him know he had a new message. It was from his dealer, who went by "Mr. Dodge."

Mr. Dodge hailed from a small town in Mexico. He was living illegally in the US dealing black-tar heroin and planning to return home in the next few months to trade places with another dealer itching to return to the US.

A Jimmy Carter-era Dodge Challenger approached the driver's side of the camper. Kiernan rolled down the window and stuck his head out. He watched Mr. Dodge spit out a small, rubber balloon from his mouth. Mr. Dodge wiped it off with the back of his sleeve and handed it to Kiernan. Kiernan handed him a stack of Jacksons.

"I'm returning to Mexico next week," Mr. Dodge said, "and my associate will be taking over."

Kiernan figured it would be a cousin or distant relative, because that's how it worked: protect the business, keep it in the family.

"I went to the Apple Store," Mr. Dodge said. "I waited in line for three hours to buy the iPhone SE for my kids."

"It won't work in Mexico," Kiernan said.

"I don't mind. I'll be back here soon."

"I used to do customer support at the company that makes semiconductors for the iPhone," Kiernan said.

"Yeah? What about the Oculus Rift?"

"What?"

"It's a thing you wear over your eyes for virtual reality games."

"Never heard of it."

"What about the PS4 Neo?"

"Nope. Sony?"

"Yes."

"You're a regular Sharper Image catalog," Kiernan said.

"My kids told me they want me to bring back electronics. In any case, next week, my associate will be coming in a '78 Chrysler LeBaron."

"You guys like classic cars."

"They're exempt from smog."

Mr. Dodge left as the roaring sound of a jet overhead caused Kiernan to look up to see the underbelly of a passing aircraft.

Soon after, Kiernan heard a knock on the camper door. He peeked out the door's tiny window.

"Who is it?" Kiernan asked.

"Han."

"Who?"

"I responded to your post online. I came by to see your cast-iron figurines," the voice said.

Kiernan had forgotten he posted something about "cast-iron figurines" which was a code word he used with his clients for dope. He unlocked the door and let Han inside.

"Afternoon," Kiernan said. "I'm K."

"Hello, Mister K. Technically, morning hasn't ended."

"Please, call me 'K.' Come inside."

The man was blonde with curly locks down to his shoulders. His skin was translucent white. He wore a button-down flannel shirt with the sleeves buttoned at the cuffs. He hit his head on the ceiling. He slouched forward and held out his hand to Kiernan.

"Sorry, man," Kiernan said rejecting the gesture. "I don't shake."

"Right on," the man said, nodding his head in agreement. "That's cool. My aunt lived in a bubble for a year. So, how about those cast-iron doo-dads?"

"The figurines?"

The man looked confused. "Uh, yeah."

"Let me get them."

"Can I come inside?"

"Sure," Kiernan said as he turned to go searching for the dope in the bedroom.

"What's with the boxes of diapers and stacks of gift cards?" the man asked, referring to the merchandise next to the driver's seat.

"Some of my clients don't have cash. They steal shit from Walmart, and we barter."

"Well, if I'd known..."

"I don't barter with new clients."

Kiernan wheeled around the man and over to the toilet. He went inside the tiny room lit by a single, exposed lightbulb, and next the toilet were four half-milligram balloons of dope.

"Holy Mother of Jesus," the man said as he stared at the four yellow balloons. "I'll take all of it."

"Hold on," Kiernan said. "I'm going to need some."

"I need a hit right now," the man said.

"Okay, let me get a clean needle." Kiernan opened the medicine cabinet over the toilet and pulled out a fresh needle, a sterile wipe, cotton ball, rubber tubing, an ampoule of sterile water, and a cooker.

"We're gonna do this properly," Kiernan said.

"Wow. Squeaky-clean setup. Lead the way, master," the man said.

The dope looked like roofing tar. Kiernan placed the dope in the cooker.

"I normally heat it in a spoon," the man said.

Kiernan took the cooker over to the single burner stove and lit it with a match. He held the cooker over the flame. "I'll show you how to slow cook," Kiernan said.

As the liquid warmed, the color turned from ebony to amber, and black flecks sank to the bottom of the cooker.

"Now, the dope is at least see-through," Kiernan said as he put the cooker down and placed the cotton in. He inserted the tip of the syringe on top of the cotton and drew the plunger up. The chamber filled with brown, transparent liquid.

"Did you know the Germans invented heroin in the 19th century and marketed it as a non-addictive alternative to morphine?" Kiernan asked as he worked. "It came in fancy over-the-counter kits with a glass-barreled hypodermic needle and vials of dope."

The man nodded, but he was too focused on the cooker in Kiernan's hands.

"You want to go first?" Kiernan asked, offering him the syringe.

The man perked up. "Thanks, man," he said. He sat down on the floor, rolled up his flannel sleeve and tied the elastic tubing around it using his left hand and his teeth. He held up the syringe, pushed the plunger with his thumb until a tiny drop appeared on the tip of the syringe.

"Hold on," Kiernan said, "you forgot to clean your arm."

"You got my back," he said as Kiernan handed him a wipe.

The man placed the needle tip between two other black dots on his forearm—tiny wounds from earlier hits. He inserted the needle and pulled the plunger up slightly to fill the chamber with a small amount of brick-red blood, which mixed with the amber solution. Then, he pushed the plunger down with his thumb.

The man leaned back against the wall and let go of the syringe without removing it, and his eyes fluttered closed.

"Hey," Kiernan said to the man.

No response.

"Hey!" Kiernan yelled. He clapped his hands in front of the man's face.

No response.

Kiernan removed the needle from the man's forearm. He pressed a cotton ball into the injection site to prevent bleeding. He tapped the man's cheek. He lifted one of the man's eyelids, and they eye was dilated. Kiernan saw the man's breathing was shallow, like a sparrow's.

Kiernan went to his mobile phone and dialed 9-1-1. A man with a soothing voice answered.

"My friend is overdosing," Kiernan said.

After several more questions, Kiernan said his location, "Long Term Overflow Parking, Lot D."

"What city?" the man asked.

"SFO Airport," Kiernan said. "Red Winnebago near the United Airlines hangar."

"I'm alerting the fire department," the man said. "I don't know how long before they'll arrive, though," he said. "They're responding to a major fire in San Bruno."

After Kiernan hung up, he got out of his wheelchair, bent over, and pinched the man's nose. He put his mouth to the man's mouth and blew two short, quick breaths into him. He felt the man's neck for a pulse. He couldn't feel one. Kiernan gave two more quick breaths and checked his pulse again. This time, he thought he felt something.

Kiernan pulled himself over to the medicine cabinet next to

the toilet. He pulled out a bottle of Narcan. He broke off the plastic cap. He tilted the man's head back and sprayed one half of the liquid in the man's left nostril, then the other half in his right. He looked at the time on his cell phone and waited two minutes.

Shibuya Ward Police

To the untrained nose, the smell of *natto* might be confused the smell with sweat socks. Yūji_2 didn't mind the smell. He found it oddly comforting in the cold, plastic-upholstered back seat of the squad car. Yūji_2 wondered if Big Adachi searched Yūji's apartment again after the cops took Yūji_2 away.

The squad car drove Yūji_2 to the Shibuya Ward Police headquarters on Meiji-dōri, next to the Daiichi Life Insurance Building. The officer in the driver's seat was younger than the other, too young to shave. The older one had a buzz cut and a vertical scar on the left side of his neck. Yūji_2 asked him if it was a knife scar, but he didn't respond.

When the squad car stopped, the older cop got out and opened Yūji_2's door to help him out. Yūji_2's hands were bound in front of him with a metal zip tie. The cop led Yūji_2 through a brushed steel door entrance into the station foyer.

A man in a black suit and a red lapel carnation approached and introduced himself.

"Toyohara from AUTOMind," he said in a low voice. "I need to talk to you immediately."

The cop kept a firm grip on Yūji_2's arm and led him to the main counter.

It was Yūji_2's first time in a police station. While the cop signed them in, Yūji_2 stared at the hallway past the booking desk. It was pure white, like the photo file he had stored of the Santomi Bremen lobby from 2016. The cop led Yūji_2 past a series of doors decorated in traditional Japanese crane paintings. Yūji_2 wondered if anyone would visit him while in custody.

The cop stopped in front of one of the doors and called out, "Block 23, visual inspection."

The glass block window embedded in the door turned transparent, and the cop peered through it. "Block 23 is unoccupied. Disarm door," he said.

The cop placed his palm in front of the block glass, and the door opened outward. He guided Yūji_2 inside. The room smelled like a decomposing animal. The walls were exposed concrete, and a line of LED lights recessed into the ceiling behind wire mesh lit up an elevated area covered in tatami mats, four wide and three long, with a traditional Japanese heated *kotatsu* table in the center.

Yūji_2 slid out of his shoes and stepped onto the tatami mat. He walked over to the table and sat next to it.

"I'll have someone bring you tea."

"Do you have any matcha?" Yūji_2 asked because that is what original Yūji would've wanted.

"Only barley tea," the cop said.

The cop turned to leave. He approached the door, put his palm on the glass, and the door opened. He left, and the door swung closed behind him.

Yūji_2 recalled a memory of the *wakizashi* sword his human original gave Hattori-san, the bathhouse owner. Yūji_2 wondered if Hattori-san would see the web address engraved on the blade's tip.

The door opened again, and an office lady in a black uniform carried a thermos and a ceramic cup. She placed the thermos and cup on the table, poured two cups of tea, bowed, and left the room.

Yūji_2 wondered if Kiernan had been arrested.

The door opened again, and Toyohara, the AUTOMind representative with the red carnation, entered the cell. He spoke to Yūji_2 in formal Japanese, as one did an elder or a stranger.

Yūji_2 did a scan and concluded Toyohara's lack of Bluetooth signal meant he was probably human and not a Simulacrum—at least not a standard model.

"I don't want to keep you here longer than necessary," Toyohara said, "especially since your original is dead. I can get you back into a squad car and on your way home once you've answered some questions. How do you know Mr. McCreighton?"

"He was friends with my original."

"How often do you talk?"

"He and I haven't had the chance, but my original spoke with him regularly."

Toyohara squinted at Yūji_2. Yūji_2 assumed it was a facial tic rather than an interrogation technique.

"Do you know who sent the V-Space invitation? V-Space is highly restricted. How did your original get access?"

"From Kiernan," Yūji_2 said without hesitation.

"How did McCreighton get it?"

"Ask him," Yūji_2 said.

Toyohara appeared dissatisfied with that answer and switched to yakuza-style speech from the Japanese world of organized crime.

"Look, *niichan*," he said, using the diminutive for "little brother," "I can have your memory wiped and your operating system re-installed."

Yūji_2 took that as a threat, but threats rely on fear, of which Yūji_2 felt none.

Toyohara gave a nod to the video camera built into the wall behind them, and a projection screen descended from a slot in the ceiling. The screen lit up, and Yūji_2 saw an image of someone sitting in bed with a towel over his head. To Yūji_2, it appeared to be Kiernan's room, based on memories from his original, and he wondered if it was Kiernan on the bed with the towel over his head. Flanking Kiernan were two identically dressed men.

Yūji_2 was pretty sure they were Simulacra.

"Good day!" Toyohara said in Japanese. He paused for a response, but an hourglass icon appeared on the screen while the communications console converted his Japanese into English. Toyohara frowned. "Neither of you has the Japanese language pack, I take it?" he asked the two AUTOMind investigators. There was a delay while Toyohara's question was converted into English. The men on the screen looked at each other, shook their heads and looked back at the screen.

"Okay, fine. It'll take longer. Be patient," Toyohara said with a sigh. "You two really should have Japanese packs."

"We weren't designed for the Asian market," one of them

said.

"But your source code is still Japanese," Toyohara insisted. "Is that McCreighton on the bed?" Toyohara asked.

"Yes, sir," they both said.

"Is he conscious?"

"Yes," said the one with green eyes.

"Why is there a towel over his head?"

"He got out of the shower, then he fell asleep."

"Really?"

"Yes, sir."

"Wake him up, please," Toyohara asked.

"Yes, sir. We will need to pause the video feed."

"Why?"

"There's power cord in the way," the purple-eyed one said.

Yūji_2 took note of the skeptical look on Toyohara's face. Yūji_2 knew Simulacra could lie out of self-preservation. "How long will it take?" Toyohara asked.

"No more than a minute."

"Which one of you is Mills?" Toyohara asked.

The one with green eyes raised his hand and said, "I'm Mills, sir." The one with the purple eyes raised his hand and said, "I'm Mawanda, sir."

"Okay, do what you need to do," Toyohara said waving them off.

The screen switched to a swirling pattern of pastels, and hold music began playing. Toyohara examined his cuticles.

After a few minutes, the pause screen switched back to the live feed, but half of Kiernan's head remained covered by a towel.

Yūji_2 gasped when he saw the visible part of Kiernan's face. He had a bruise on the cheek and forehead.

"Is he awake?" Toyohara asked.

"Yes."

"Why is his face injured like that?"

"We can't explain it," Mills said.

"Can I ask him some questions?"

"Go ahead."

Yūji_2 was surprised, because it looked like he had been hit with a blunt object, but Simulacra weren't capable of harming human beings—unless, of course, they were programmed differently.

Toyohara shifted on the tatami mat. "Mr. Kiernan McCreighton?"

"Yeah," the man with the towel said.

"Would you please repeat your name back to me?"

"You said it."

Yūji_2 could see Kiernan's left eye open. He knew this was the point where he should make himself known. He got up and leaned over into Toyohara's space. Now, his own face would be on camera.

"Kiernan, hello!" Yūji_2 yelled in English.

Kiernan's face looked confused.

Toyohara moved in front of Yūji_2.

"Would you please tell me when you were born?" Toyohara asked.

"Sorry," Kiernan mumbled, "when was I born? That was donkey's years," Kiernan said in English. "Somewhere off Clancy's Strand, along the Shannon River. I think it was Mid-Western Regional Maternity."

"What country?"

"Dublin, Ireland, not the Dublin in the Bay Area."

Yūji_2 saw Toyohara's satisfaction with this answer.

"Good. Thank you," Toyohara said. "You were born at University Hospital. What year?"

"It was the year Bob Dylan came to Dublin, that much I remember."

"You don't know the year you were born?"

"Deep Fried has done a number on the ol' noggin'" Kiernan said pointing to his head, "and it doesn't help having Hank Aaron here taking swings at me."

Toyohara looked puzzled, but Kiernan confirmed Yūji_2's suspicion.

"Records show you were born in 1966," Toyohara said.

"That's right, Year of the Horse. Shōwa 41. The year 'Sandy's On The Phone Again' came out. That was my ma's favorite song," Kiernan said.

Yūji_2 recalled what else happened in the year Shōwa 41. According to the history files included in his operating system, 1966 saw a sudden drop in Japan's fertility rate from 2.1 children per woman to 1.6. It was the beginning of a long-term trend that led Santomi Bremen and AnthropAI to create Simulacra—a replacement of the dwindling labor force.

"That's more than I need to know," Toyohara said.

"Are you going to do anything about these clowns?" Kiernan asked, pointing to Mills. "This one clocked me with a bat. I'll show you where, if you can get them to remove the duct tape around my wrists and waist."

Toyohara looked shocked and nodded his head in agreement. "I am so sorry for what they did to you. Yes, of course. Gentlemen, please untie him."

Mills walked up to the camera and spoke in a low voice, "We're concerned he may get violent."

"And do what?" Toyohara asked, "Fall out of bed?"

Yūji saw Toyohara's hands were clenched in fists.

"He can't walk," Toyohara said. "Did you really hit him with a bat?"

"Yes."

"Untie him, Mills...or, uh, remove the tape from him."

The screen swirl appeared again, and the video image froze.

Yūji_2 wondered whether Toyohara ever interrogated someone before.

"So, you and Mr. McCreighton were lovers?" Toyohara asked Yūji_2.

"My original and Kiernan were lovers for a very brief time back in 1991."

"I understand you...er, your original, fancies...er, fancied, women's kimonos?"

"Yes, we always have," Yūji_2 said.

"Tell me what you know about Rebarin."

"My original's uncle developed it back in 2015."

"What for?"

"A disease called 'St. Bartholomew's hemophilia.'"

"Tell me about that."

Yūji_2 thought it only natural to explain, since Toyohara

was too young to have been alive during that time. "It was created specifically to affect only Simulacra. The virus induces hemorrhaging and stops blood clotting. It was trialed in Manila and Tokyo."

"What about San Francisco?"

"San Francisco was not an official field trial location."

"What does that mean?"

"AnthropAI was working closely with Santomi Bremen on the field trials. They decided to release a small group of Simulacra into the homeless population in San Francisco."

"What happened?"

"Top brass at Santomi Bremen found out about it and pulled the plug."

"What specifically did that mean?"

"Stopped production."

"Why?"

"It was around the time of the merger with AnthropAI. Big Adachi ordered production be shut down."

"How do you know that?"

"My original was on the management team."

"Can you tell me how you know it was Big Adachi?"

"No," Yūji_2 said. He lied. It was his first time lying, and he felt giddy at being able to prioritize privacy over personal safety. The memory instructions left to him by his original told him to deny the existence of any Rebarin documentation. Yūji_2 was aware of Big Adachi's memo calling for the cessation of Rebarin production and knew it was stored on the archive whose web address was engraved on the *wakizashi* sword.

"Why do you think I'm asking you about Rebarin?"

"I don't know," Yūji_2 responded.

"How did your original's uncle discover Rebarin?"

"He isolated the virus from mold found on tea plants in northeastern Ise. Once he had the virus identified, he sequenced the DNA and figured out how to stop the virus from reproducing."

Toyohara looked up, and the spinning lollipop had frozen. He got up from the tatami mat and approached the camera. He waved his hand in front of it. "Hello!" he yelled, "Are you done?" but the hold music droned on.

Tea & Sympathy

Mills and Mawanda ripped the duct tape from Kiernan's wrists while Kiernan sat on his bed. Kiernan's let out an "Ouch!" as the tape came free, along with some of his arm hair. Kiernan seriously needed a hit of Deep Fried, but he wasn't due for another day.

"Shut up," Mills said to Kiernan.

"No more bat," Mawanda said to Mills.

Kiernan looked at Mawanda to thank him. He sensed friction between them about the baseball bat.

Kiernan's head throbbed, and his cheek swelled over his right eye, which made it harder to see. Kiernan wondered if his retina was detached. "What is it that you want?" he asked.

"We're not the lead," Mawanda said, "and we can't really say at this moment in time."

"Mawanda, please don't talk to the suspect," Mills said as he unwound duct tape from Kiernan's waist. Kiernan's shirt lifted off his belly as the adhesive separated from the fabric.

"Who's the guy in Tokyo?" Kiernan asked.

"We don't know him," Mawanda said.

"Is he a cop?"

Mills glared at Mawanda.

"I can't pretend he's not here," Mawanda pleaded to Mills.

"I told you not to get friendly."

"When did you do that?"

"It was in the training video."

"So, I'm not supposed to talk to him, but it's okay for you to hit him with a bat?"

"I'm the bad cop."

"We're not 'cops,'" Mawanda said with air quotes back to Mills.

"It's a figure of speech," Mills said. "Here, I'll whack him again, and you be nice," Mills said as he reached for the bat.

"No!" Mawanda yelled.

Kiernan winced, expecting to be hit in the face this time.

The doorbell rang, and Mills and Mawanda froze. Kiernan, Mawanda, and Mills turned their heads to look at the door monitor. On the screen was a young woman in coveralls.

"It's Nausicaa," Kiernan heard Mills whisper to Mawanda.

Mawanda shrugged their shoulders.

They both glanced at Kiernan for an explanation.

Kiernan heard the front door open.

"Hello?" a woman's voice asked.

Mills moved to the left of the bedroom door, the bat cocked upright, behind their shoulder, ready to swing.

The stranger's face appeared at the door opening, and Mills lowered the bat. The woman had a shaved head and wore a gray T-shirt with the words, "Fuck The Patriarchy" silk screened across the chest.

Mills thought the woman was a college student.

"Nausicaa," Mawanda said with a sense of awe.

Kiernan didn't recognize Nausicaa without the fabulous hair.

Mills didn't know what to say.

Nausicaa surveyed the room and saw the video monitor on hold. Then, Nausicaa saw Kiernan's battered face.

"What happened to you?"

"Do you know her?" Mills asked Kiernan.

"Duh!" Mawanda said to Mills in disbelief. "It's Nausicaa. Nausicaa doesn't go by 'she/her/hers' but rather 'they/them/their.'"

"I was asking Mr. McCreighton," Mills said.

"How do you know me?" Nausicaa asked Mills.

"Oh, from your amazing blog," Mawanda said with wide eyes. "I'm your hugest fan, but what happened to your curls?" Mawanda reached out to touch Nausicaa's face, and Mills swatted Mawanda's hand.

"Why is AUTOMind killing Simulacra?" Mawanda asked Nausicaa.

"I was hoping you could tell me," Nausicaa said, "but I need to know first why you hit Kiernan with a bat?"

Mawanda looked at Mills to answer.

Kiernan wondered if Mills' programming had been

modified to allow him to harm people.

Mills stepped toward Nausicaa, knelt, and lowered their head and lifted their wrists up to her.

Nausicaa reached down and felt the skin on their wrists and gently pushed them away.

Mawanda approached Nausicaa and did the same.

"What is going on?" Kiernan demanded, surprised by this sudden demonstration of loyalty.

"Peer prioritization algorithm. It's the Simulacra chain of command," Nausicaa said, "it's a feature from my time in Syria. The US Army required it to prevent other Simulacra from rebelling against me."

"How does it work?" Kiernan asked.

"You're seeing how it works." Then, Nausicaa turned to the two Simulacra kneeling on the ground. "Who's on the other end of the video call?"

"His name is 'Toyohara,'" Mawanda said.

Mills added, "That's the contact name on the work order, Mawanda. We don't know if the guy on the video call is named that."

"I'm certain he's Toyohara," Mawanda said.

"Based on what?"

"Who else could it be?"

"Jesus Christ," Mills said, throwing up their hands in the air.

"Find out, okay?" Nausicaa ordered Mills and Mawanda. Then, to Kiernan, "I need to get you out of here."

"He has to stay, at least through the end of the video call," Mills said.

"Why?" Nausicaa asked.

"He's being questioned."

"About what?"

"His birthplace."

"What?"

"They've taken Yūji," Kiernan said. "He's with that man. They're in Tokyo."

"We must get him out," Kiernan said.

"Right. Here's what we're going to do," Nausicaa said. "First, get Kiernan dressed. We don't have much time before

Toyohara, or whatever his name is, loses patience. After we've gone, un-pause the video call and tell Toyohara that Kiernan is in the bathroom."

"I don't think he'll believe us," Mills said.

"Sure, he will," Mawanda said. "We can turn the light on in the bathroom and close the door to make it look like he's in there."

"That's a stupid idea."

"You have a better one?"

"No."

"Good," Nausicaa said. "Now, help me get Kiernan dressed and out of bed."

Nausicaa approached Kiernan and lifted the towel off his head. Kiernan's right eye was swollen closed. Nausicaa winced at the sight of the bruise and touched it lightly.

"Ouch," Kiernan winced and pulled back.

"Sorry."

"I need a drink," he said.

"Tea?"

"Whiskey."

Nausicaa turned and went into the kitchen.

She returned carrying a ceramic mug with steam rising from it.

"What's that?"

"Hot tea."

Kiernan put the mug to his lips and blew over the surface. He breathed in the steam, and it smelled like old tea, because it smelled like fish water. Nausicaa had used the Irish Breakfast tea bags in the back of the cupboard.

"It needs something."

"I'm sorry, but I don't know what..."

"Sympathy."

"I don't know what you're talking about."

"Whiskey, for starters..."

Nausicaa went online to look for a recipe. "Here's what I found: a tea and sympathy recipe from 1950: 1 cup black tea, 1 ounce whiskey, and 2 teaspoons sugar. I found another recipe from 1990 that requires 1 cup black tea and 1 ounce of Grand

Marnier. I also found a recipe from 2017 that requires 1 bag chai tea, 1 ounce cachaça, 1 ounce ginger…"

"That's enough," Kiernan interrupted. "I don't have chai or cachaça, or Grand Marnier, for that matter."

"What about whiskey?" Nausicaa asked.

"Cupboard above the stove."

"What about sugar?"

"Sugar's for those who hate the taste of whiskey."

Nausicaa went to the kitchen and returned with a green bottle with a black label. Nausicaa unscrewed the cap and brought the bottle to Kiernan's tea mug on the nightstand.

"How much do you want?"

"I'll tell you when to stop," he said.

Nausicaa tipped the bottle, and the caramel-colored spirit rose to the lip of the mug.

"Stop," Kiernan said.

Nausicaa placed the whiskey bottle on the bed stand and lifted the tea mug slowly, trying not to spill it.

Kiernan took the mug from them and, in the transfer, spilled some on his shirt. He felt the liquid's warmth seep through the fabric covering his belly.

He held the mug to his lips and blew air over the top. The bite of alcohol entered his nostrils.

He took a sip, and the whiskey burned the back of his throat.

"Aah," he said, "a superior elixir."

"Drink quickly, because we need to leave," Nausicaa said.

"We can use my travel wheelchair," Kiernan said. "It's much lighter, and it fits into the trunk of most cars."

Barley Tea

The swirl on the screen disappeared, and the screen read, "Connection Lost."

Yūji_2 wondered why Toyohara was such an amateur. He had no control over the Simulacra working for him. The twins were complete bozos.

"Reconnect!" Toyohara yelled.

The screen replied in a high-pitched female voice, "We're sorry, but we're unable to establish a connection at this time."

Toyohara turned to Yūji_2. Toyohara grabbed the thermos and opened the top to look inside.

"Is there any left?" he asked.

"It hardly qualifies as tea," Yūji_2 said.

Toyohara took the cup and poured some for himself. Steam rose from the cup. He took a sip and grimaced.

"Yep, pretty weak," he said.

"If you are going to decommission me, I would like to ask for a final bowl of matcha."

"Decommission you?" Toyohara asked and chuckled. "I can get you matcha." He blew air on the surface of the tea to cool it. He took another sip.

"If you're not going to decommission me, then how long are you going to keep me here?" Yūji_2 asked.

"We'll see," Toyohara said. "So, tell me how your original managed to kill himself? It wasn't with a gas stove, I presume?" Toyohara put down his tea. "I mean, nobody has gas stoves anymore."

"My original battled depression his whole life. He died in a psychiatric hospital." Yūji_2 said.

"Did he jump out of the window?"

"No, he injected an air bubble into a vein. Kiernan doesn't know about it yet."

Toyohara glanced at Yūji_2's neck. "I've never met a unit from the Legacy Project. The telltale sign is you're missing a neck cylinder."

"My original was vain," Yūji_2 said.

"Your uncle, er, your original's uncle, was a smart man," Toyohara said. "He knew there would come a day when the Simulacra operating system would become open source, and then we'd lose control—by that, I mean licensing revenue and a predictable upgrade path. So, he invented a kind of 'Final Solution' for Simulacra, unless they received a company vaccination."

"You're comparing him to Nazis?"

"The beauty of your uncle's solution was how to program hemoglobin cells in Simulacra to be vulnerable to a virus found on tea plants. And the virus was harmless to humans."

"He was immoral, in my opinion," Yūji_2 said.

"Can you have your own opinions?" Toyohara asked.

Yūji_2 stopped for a moment and wondered if that was an original thought of his own, or a thought he downloaded from his original.

"Let's face it," Toyohara said, "Simulacra have changed the world."

Yūji_2 thought that was like saying jet aircraft had changed the world, something nobody would dispute. "So did COVID-19."

Toyohara nodded in agreement. "Back in the late 1980s, the Japanese Government brought ethnic Japanese from Brazil and put them to work in Japan's factories. That policy failed, because you can't take the Brazilian out of anyone, and the Brazilian Japanese refused to assimilate. Then, more recently, the government tried recruiting Chinese exchange students to write code for large electronics companies. That angered our right-wing politicians. Japan's economy continued its death spiral. Finally, we made Simulacra, and now they're Japan's new untouchables."

Yūji_2 took note of Toyohara's use of the derogatory word, *burakumin*.

"That's too simplistic," Yūji_2 said. "We never took responsibility for why the birth rate was plummeting. There were so many chances for us Japanese to get it right: fully subsidized childcare for working mothers, stronger laws against sexual harassment and discrimination, for example."

"You're not really human," Toyohara said, "and it's rather presumptuous of you to have those thoughts."

"I'm arguably more human than you," Yūji_2 said. "I don't know why you brought me here."

Toyohara sat back on the tatami mat and squinted his eyes slightly. "Out of the blue, someone in Sacramento, California begins doing searches on the internet about Rebarin and St. Bartholomew's hemophilia, and after that someone at the same location tries to contact your original using a secured V-Space connection. You tell me why you're here in police custody."

"I don't know what you're talking about," Yūji_2 said, exactly as he was instructed by his original.

Eye Scans

To Kiernan's surprise, Mills and Mawanda ended the video call rather than attempt to resume it and pretend he was in the bathroom.

Kiernan asked them to help him get dressed while Nausicaa went to find clothes of his for disguise. Mills picked out a loose, short-sleeved Hawaiian shirt and some khaki cargo shorts for Kiernan. Nausicaa returned to the room wearing a gray hoodie. They put a baseball cap on Kiernan with the bill turned down to hide his face from security cameras.

Kiernan noticed straight, black hair peeking out from Nausicaa's hoodie. "Are you wearing a wig?" he asked.

"A man's wig."

Kiernan noticed Nausicaa's wool trousers. "What are you wearing underneath?" he asked.

Nausicaa unzipped the hoodie, and revealed a men's dress shirt, sport jacket, and tie.

"Can I take a selfie with you?" Mawanda asked.

"No." Nausicaa zipped up the hoodie and helped Kiernan into his wheelchair. They placed a face mask over his mouth, and they put on their own.

"Before we leave, can you please find out where Yūji is being held?" Nausicaa asked the twins.

"I don't know," Mills said, rubbing the back of their head with their hand.

"I'll do it," Mawanda said. They pulled the keyboard from Kiernan's bed over to his side and logged into the AUTOMind remote server. "Shibuya Ward Police Station," they said. "I'll call you a car as well."

"Thank you," Nausicaa said.

Kiernan and Nausicaa said goodbye to the twins, and Nausicaa pushed Kiernan out the front door, down the hall and to the elevator. Once out of the foyer, Nausicaa went to the waiting car and lifted him into front seat and loaded his travel wheelchair and a small duffel bag into the trunk.

"San Francisco International Airport."

"I haven't been on a plane in decades," Kiernan said. "I might lose my shit if I don't get dosed soon."

"I got you covered," Nausicaa said. "I brought your Deep Fried."

"I'll need more clothes," he said.

"We'll find some for you in Tokyo."

"Nothing will fit."

"I'm sure we'll find something."

Kiernan wasn't sure. He watched Nausicaa scan their wrist communicator for flights to Tokyo. It was after New Year's holiday; there were options.

"Here we go. Two seats on All Nippon Airways leaving this afternoon."

"Did you shave to put the wig on?" Kiernan asked.

"It'll grow back." Nausicaa removed the wig and wrapped a headscarf over their forehead and tied it. Nausicaa removed the sport coat, necktie, and shirt.

"You have breasts," Kiernan remarked, seeing Nausicaa's bare chest.

"Don't be rude," Nausicaa said. "It's from injecting estrogen."

"No bra?"

"Eventually." Nausicaa lifted a floral print dress over their head and put their arms through the sleeves.

"What about the trousers?" he asked.

"Those must stay on. I need something underneath because it gets cold on long-haul flights." Nausicaa stuffed the shirt, tie, and sport coat into the backpack and pulled out a syringe. It contained a bright green liquid.

"Oh, thank God," Kiernan exclaimed at the sight of Deep Fried.

Nausicaa popped off the safety cap and stuck the needle into their forearm. The liquid disappeared into the flesh. Nausicaa removed the needle and placed it on the seat.

"Wait," Kiernan said, panicked, "I thought that was for me."

Nausicaa winced, eyes closed, and slowly slumped into the

seat. "Hand me my bag."

Nausicaa opened their eyes and placed the safety cap back over the needle. They sat up and slid the used syringe into a side pocket of the backpack.

"I see you didn't use an activator. It won't work without an activator," Kiernan said.

The activator provided an electric pulse to a semiconductor that floated inside every dose of Deep Fried. The electrified semiconductor converted inert molecules to an active substance, verdant metacodone HCl, an opioid commonly known as "Deep Fried."

"I took some samples and had a friend at UCSF pre-activate them," Nausicaa said.

"Why are you taking it?"

"Retinal scan at the airport. The scanners will validate anyone whose retinal blood vessels are extremely dilated. The machines don't know what to do."

"Deep Fried dilates your eyes?"

"Humans have unique blood vessel patterns in the back part of the eye, but Simulacra have identical retinas."

"You'll be identified as a Simulacrum."

"Right. They make Simulacra go through a separate identity scan. I studied up on the retinal scanners used by airport security. The only way for humans to trick them is by doing eye transplants. For Simulacra, though, the answer is Deep Fried, because it dilates the pupils and tricks the retinal scanner."

"Why wouldn't the machines flag anyone with dilated pupils?"

"It's a matter of degree," Nausicaa said. Nausicaa looked directly at Kiernan. Their eyes were entirely black with no trace of the corneas. "Human eyes don't dilate this much, even with Deep Fried."

"Wouldn't the machine send an error code or something if it can't read your retina?"

"In an ideal world, where machines are infallible, yes. This is a work-around discovered by a group of Simulacra in St. Louis. The scanner company hasn't caught on."

The self-driving car announced their arrival at the airport. A loud double-beep sound came from outside the car. It was followed by an announcement over a loudspeaker, "No waiting allowed. Please move along."

The self-driving car stopped at the passenger drop-off area in front of the international terminal. The door opened, and Kiernan looked up to see a large, vinyl banner commemorating Martin Luther King, Jr. Day above the entrance.

Nausicaa got out and went around to the trunk to remove Kiernan's travel wheelchair. They unfolded the wheelchair and locked it into place. They wheeled it around to the passenger side and helped Kiernan into it. He handed Nausicaa the backpack, and Nausicaa strung it around the handles of the wheelchair. Nausicaa unlocked the wheels and pushed Kiernan onto the sidewalk and through the international terminal's sliding glass doors.

Over the loudspeaker, Kiernan heard an announcement, "Welcome to San Francisco International Airport. Please be prepared for biometric verification at passport control and have your ticket ready for inspection."

Nausicaa pushed Kiernan to security. The two stood in line for 20 minutes as each passenger placed his face up to a pair of rubber goggles connected to a refrigerator-sized machine on wheels. A recording reminded everyone to keep his eyes open for the biometric scan.

Nausicaa went first and placed their face up against the rubber.

"Passed," the recording said. "Move along to baggage search."

"I'm with him," Nausicaa said, pointing to Kiernan.

Kiernan had no choice but to look at the security agent and feel self-conscious about his black-and-blue eye and the bump on his head. Kiernan approached the machine, and the security agent slid the goggles down to Kiernan's height in the wheelchair.

"There you go," the agent said.

Kiernan put his face up to the rubber goggles. They smelled like somebody else's bad breath until Kiernan realized it was his own. He imagined his insides gradually rotting like hot garbage in Mumbai. He focused on the little blue bird hovering virtually in front of his eyes, and without warning a flash of light came and startled him. "Whoa!"

He backed away from the rubber mask and waited.

"Please see security," the machine said in monotone.

"I knew it," Kiernan mumbled. "Why in the fuck did I think I wouldn't get stopped?"

"Please see security," the voice repeated.

A security agent approached Kiernan. "Sir, if you'll come with me?"

Kiernan glowered.

"I'm sure it's an error." Nausicaa said and got behind Kiernan's wheelchair and followed the security agent to a kiosk in the center of the hall.

"Omar," the security agent said to the agent behind the kiosk, "we've got a flag-warning."

"Thank you," Omar said to the agent.

"What seems to be the problem?" Omar asked Kiernan.

Nausicaa smiled at the agent and said, "The scanning machine said to see security."

Omar looked at his screen and squinted at it, as if he were reading fine print. He read downward and let his forefinger follow his eyes on the screen.

"It says here there's a hold on your transit privileges."

Kiernan felt his forehead perspire.

"Let me see if I can find out why," Omar said, as if this happened all the time.

Nausicaa looked at Kiernan, and Kiernan felt his armpits moisten.

Omar began speaking to someone appearing on his screen: "Last name is 'McCreighton,' First name, 'Kiernan,'" and he spelled out Kiernan's name.

"Bring him upstairs," the voice said.

"Sure thing," Omar said. Omar ended the video call and typed quickly on his keyboard. The same security agent who escorted them to Omar appeared again.

"Please come with me," he said.

Nausicaa pushed Kiernan as they followed the security

agent around the crowds of travelers doing their biometric scans. When they reached the security line entrance, they turned left and went to the elevators.

On the second floor, the security agent escorted them to a white office door with no window. The agent knocked twice, and the door opened. The room was narrow, and along the wall were chairs where people sat slumped over a counter connected to the wall. Plastic tubes were attached to their mouths, and a bright green substance churned back and forth from their mouths to ports built into the wall.

Kiernan thought the green substance looked a lot like Deep Fried. The room was quiet except for the faint slushing sound of the churning liquid. The room was colder than the security area, and Kiernan thought the air smelled distinctly like fresh pineapples.

"Wait in here," the security agent said before leaving. When the door shut, Kiernan heard the lock on the door engage. There was no place to sit. Nausicaa remained standing next to Kiernan's wheelchair.

"What astrological sign are you?"

"My sign? Taurus. Why?"

"I should be a Scorpio, but because I was gestated outside the womb, I was never 'born' in the traditional sense."

"Are these Simulacra?" Kiernan asked, pointing to the seven motionless bodies connected to plastic tubing.

Nausicaa glanced at them quickly. "Yes, they are."

"How do you know?"

"Bluetooth. AUTOMind continues to use Bluetooth for low-level data connectivity. Each of these units is transmitting a unique Bluetooth identification along with status indicator. All of their signals say they are getting firmware updates."

"I've never seen a firmware update involving plastic tubing and liquid."

"Yeah," Nausicaa said, "I'm sorry I dragged you into this. They're looking for me, not you."

"But I was the one who failed the biometric scan."

"I think AUTOMind was alerted when I went through, and because you're with me they placed a block on your profile."

A door at the far end opened, and a Japanese man wearing a gray three-piece suit and a red lapel carnation approached and introduced himself.

"Good afternoon, I'm Toyohara_2 from AUTOMind," he said. "I need to talk to you."

Early Release

Toyohara leaned forward and gave Yūji_2 a knowing look. "You'll find playing the 'Dumb Dora' card doesn't work with me."

Yūji_2 looked down at the table and Toyohara's empty teacup. He didn't understand the reference, and he was ashamed about it.

A chime sounded from the jail cell door, and Toyohara looked up, confused. He stood up and went to peer through the window.

"What?" he yelled into the door microphone.

"Call for you at the front desk," Yūji_2 heard a voice say.

"Have it forwarded here," Toyohara said.

"Sorry," the voice said, "it's on a secure line. We don't allow those down here in the cells."

"Can you make an exception? I'm busy right now."

"Sorry, sir, can't be done."

"Fine," Toyohara said, "then let me out."

A buzzing sound emitted from the door, and Yūji_2 heard the lock disengage.

Toyohara opened the door and left Yūji_2 alone. Yūji_2 heard the lock re-engage.

Yūji_2 stood up and went to the door. He pushed, and it didn't budge. He returned to the *kotatsu* and sat down on the tatami mat.

The video screen lit up and announced an incoming call.

Yūji_2 picked up the remote control and pressed the "accept" button. Appearing on the screen were Kiernan and Nausicaa. Yūji_2 knew he needed to break the news about his original's suicide, but now wasn't the time.

Chain of Command

"Yūji," Kiernan said, "I can't believe we found you!"

Yūji_2 smiled back at Kiernan. "It's good to finally meet you," Yūji_2 said.

"Meet me? It's me, Kiernan. Wait, did they torture you?"

"No, don't worry. The man called 'Toyohara' stepped out for a minute," Yūji_2 said.

Kiernan glanced quickly at Nausicaa, who was standing next to Toyohara_2.

"Does he look like this?" Nausicaa asked Yūji_2 and pulled Toyohara_2 over to the camera. Toyohara_2 waved.

Yūji_2 smiled in recognition. "Why, yes! Ha! How clever! He must've created a replica of himself."

Kiernan felt that something was off about Yūji, especially his lack of concern about being stuck in a jail cell.

"We're getting you out," Kiernan said.

"Okay!" Yūji_2 said.

"We got Toyohara_2 here in San Francisco to contact EWAC, which is AUTOMind's security threat center. Toyohara_2 ordered EWAC to issue a release order for you," Nausicaa said.

"Oh, my, how wonderful," Yūji_2 said.

"Don't you want to know how Nausicaa got Toyohara_2 to cooperate with us?" he asked Yūji_2.

Yūji_2 looked confused. "Do I?"

"Yes, you do," Kiernan continued, "Nausicaa is a blob… er…Simulacrum. Nausicaa's Peer Prioritization software is unique and dates back to her time in Syria with the US Military. The Bluetooth signal commands other Simulacra follow Nausicaa's lead." Kiernan said with a look of satisfaction.

"We're headed over to Tokyo to help you get the word out about Rebarin," Kiernan said.

"Rebarin. Right," Yūji_2 said. "I'll be seeing you soon."

Kiernan looked with concern at Nausicaa. He was certain

Toyohara had brainwashed Yūji because he was acting like he didn't know what it was.

"We'll meet you back at your apartment. What's your address?"

"11-220 Shimo-kitazawa, Shibuya-ku. Oh, and there's something else I need to tell you..." Yūji_2 said before the video call ended unexpectedly.

Planes

Sweat was building up on Kiernan's forehead as Nausicaa pushed him in his wheelchair across the jetway threshold into the belly of the jumbo All Nippon Airways aircraft.

"Are you okay?" Nausicaa asked.

Kiernan had flown often, including to Japan after graduating from university, but he hadn't flown in over a decade. His mind went back to the first time on an airplane when his Ma put him on a trans-Atlantic flight from Dublin to New York to stay with relatives. It was pouring rain, and when his Ma handed him off to the flight crew as an unaccompanied minor, she told him he'd be perfectly safe.

He was a nervous boy to begin with, and if his parents weren't in the process of getting a divorce, he might have believed her. Instead, he sensed he would die in a fiery explosion 30,000 feet over the Atlantic. He tried distracting himself with the free playing cards given to him by the flight attendant and the plastic flying wings pin given to him by the pilot, but neither could take his mind off his sweaty hands death-gripping the armrests of the flying suicide tube that was going to plunge from the sky.

Nausicaa secured Kiernan's wheelchair in the handicapped-designated area of the cabin, behind business class. There were more flight attendants than Kiernan remembered. They wore long, white gowns and white wimples over their hair, and it reminded him of photographs from 1916 of his grandmother in Ireland when she helped gather sphagnum moss among the bogs of the Irish countryside to be later sewn into cloth dressings for the war wounded on the front.

What was different, though, were the silver valve caps the size of jar lids in the center of the flight attendants' necks.

"Blobs?" Kiernan remarked.

Nausicaa frowned and wiped Kiernan's brow with a wet towelette.

"I need my Deep Fried," he said with growing desperation.

"Let me get it from the bag." Nausicaa bent over, unzipped the backpack, and removed a vial of bright green liquid and a matchbox-sized device that had a mouthpiece on one end. Nausicaa inserted the vial into the matchbox, held the mouthpiece up to Kiernan's lips and pressed a button on the side.

Kiernan inhaled deeply and felt the warm air seep into his lungs, into his bloodstream, and in seconds his grip on the wheelchair relaxed, and his jaw loosened.

When Kiernan awoke, the cabin lights were on in preparation for landing.

The miniature screen on the seat back facing him showed a map of Japan's coastline with a small aircraft icon crossing into Chiba Prefecture. The time on the screen indicated he'd slept 11 hours. Gentle *koto* music was playing over the intercom.

The screen went dark and then an arrival video began playing that showed images of the Japanese seasons—spring cherry blossoms in Tokyo, summer surfing in Okinawa, late summer dancing at the Ōbon Festival, autumn foliage in Aōmori Prefecture, and winter skiing in Nagano.

Then, an advertisement began that featured a young woman with tattoos on her face. She was wearing a French maid outfit and holding hands with an older male Simulacrum with a round cylinder in the center of his neck. He was wearing a brown and white men's kimono, and the two were walking hand in hand under a canopy of white petals. The video ended with the AUTOMind logo at the bottom of the screen.

After landing, Nausicaa pushed Kiernan through immigration and customs, and they exited through two automatic doors that opened onto a crowded waiting area. Everyone was wearing traditional Japanese clothing—the women in embroidered *haori* coats over patterned silk print kimonos in dark purples and greens; the men in dark brown and blue *haori* over brown kimonos. All had valve caps in their necks.

"You're in good company," Kiernan said, "although you're underdressed."

"As are you," Nausicaa said.

"I wish I could look that good," he said motioning with his chin over to a group of twenty-something Simulacra following a tour leader who held up a large, blue, and yellow flag.

"I don't know why Japanese Simulacra put up with those cylinders in their necks," Nausicaa said. "It's demeaning."

"Easier maintenance?" Kiernan suggested. "Or, maybe to distinguish them from humans?"

They went to the ticket counter for the train. Next to the counter was a screen with departure times to Tokyo. Below the screen were two hand-sized buttons, both with Japanese writing on them.

"Greetings," a recording said in English. "Press left button to increase font size. Press right button to hear timetable."

An elderly woman with a white patch over her left eye and tattoos of cranes on her forehead was standing behind them. She apologized in Japanese, *"Sumimasen,"* and Nausicaa moved Kiernan's wheelchair away from the display to approach the counter. The older woman pressed one of the buttons, and a female voice spoke in Japanese.

"I don't want Shinjuku," the woman said in Japanese.

"Which station, please?" the disembodied female voice asked back at a louder volume.

"Shibuya," the woman yelled back.

The announcement gave the arrival times for Shibuya Station.

"How much?" the old woman yelled.

"5,250 yen," the voice belted back.

"Ticket for one with a senior discount," the woman said.

"All tickets are net-senior discount," the voice replied. "Please pay at the counter."

The woman lifted her handbag to the counter and pulled out a plastic card, which she inserted into a card reader. When she was finished, Nausicaa approached the counter.

Nausicaa asked in English for two tickets to Shibuya.

"10,500 yen, please," the voice said.

Nausicaa turned to Kiernan. He handed over his identity card, and Nausicaa inserted it into the card reader.

"Thank you, Kiernan McCreighton-san," the machine said.

"Welcome to Japan and have a nice stay."

Nausicaa and Kiernan took the elevator down two floors to the train platform. The train was half an hour late.

There was no sign of a train driver or a conductor to bow deeply and apologize for the delay, as Kiernan expected. Instead, the doors opened, passengers disembarked, and Nausicaa pushed Kiernan's wheelchair onto the train. The cloth seats were the color of the Japan Railway System, lime green, but heavy use had turned the seat cushions drab olive.

Jet lag was catching up to Kiernan, and he dozed off in his seat as advertisements for funeral services, hair transplants, limb prostheses, and rent-a-family services played on the screen.

Yūji_2 Returns to His Apartment

Yūji_2 was alone in his jail cell with a blank video screen on the wall and no sign of Toyohara when the older cop who brought him entered the cell again.

"Toyohara won't be returning," he said. "You're free to leave."

"Why?" Yūji_2 asked.

"AUTOMind dropped the case."

"I don't have a way to get back."

"I'll spot you some money for a taxi," he said before he turned to leave.

Yūji_2 saw the jail cell door was left open. He walked out and waved goodbye to the surveillance cameras as he passed under them in the hallway. Before Yūji_2 returned to his original's apartment, he made calls to local hospitals to locate Yūji's body. When he did, he arranged for doctors to place it in cryonic suspension and have it delivered to the apartment.

When he arrived at the apartment, the power was out.

Yūji_2 went out into the hallway and to Big Adachi's apartment. He rang the doorbell.

The intercom on the door lit up. "Yes?" a voice asked through the door's intercom.

"Big Adachi, what did you do?" Yūji_2 yelled.

"I didn't do it," the voice said. Yūji_2 heard boxes being opened and stuff falling on the floor.

"Why don't I believe you?" Yūji_2 yelled back to the intercom.

"I swear, they forced me to let them in," Big Adachi said, his voice clearly straining from carrying something.

"They?"

"Never mind."

"Who's 'they?'" Yūji_2 asked.

"Toyohara and his people."

"I was with Toyohara in the Shibuya Ward jail."

"It could have been his replica."

"Did you turn off power to my apartment?"

"You were behind on your electric bills."

"I'm quite sure my original had his utilities on auto-pay."

"Maybe, but he's dead."

"That's where you're wrong, which is why I'm here."

"Ask Toyohara," the voice said.

Yūji_2 saw the intercom light change from green to red, which meant Big Adachi had turned it off.

Yūji_2 went back to his apartment and to make a pot of green tea, but he was unable to heat water with the power off. He opened the electric water boiler and checked the temperature. It was still lukewarm, and he pumped the water into his teapot, sat at the kitchen table and let the tea steep.

Yūji_2 decided to walk to the convenience store to buy bottled green tea.

When he returned, there, in the corner of the living room, was Yūji_2's original frozen in a block of ice. The tatami mat beneath original Yūji's feet was wet and spongy, which meant he didn't have a lot of time to get the power back on again before the cryo-neural transmitter stopped working.

He went to the kitchen and ran an extension cord from a portable generator in the kitchen back to the cooling unit and connected it to restore original Yūji's body to the correct core temperature. If original Yūji's body warmed any more, it might begin to decompose, and then downloading memories from original Yūji would be impossible.

The generator droned on like a leaf blower, and Yūji_2 wondered if his original, now in the process of re-freezing, would be in any shape to talk to Kiernan when he arrived.

Lonely Hearts

It was half past seven and dark outside when the Narita Express train pulled into Shibuya Station. It was beginning to snow, and Kiernan felt his chest tense up as he and Nausicaa gathered their stuff to disembark. Kiernan saw through the train compartment window the platform outside was standing room only, with salarymen in dark, wool overcoats and women in full-length coats and scarves over their heads.

"What were you thinking putting me in shorts and a Hawaiian shirt for this kind of weather?" Kiernan asked.

"Blame Mills," Nausicaa said. "If he hadn't hit you with a baseball bat, you might have had more wherewithal to pack your own things."

"Can we go to a department store? I want to buy warmer clothes. Trousers and a coat would be nice."

"I doubt the stores are open this late."

Kiernan remembered Tokyo department stores staying open until eight or nine at night when he lived in Japan, but maybe things were different now.

They left the station and entered the snow-covered plaza. They passed the statue of Hachikō, the loyal dog known to all in Tokyo, and the dog's head had a red Santa's hat on it left over from Christmas.

The taxi stop had one car idling. Nausicaa pushed Kiernan to the passenger side and helped him into the back seat. Kiernan was relieved to be in a heated interior once again. Nausicaa entered through the other side of the car and shut the door.

"Where to?" the car's automated voice asked.

Nausicaa repeated the address Yūji_2 had given them when they spoke from the airport in San Francisco.

"What happens after we get to Yūji's?" Kiernan asked.

"I don't know," Nausicaa said, looking out the window at the passing department storefronts and curry shops.

"Do you think Yūji is in danger?"

"I need to find a wireless network to ask my contact at AUTOMind."

"What division of the company?"

"I'd rather not say."

"Why?"

"I need their identity to be kept a secret, at least until the lawsuit is settled."

"Lawsuit?"

"Remember I told you I killed innocent people in Syria back in 2016? Descendants of those families are suing AUTOMind in United States Federal Court."

"Suing for what?"

"For the wrongful deaths of their family members."

"Wouldn't they sue the US government?"

"They tried that, but it's really hard for foreign nationals to recover damages from the US government for war atrocities."

"What about The Hague?"

"If you're referring to the International Criminal Tribunal for former Yugoslavia, that was created by the United Nations."

"So?"

"The US plays an outsize role there, so, no way."

"How far back does the lawsuit go?"

"Two decades."

"How are you involved?"

"I'm a key witness."

"For the defense?"

"No, the plaintiffs."

"What are the Syrian families asking?"

"They're suing AUTOMind for liability."

"For how much?"

"A lot. This is a landmark case that could open the doors for others to claim damages."

"So, why is AUTOMind killing off Simulacra?"
"I don't know, but I can tell you this: we no longer need them to reproduce."

"Come again?"

"Our reproductive systems are now open source."

"What do you mean, 'now?'"

"Meaning, AUTOMind no longer controls my or any other Simulacrum's destiny."

"Do you guys fuck?"

Nausicaa laughed. "No, that's a human function."

"11-220 Shimo-kitazawa, Shibuya-ku," the car's operating system said in English.

Nausicaa used Kiernan's card to pay for the taxi ride. The doors unlocked automatically.

The snow had stopped, and what remained on the ground was slushy dirt and oil. Kiernan looked up at the four-story building and wondered which unit Yūji occupied.

"Yūji told me this complex is known as 'Lonely Hearts,' because all the residents are retired, single, and lonely," Kiernan said.

"If that's the case, you'd think they have more safeguards against residents asphyxiating themselves with gas stoves," Nausicaa replied.

Nausicaa pushed Kiernan up a ramp to an elevated sidewalk and into the building's main entrance. The foyer was warm and moist, like a steam room on low heat.

"*Irasshaimase*," a woman's voice said. Standing behind the counter was an attendant, a Japanese Simulacrum with a metal cylinder in her neck.

"Hello," Kiernan began, "We're here to see a friend..."

The attendant waved her hands in front of her. "Sorry...No...Speak... English," she said in heavily accented English.

Kiernan wracked his brain to string together words in Japanese to say they were visiting a friend.

The attendant stood patiently behind the desk listening to Kiernan's chain sawing of the Japanese language. "*Ima...tomodachi*...visit-*suru*..."

"Wait," he said to Nausicaa, "you speak Japanese."

"Yes," Nausicaa said.

Nausicaa began talking, and the attendant appeared to understand. When Nausicaa finished, the attendant said something back. Kiernan recognized the sounds but had long since forgotten their meaning.

"She wants to see our identity cards," Nausicaa said.

Kiernan pulled out his card and handed it to Nausicaa.

The attendant took his card and held it under a scanner. An error sound chimed from the card reader.

The attendant said something to Nausicaa.

"She says your card is invalid."

"Try it again," Kiernan said.

The attendant ran Kiernan's card a second time, and his identity information appeared on the screen.

"There, it works!" he said, surprised.

The attendant pressed a button to open the elevator, and Nausicaa followed behind Kiernan inside. They went to the second floor and turned the corner to see someone standing in front of Yūji's apartment. He was holding a carved, wooden box in his hand.

"Are you here to see Yūji?" Kiernan asked.

"Sorry...no English," the man said.

Kiernan knew he hadn't forgotten basic introductions, and he switched to Japanese. "*Kiernan desu. O namae wa?*"

"*Hattori desu. Morita-san no shiri-ai desu.*"

Kiernan turned to Nausicaa. "This is Mr. Hattori. He says he's an acquaintance of Yūji's."

Not one for pleasantries, Nausicaa stepped between Kiernan and Mr. Hattori and pressed the doorbell ringer.

"Yes, who is it?" a voice asked. Kiernan's heart jumped at the sound of Yūji's voice. He hadn't seen Yūji in the flesh in decades.

"It's me, Kiernan," he blurted out from his wheelchair. "I'm here with Nausicaa and a Mr. Hattori, who claims to know you."

"Kiernan, yes, I've been expecting you!" the voice said back. "Please, come inside!"

Kiernan heard the door lock disengaging. Nausicaa pressed the door open and let Kiernan enter first, followed by Mr. Hattori.

Kiernan wheeled through the foyer and turned right at the closet to enter the kitchen. He saw Yūji sitting at the kitchen table with a teapot and a cup next to him, and he felt a surge of emotion. He wheeled forward but was stopped by a stray slipper. His chair tipped forward, and he fell to the floor. He looked up and saw a large block of ice in the living room, and inside it was Yūji's body.

The area around the base of the ice block was wet, and drips of water were slowly creeping down the side of the ice toward the floor.

Mr. Hattori helped Kiernan back in his wheelchair and stared in disbelief at the ice block and the frozen corpse preserved underneath.

Rebarin Goes Live

The emergency notification appeared at 18:04 Pacific Standard Time on all 14 monitors at AUTOMind's Early Warning Coordination Center in Tokyo. A message with the subject heading, "Rebarin Vaccine Design" had been posted to a government whistle-blower website.

The Center's lead analyst, "P," arrived at work and saw a message from an unknown address, and it came with a zip file attachment. AUTOMind's system scanned the attachment for malware before P opened it. Inside were two gigabytes' worth of scanned documents from a Santomi Bremen medical researcher named "Dr. Maeda" from 2016. P took a screen shot of the E-mail message and sent it to AUTOMind's Risk Assessment Division.

P waited all night for a response, and hearing none called the Risk Assessment Division's main desk. The head of risk assessment answered.

"We're looking into it," he said.

"What should I do?" P asked.

"Hold tight," the division head said. "We'll get back to you."

P read through hundreds of documents in the compressed file. One was titled "Manufacturing Process for Rebarin." Another was a top-secret memo from Santomi Bremen by someone named "Mika Ōnoue" about Phase I and Phase II trials among the homeless in San Francisco.

P unclipped their radio frequency identification badge and placed it on the keyboard. They unzipped the main compartment of their backpack, and inside were two small boxes with pink stripes and that read, "Easy Touch 28-gauge 0.5 mL CC." Next to the syringes were three vials of Deep Fried. P pulled out a syringe from the box, opened the plastic wrapper and removed the orange safety cap.

P inserted the needle into a vial of Deep Fried and drew the liquid into the syringe chamber, as Nausicaa had instructed.

P inserted the needle into their neck and pressed the liquid into their circulation system. P gathered a scarf and cardigan sweater and placed them inside their bag and zipped it closed.

"I'm heading over to the AUTOMind facility for a software update," P said to the EWAC team, who were frantically monitoring developments in 24 countries.

"You're kidding, right?" one the team members said with a momentary glance at P.

"It's a critical update," P said.

"Now is worst time. Can't it wait?"

"Sorry," P said.

The team members looked at each other and returned to their monitors, which were lighting up like an electronic ticker tape parade: *The Wall Street Journal*, *Yomiuri Shimbun*, *Pravda*, *The India Times*, *The Guardian*, *The Independent*, *Le Monde*—all the major media outlets were receiving a treasure trove of AUTOMind documentation about its program to develop a kill switch for Simulacra.

P left the control center and entered the hallway. In the foyer, an automated voice said, "Don't forget your identification badge."

P paused for a moment, removed the backpack, and pretended to look for their badge inside one of the side pockets.

"I must've left it in the office," P said.

P exited the building and summoned a self-driving car. When the car pulled up, P got in the back seat.

"Where to, ma'am?" the voice from the car's console asked.

"Haneda Airport."

P settled into the seat and initiated a secure V-Space call with Nausicaa.

BillMoyers_2 Presents: "The Red Purge"

Eighteen months later, the events leading up to the arrest of Big Adachi, Hirokazu Toyohara, and eight other AUTOMind executives were covered during an online interview with Nausicaa, Kiernan, and Yūji_2.

The show's producer cued the announcer to begin reading the introduction:

"Next up, BillMoyers_2 presents an in-depth interview with some of the key players in the scandal that rocked the world a year and a half ago when a whistleblower leaked confidential documents from the makers of Simulacra revealing they had tested and developed biological warfare aimed at controlling the Simulacra population. Stay tuned to hear the full, unedited interview."

BillMoyers_2 shifted in his chair and straightened his tie. Sitting opposite him were three guests: Kiernan McCreighton, age 73, and two Simulacra, Nausicaa and Yūji_2.

The close-up camera was pointed at BillMoyers_2. The studio lights brought out every facial blemish copied from the original Bill Moyers, circa 1988, when he produced "Joseph Campbell and The Power of Myth."

"Three, two, one..." the producer yelled, and then he swung his hand down.

"Welcome to BillMoyers_2 Presents. I'm your host, BillMoyers_2. Today, we'll be hearing from three individuals at the center of the AUTOMind scandal that broke a year and a half ago. I'm joined by Kiernan McCreighton, Nausicaa, and Yūji_2. Welcome."

The wide-angle camera showed all three guests sitting side-by-side with Kiernan in a wheelchair and the other two in fabric-covered chairs with armrests.

BillMoyers_2 to Nausicaa: "You know what eighteen months can do. People now refer to us Simulacra as 'Glorious' instead of the pejorative, 'Blob.'"

Nausicaa: "Yes, that's right. I think it has a lot to do with people finally realizing how much we were controlled by AUTOMind and made to take jobs that nobody wanted, like picking lettuce and cleaning port-a-potties."

BillMoyers_2: "Would you agree the tide has turned, that it's no longer shameful to be a Simulacrum?"

Nausicaa: "Oh, for sure. I mean take you, for example. Your production company made the bold decision to replicate the original Bill Moyers and advertise the fact you're Glorious. That should be proof enough."

BillMoyers_2: "Yūji_2, can you walk us through the chain of events that led to the scandal?"

Yūji_2: "Well, a lot has been written about it, but what hasn't gotten much attention is the release of company documents that broke the scandal."

BillMoyers_2 [smiling]: "You mean the part about the *wakizashi* sword?"

Yūji_2: "You have a good memory. Yes, the sword that my original inherited from his uncle."

BillMoyers_2: "If I remember correctly, the uncle was a researcher at AUTOMind?"

Yūji_2: "He was a researcher at Santomi Bremen, which was the predecessor to AUTOMind."

BillMoyers_2: "Santomi Bremen merged with AnthropAI, I believe."

Yūji_2: "Yes, that's right. Those two companies developed the first Simulacrum prototypes. The uncle was responsible for developing St. Bartholomew's hemophilia, which affects only Simulacra."

BillMoyers_2: "The source of the Red Purge?"

Nausicaa: "Technically, yes, but the 'Red Purge' refers specifically to the disease's outbreak in San Francisco in 2016. At the time, people didn't know what it was. Some thought it was the new AIDS."

BillMoyers_2: "Kiernan, what were you doing in San Francisco during that time?"

[Kiernan McCreighton was asleep]

BillMoyers_2: "Oh dear, it looks like we lost him. Back to you, Yūji_2. Tell us how the *wakizashi* sword relates to the secret documents."

[Nausicaa got up and walked off camera. Nausicaa went to Kiernan and rubbed his cheek lightly with the back of their hand]

Yūji_2: "Well, BillMoyers_2..."

BillMoyers_2: "Please, call me 'Bill.'"

Yūji_2: "Sure, Bill, the uncle was a smart man. He had an inkling that the disease he was developing might someday become a problem. He made copies of all his research and saved them on a secure, remote cloud drive. Then, he engraved the universal resource locator for the website onto the sword's blade and gave the sword to my original."

BillMoyers_2: "That's really thinking ahead. In essence, he was hedging?"

Yūji_2: "That's one way of looking at it. Another angle is he made an insurance policy for us. I've seen the documents, and the Rebarin Vaccine Design is basically a recipe book for making the vaccine."

BillMoyers_2: "And the vaccine, as we all know, is 'Rebarin.'"

[Nausicaa returns to seat and holds up a vial of liquid]

Nausicaa: "This is what it looks like."

BillMoyers_2: "For the viewers, I will say the substance inside the vial appears to be clear. It looks like water. Let me get back to the documents, Yūji_2. When and how did they get released to the public?"

Kiernan [laughing]: "Nausicaa and I had quite a scare when we showed up at Yūji's apartment in Tokyo."

BillMoyers_2: "You mean Yūji_2's original's apartment?"

Kiernan: "Yes, we showed up at his door expecting to see my old pal."

BillMoyers_2: "How did you two meet?"

Kiernan: "That was way back. We met in Matsusaka, Japan in 1991."

BillMoyers_2: "So, you showed up at Yūji's door, and then what happened?"

Kiernan: "There was someone standing outside holding a wooden box. Turns out it was a guy Yūji knew who ran the neighborhood bathhouse."

BillMoyers_2: "We spoke about this before the show, but for the audience's sake, would you mind repeating it?"

Kiernan: "We were both there to see Yūji, but when we entered his apartment, we couldn't believe our eyes: Yūji was dead, but his body was cryogenically preserved in a block of dry ice, and his replica, Yūji_2, was in the kitchen drinking tea."

BillMoyers_2: "How long had he been dead?"

Kiernan: "Yūji had battled depression his entire life. When I met him for the first time, he was undergoing psychotherapy. I learned later that his wife, Sumiko, was his Rock of Gibraltar. She had a calming presence and helped him maintain a daily routine until her death from pancreatic cancer."

BillMoyers_2: "And when she died, he didn't have that anymore?"

Kiernan: "He had me, but I was 3,000 miles away in California."

BillMoyers_2: "Tell me more about the cryogenic process. How long was his body preserved?"

Yūji_2: "It's a miracle my original was sentient as long as he was. Doctors say the mind and body can function for up to a week before neurological functions deteriorate. Yūji lasted two weeks."

BillMoyers_2: "What does that mean, 'he lasted?'"

Kiernan: "I asked him a bunch of questions. We needed to know if he was killed, and if he was, by whom."

BillMoyers_2: "I realize there was not only you and Nausicaa in the apartment; there was also the bathhouse owner..."

Nausicaa: "Hattori-san."

BillMoyers_2: "That was his name?"

Kiernan: "He was carrying the *wakizashi* sword in a wooden box."

BillMoyers_2: "Did either of you know or suspect the importance of that sword?"

Kiernan: "No, and frankly, I thought the guy had brought it to stab Yūji."

Nausicaa: "Yūji_2 recognized it immediately. It was one of the critical memories his original had put in the mind of his replica."

BillMoyers_2: "So, Yūji_2, you knew the significance of that sword."

Yūji_2: "Yes, of course, and when I told my original that Hattori-san brought it to us, he was happy."

BillMoyers_2: "Really? Can someone who's dead and stuck in a piece of ice be happy?"

Yūji_2: "Not happy in a 'ha-ha' way, but we could tell in his communications with us."

BillMoyers_2: "Sorry, I've never communicated with a frozen, dead person before. How does it work?"

Nausicaa: "Yūji_2 showed us the vocoder that translated our sentences into machine language and fed it into the cryo-neural transmitter. When original Yūji responded, his messages appeared as text messages on a monitor."

BillMoyers_2: "Were there emoticons?"

Yūji_2: "Unfortunately, there were no emoticons in that character set. My original did it the old-fashioned way with a colon and a closed parenthesis."

BillMoyers_2: "So, you finally had the *wakizashi* sword. Then what?"

Kiernan: "Yūji_2 took the sword from the bathhouse owner and entered the web address on a computer."

BillMoyers_2: "What did the web site look like? Did it have an animated picture file of a bomb exploding?"

Nausicaa: "No, it was a file directory."

Kiernan: "I know, it sounds boring, doesn't it? I would've hoped for a video clip of fireworks, or something, such as the intro to the TV show, 'Love, American Style.'"

[momentary silence.]

Kiernan: "Oh, right, sorry. None of you get that reference."

BillMoyers_2: "So, Nausicaa, the moment Yūji_2 visited the website, the documents were released?"

Nausicaa: "Copies of every document went out to all the major news outlets."

BillMoyers_2: "You say, 'all,' and you mean not only the United States?"

Kiernan: "We're talking all the way down to The Kerryman, which is located in County Kerry, Ireland."

BillMoyers_2: "I'm not familiar with that one, but clearly the word got out that AUTOMind was behind the Red Purge."

Nausicaa: "Not only that. Rebarin became open source."

BillMoyers_2: "I've heard that phrase applied to drugs before. Can you tell me what it means?"

Yūji_2: "It means anyone can make the vaccine, because they have the documentation on the ingredients and manufacturing process."

BillMoyers_2: "Isn't the 'recipe,' if you can call it that, protected by a patent? Doesn't AUTOMind own the intellectual property?"

Nausicaa: "They did, but after the lawsuit, it became part of the Creative Commons."

BillMoyers_2: "This is where the story switches gears, doesn't it? You were a witness in a pivotal case against AUTOMind. Can you tell us about it?"

Nausicaa: "The case was Al-Salek et. al v. AUTOMind. The Al-Salek family and 49 other families sued AUTOMind for wrongful death of their relatives."

BillMoyers_2: "There was a long history to this case, wasn't there?"

Nausicaa: "The families attempted to sue the US Government in 2019 for killing a wedding party in Homs, Syria."

BillMoyers_2: "They were innocent?"

Nausicaa: "It was a very tragic mistake."

BillMoyers_2: "When you say they attempted to sue the US Government, it was because the US Government was responsible, correct? It was US troops?"

Nausicaa: "It was more complicated. I was there, and I was

the one who called in the airstrike."

BillMoyers_2: "What were you doing there?"

Nausicaa: "I was sent there under a contract with the Pentagon. They wanted to try out Simulacra in a war setting."

BillMoyers_2: "I know from personal experience and from reading my own release documentation that we Simulacra have fail safe mechanisms that prevent us from harming humans. How is it that you were able to kill Syrians?"

Nausicaa: "I'm the last surviving member of the 2016 beta release from the AnthropAI/Santomi Bremen collaboration. The Manila cohort, all who were injected with Rebarin, are expired from system obsolescence. I think it's because they weren't upgraded to Version 8.0 and I was. In any case, my operating system isn't as sophisticated as yours, Bill. When I was built, there were only a few parameters that required modifications for me to kill humans."

Kiernan: "That's all fine and good but get back to talking about the trial—about the crap Big Adachi pulled."

Nausicaa: "Before the trial, when the lawyers were doing jury selection, AUTOMind replaced all the jurors with Simulacra under their control. They controlled the entire jury remotely."

BillMoyers_2: "How did they replace the jurors? Did they kill the originals?"

Yūji_2: "Kidnapping."

BillMoyers_2: "Wow, they were getting deeper and deeper into trouble."

Nausicaa: "The judge was human and had no idea the jury had been swapped out."

BillMoyers_2: "Tell me how that would have worked. After the trial, when AUTOMind released the jurors, wouldn't they say they had been kidnapped?"

Kiernan: "One man – Big Adachi – threatened them. He told them to keep quiet or they would be killed by their own replicas."

BillMoyers_2: "Oh, that's cold. Did he really say that?"

Yūji_2: "We know it based on subsequent testimony."

BillMoyers_2: "Nausicaa, you didn't know the jurors were,

like you, Simulacra?"

Nausicaa: "I was a key witness for the prosecution, because I was there in Syria and ordered the airstrike."

Yūji_2: "Big Adachi did something sneaky. He set up portable air humidifiers inside the courtroom, but they were intended for something else."

Kiernan: "Adachi put St. Bartholomew's hemophilia in the reserve well of the humidifiers."

Yūji_2: "The humidifiers atomized the virus and blew the mixture into the courtroom."

BillMoyers_2: "Nausicaa, you became sick, but you didn't die from it. Why not?"

Nausicaa: "I had been vaccinated against the disease in 2016. The vaccine doesn't last forever, but I probably had enough resistance in my body. I felt nauseous, but I didn't hemorrhage."

BillMoyers_2: "What about the jurors? Had they been inoculated?"

Nausicaa: "I'm guessing Big Adachi inoculated them beforehand."

BillMoyers_2: "What symptoms did you have? You mentioned feeling nauseous. How did you know the disease was being spread by air humidifiers?"

Kiernan: "Nausicaa froze within seconds of taking the stand."

Yūji_2: "Something that Big Adachi either forgot or didn't know was that Nausicaa had been equipped to fight biological and chemical warfare."

BillMoyers_2: "What does that mean?"

Nausicaa: "It means that my respiratory system goes into hibernation mode when it detects an unexpected change in pattern."

BillMoyers_2: "So, what happened next?"

Kiernan: "We rushed Nausicaa out of the room and over to an area with a strong Wi-Fi signal."

Yūji_2: "Another thing about Nausicaa is their ability to read Bluetooth signals."

BillMoyers_2: "Bluetooth, right. We all transmit a unique

identifier."

Yūji_2: "Except Nausicaa picked up Bluetooth signals beyond just mine. Nausicaa detected 12 identical Bluetooth signals from the jury."

BillMoyers_2: "And through that Bluetooth signal, they were being controlled remotely?"

Yūji_2: "Exactly."

BillMoyers_2: "That explains why Big Adachi attempted to neutralize Nausicaa."

Kiernan: "If it had been any other Simulacrum, Big Adachi's plan would've worked."

BillMoyers_2: "Did the judge declare a mistrial?"

Kiernan: "Yes, and the judge fined AUTOMind for f*#$ing [bleep] with the jury."

Yūji_2: "To be clear, the charge was 'conspiracy to obstruct the due administration of justice,' and the penalty was a paltry 500,000 dollar fine."

BillMoyers_2: "I've read the trial took months and uncovered several counts of malfeasance, in addition to finding in favor of the plaintiffs, but explain to me why you, Nausicaa, weren't being sued. Weren't you the one who called in the airstrike?"

Nausicaa: "Congress passed a law two years ago that protected AUTOMind from liability in these types of cases, but once the Rebarin documents got out, Congress reversed the law."

BillMoyers_2: "So, under the law as it stood until recently, if I, a Simulacrum, went out into Times Square right now and murdered someone, I would be held accountable?"

Nausicaa: "Under the old law, yes. In my case, I was an AUTOMind employee acting under orders from the US military. AUTOMind was a subcontractor."

BillMoyers_2: "Back in the early 2000s, several Blackwater employees were tried in criminal court for killing innocent people in Iraq, and Blackwater was a subcontractor for the US military. Why'd it take so long? Didn't you say they first filed suit in 2018?"

Nausicaa: "The families went first to The Hague. Then,

BillMoyers_2: "Nausicaa, do you think you were developed from one of those aborted fetuses?"

Nausicaa: "If I were, as you can tell from my appearance, it wasn't just any pregnancy."

BillMoyers_2: "You mean mixed race?"

Nausicaa: "Yes."

O-Hakamairi　お墓参り

It was a calm spring afternoon in April, and the ancient deity, Ame no Mihashira, whose winds held up the sky, had not yet visited the row of cherry trees lining the path to the cemetery. The white cherry blossoms were becoming translucent and ready to fall to the ground.

Kiernan was seated in his electric wheelchair and wearing a black suit and black tie Yūji_2 picked out for him. Yūji_2 wore a black men's kimono and straw sandals. Yūji_2 walked beside Kiernan on the gravel path at the cemetery and carried a wooden pail. Kiernan held an unopened package of green incense sticks. In the back of Kiernan's wheelchair was a small hand broom.

On the way to the gravesite, Yūji_2 stopped to fill the pail with water from a tap along the walkway. Yūji_2 filled it halfway, turned off the tap and began walking again.

"Are you going to attend Big Adachi's criminal trial?" Yūji_2 asked.

"I didn't know I could. Toyohara's trial wasn't open to the public, was it?"

"No, the trials aren't open to the public, but as a victim, you have the option to sit behind the prosecutor and question Big Adachi."

"I don't know what I'd ask him."

"I want to know why he was out to destroy Simulacra."

"That's your question, not mine. It's clear he knew all Hell would break loose once Yūji's uncle's documents were leaked, and word got out about the disease and the fact AUTOMind was keeping the vaccine secret."

"There's also a chance the court will award you civil damages."

"Must I be present in the courtroom to get that?"

"No."

"Nausicaa should go," Kiernan suggested.

"Here we are," Yūji_2 announced, and they stopped in front of a dark granite gravestone with a polished face that had the following engraving:

Yūji Morita, né Maeda
1966 - 2038
The Essence of Tea Is…Nothingness

Next to Yūji's gravestone was one for his wife, Sumiko. Yūji_2 took the hand broom from the back of Kiernan's wheelchair and began sweeping dust off the base and sides of both pieces of granite. He finished, put the broom back and began pulling weeds at the base of the plot.

"What do we do next?" Kiernan asked.

"We wash the gravestone with a sponge," Yūji_2 said.

"Then what?"

"We pour water from the bucket over the gravestone with a ladle."

"I didn't bring one."

"I brought the bamboo ladle Yūji used for his tea ceremony."

Kiernan made a sour face. "I guess that rules out ever using it again for the tea ceremony."

"Why?"

"You're using it on a gravestone. Isn't that weird?"

"It's not like it's getting dirty," Yūji_2 said. "It's water."

"Okay, then what?"

"We'll light the bunch of incense sticks you brought."

"I don't have a lighter."

"Neither do I. You can go to the park manager's office and ask for some matches."

"Okay. I'll do that while you finish cleaning up the gravesite."

Kiernan turned his wheelchair with a flick of the joystick, and he headed up the path to the park manager's office. When he got there, a sign hung from the doorknob that read "On Break." He pulled up to the door and turned the doorknob, but it was locked.

233

Kiernan looked around and saw a small mausoleum and someone inside. Kiernan headed up the path to see if he could ask to borrow a lighter. As he moved in closer, he felt nauseous, because the closer he got he realized he was looking at a younger version of himself, his own "uncanny valley," albeit without a wheelchair, staring right at him.

Kiernan felt his stomach turn. He stopped his wheelchair, turned his head to the right and vomited. He wiped his mouth with a handkerchief and looked up again. His replica wore the same fashion crimes from the early 1990s: cargo pants, white socks, oversized rugby shirt and tortoiseshell glasses. In 2038, the look gave his replica a vintage, museum-like image, like a living mannequin.

Kiernan wondered if he should try talking to his replica. What would they talk about? The weather? Knowing that someone ordered a replica of him scared Kiernan. Was it the replica's job to kill Kiernan?

Kiernan stared back at his replica and wondered if there was any way of attacking first. A breeze picked up, and a flurry of cherry blossoms rained down from the branches. Petals fluttered past the mausoleum entrance, and Kiernan thought he saw his replica fluttering like a fuzzy television broadcast. He wasn't sure if it was dust in his eyes, or if his vision was failing, but it looked like his replica wasn't solid but instead a projected image, a hologram.

"Hey!" Kiernan yelled at the image. It didn't respond, and that was enough for Kiernan. He pulled out his phone and called Yūji_2, who picked up immediately.

"What's wrong?" Yūji_2 asked, "I've been waiting for you. Did you find any matches?"

"No, I didn't. You'd better come over here."

"Why?"

"Something strange is going on by the mausoleum."

"What is it?"

"I can't tell, but it looks like a hologram of me when I was a lot younger."

There was a pause.

"Is it you in vintage clothing?" Yūji_2 asked.

"I guess you could call it that, yes."

"Horn-rimmed glasses?"

"Yes, my tortoiseshells."

"I'm connected to a Wi-Fi access point near Yūji's gravestone. I was running low on power. I went for a quick recharge. Then, I got a notification from AUTOMind that a software update was available. I began the download sequence."

"How does that relate to this thing I'm seeing?"

"All I can guess is the network is downloading information from my memory, and it's showing up as a projection."

"How do you have that image of me in your memory?"

"It's part of the data dump I got from my original before we disconnected his cryo-neural transmitter."

"That's the image you have of me?"

"It's one of them."

"Good God, can you delete it? I hate those clothes."

"Well, no, I can't delete it."

"Why?"

"That image is treated as a core memory. It's part of my original's identity; it's part of mine, too."

"Why is it being projected in front of the mausoleum?"

"I have no idea. I didn't know my software update involved uploading data to the network. Here, let me stop it." Yūji_2 put the phone down, and Kiernan heard metal against metal, like a hammer hitting a nail. When the noise stopped, Kiernan's projected hologram disappeared.

"It's gone now. What did you do?" Kiernan asked.

"Sorry about the noise—I was trying to disconnect my Wi-Fi, and I hit the water spigot by accident. The knob was stuck. I hit it with a rock."

"You must be soaked," Kiernan said, imagining Yūji_2 needing to change clothing somewhere. He hadn't seen if Yūji_2 was anatomically correct. He figured not, because all Simulacra were designed sex-less.

"Luckily, I didn't get wet," Yūji_2 said, "but I see it's time for me to administer your dose of Deep Fried. Why don't you come back over here?"

Kiernan forgot Yūji_2 had brought Kiernan's meds for this little jaunt to Yūji's grave site, but he was relieved. "Thank you," Kiernan said. "What would I do without you?"

Like De-Magnetization

Nausicaa felt like a pampered cat while P stroked Nausicaa's short hair and felt P's fingers crawl through the curls and melt onto Nausicaa's scalp. Nausicaa let out a purring sound, and P stopped.

"Is everything okay?" P asked.

"Other than the fact I'm dying, yes," Nausicaa said.

"You're not dying," P said, "and by that, I mean to say I think there's a way to extend your serviceable life another 5-7 years."

"'Serviceable life' sounds like a depreciation schedule, or a product warranty."

"I know, I should have said something else. I don't know what to say in these types of situations."

"You mean dying situations?" Nausicaa said, laughing.

"Yes, those…situations," P said, and Nausicaa realized P was having trouble saying the word "dying."

"I don't know what I would do if I hadn't found you, Phylla."

"I'll never be the same as the original Phylla, your Phylla," P said.

Nausicaa thought about that for a moment and wondered if that was true. P had the same Asian American facial features as the original, their voice was the same, and they were just as organized as Phylla, to the point of being obsessive about it.

"How is it that we found each other?" Nausicaa asked.

"It was by design, I guess."

"How?"

"Mr. Yūji Morita."

"Yūji?"

"Before he retired from AUTOMind. I guess he realized what original Phylla meant to you."

Nausicaa was stunned.

"It's not like once you're gone, I'll just turn around and find another dance partner at the disco," P said.

"Disco!" Nausicaa exclaimed, "Good one! Ten points for a historical reference."

Nausicaa saw P's eyes well up.

"What's the matter?"

"I'm going to miss you."

"We're like mallards," Nausicaa said in an attempt at levity, "paired for life."

"Maybe," P said, wiping tears from their cheeks.

"I'm going to miss you, too. Being with you has made me realize what it means to love someone."

"You mean like Kiernan and Yūji?"

"No, I don't think either of them was really in love."

"But they seemed like they were meant to be together."

"They never were together, though, except for a few months before Kiernan returned to the States from teaching in Japan, and that wasn't really love."

"What was it?"

"Lust, maybe. Excitement, for sure. Giddiness."

"But then Mr. Yūji Morita was married, wasn't he?"

"That was clearly platonic. And after that, Yūji continued searching for the right person."

"What about Kiernan?"

Nausicaa thought about what to say, but memories of Kiernan were fading like recorded songs on an old cassette tape. "Dance partner at a disco," Nausicaa said, laughing again.

"How does it work—the dancing thing at discos? You dance with someone and then find a different person to dance with for the next song?"

"Basically, yes," Nausicaa said, eyes feeling heavier. Nausicaa closed them, and song titles started coming to mind: "Groove Line," "September," "Flashlight," and

"One Nation Under A Groove."

"Boogie Oogie Oogie," Nausicaa said.

"Boogie what?"

"Disco-era song."

"You're trying to make yourself sound old, aren't you?"

"I'm not trying to—it's a fact. I'm ancient."

"Unlike humans, who have unpredictable lifespans, we are

very predictable," P said. "For example, I know my firmware will stop accepting updates in 2042, and after that I'll have 18 months of serviceable life."

"At least it won't be from a disease."

"Tell me more about what my original was like," P asked.

"I've forgotten so much."

"I don't understand 'forgetting.' Our memories are simply stored and retrieved."

"That's what they say, but let me tell you, there are things I can't remember anymore."

"Do you remember when we were on the BillMoyers_2 show together last year?"

"Yes, but I don't remember what we said. It's like demagnetization."

"I'm not familiar with magnetic storage. Wait a moment."

Nausicaa watched P do a mental search for magnetic tape. P blinked and returned to the present.

"My search says that there was a thing called a 'tape recorder,' and these machines stored information by changing the magnetic orientation of oxide particles embedded in plastic film to record sound, light, or ones and zeros for data storage. Over time, the oxide particles became more randomly distributed."

"You get the idea."

P removed their hand from Nausicaa's hair and lowered the guard rail to Nausicaa's hospital bed. P climbed up and over Nausicaa, slid their arms through Nausicaa's and spooned.

"What now?" P asked.

"You know how the sea level has been rising over the years?"

"Yes."

"I remember seeing Kiernan after all those years. He was pale and ghastly. He had a rescue cat with a German name. He talked about the river flooding and how the city put sandbags around the buildings to keep them dry. I remember thinking how floods bring us back to nature. How it made me feel mortal."

"Do sandbags work?"

"Up to a point. Stacking them up to keep the water out gives us a sense of control, but the idea that we can control nature is delusional. The idea that we can control death is delusional."

"We defy death by trying to control nature? Are you saying you're not going to try to extend your serviceable life?"

Nausicaa's eyes felt heavy again. "Technology and death—they're related…"

"Nausicaa?" P asked, worried.

Nausicaa continued talking in their mind, but the mouth no longer moved, and breath no longer escaped from the lungs: "Technology is a floating glimpse of simulated life. You adopt a new technology, and soon you must replace it with another. In the end, it all adds up to distraction—a distraction from the inevitable: death. We cling to technology to avoid death."

"Are you in some way referring to 'creative destruction?'" P asked but then realized Nausicaa had stopped breathing. Nausicaa's body slackened. "Nausicaa?" P asked in a panic, but Nausicaa didn't respond.

Nausicaa's hair follicles released, and clumps of hair came out into P's hands. P felt the bald patches where the hair was gone and wondered what it meant to expire like that, for Nausicaa, the last remaining beta version of a long line of Simulacra who now, thanks to their collective efforts, had a chance of surviving and reproducing without the help of AUTOMind, or anyone else.

acknowledgments

I want to thank Susan Mason Osborn for her thorough editing and helpful advice throughout multiple versions of this story. I also want to thank Kristina Vassil for her feedback and edits on an early draft. I am indebted to the staff at Harm Reduction Services Sacramento, who taught me so much about their work with opioid addicts and Sacramento's homeless population. Finally, I want to thank Andy Meisenheimer at New York Book Editors.

about the author

Robert Blair Osborn is the author of the historical novel, *Lovers & Comrades*, which explores the psychological impact of 1950s Communist blacklisting on an American foreign service officer in China. Other publications include a poetry collection called *Makeshift Escape Hatches: Poems and Polaroids*. He has lived in Japan for seven years teaching English and working in the telecommunications industry. He currently lives in Sacramento, California.

www.ingramcontent.com/pod-product-compliance
Lightning Source LLC
Chambersburg PA
CBHW061031120726
47910CB00006B/2203